Dark Sky

A novel by Joel Canfield

"...from page one on, there was never a single moment where i wasn't entertained, surprised, intrigued, involved in both the story and the characters...funny and smart and completely unpredictable."

- Jeff Arch, Screenwriter of *Sleepless in Seattle*

"Dark Sky is a fast paced and action-packed detective style thriller...Max Bowman is a great and believable character."

- UndergroundBookReviews.org

The unforgettable debut of an unforgettable character.

Meet Max Bowman, discarded by the CIA years ago, now living on an endless stream of harmless search-and-find freelance jobs provided by his old boss. Suddenly, he's given a mission way above his paygrade — to uncover the truth about First Lieutenant Robert Davidson, the son of an American military legend and a war hero who died in combat during the Afghanistan conflict.

Or did he?

To find the answer, Max must take a road trip into the heart of America's darkness as well as his own, where he has to deal with exploding homes, a classic TV hero on a rampage, a sexy heiress, a misguided teenager and Max's girlfriend back home who's text-cursing him out on a regular basis. And, oh yeah, there's also a para-military organization that's just waiting for the right moment to kill him.

It all happens in DARK SKY, a sardonic and suspenseful mystery-thriller in which an underwhelming hero must confront an overwhelming conspiracy - not to mention himself.

Copyright 2015 © joined at the hip inc.

Revised Edition 2017

Edited by Lisa Canfield

www.copycoachlisa.com

Cover illustration by A.J. Canfield

www.ajcanfield.com

This is a work of fiction. Names, characters, businesses, places, events and incidents are either the products of the author's imagination or used in a fictitious manner. Any resemblance to actual persons, living or dead, or actual events is purely coincidental.

All rights reserved. No part of this book may be reproduced or transmitted in any form or by any electronic or mechanical means, including photocopying, recording or by any information storage and retrieval system, without the written permission of the Author, except where permitted by law. Dogs are not allowed to read content without written permission provided by owner.

Special thanks to Joshua James, who gets all of the blame for this.

Table of Contents

Mr. Barry Filer 3
The Island 12
The Davidsons 25
The Blue Toyota 45
Dinner Date 65
Gas Leak 80
Lockdown 96
Branson 119
Debrief 145
The Gallery 166
Sleepover 183
Family Time 195
Milwaukee 204
Last Stop 223
Black Sun 238
The Tank 261
Retreat 272
Homecoming 286
The Hunt 299
Recovery 322

For Leese, of course.

"It is part of the general pattern of misguided policy that our country is now geared to an arms economy which was bred in an artificially induced psychosis of war hysteria and nurtured upon an incessant propaganda of fear. While such an economy may produce a sense of seeming prosperity for the moment, it rests on an illusionary foundation of complete unreliability and renders among our political leaders almost a greater fear of peace than is their fear of war."

>General Douglas MacArthur, Speech to the Michigan legislature, May 15th, 1952

"Out here, due process is a bullet."

>John Wayne, *The Green Berets*

Joel Canfield

Mr. Barry Filer

Mr. Barry Filer was not a pretty man.

That's not a judgment on who he was as a human being, because I had just met the guy five seconds ago. And I don't believe in all that ugly duckling shit – you know, that they're really secretly swans. You better believe somebody ugly wrote that goddamn fairy tale.

The truth is sometimes God turns the ugly inside out to warn everybody else about what they're dealing with. And I had that kind of feeling about Mr. Barry Filer. But there I was, in the hotel lobby bar sitting across from this guy. And, because business was business, I *had* to look at him.

Unfortunately, I couldn't be sure if he was looking at me.

Because part of what made Mr. Barry Filer such a feast for the eyes was the fact that one of *his* eyes was what they call "lazy." Make that extremely lazy. You couldn't actually look Barry in the eyes, you could only look him in the eye – because its mate was always staring off towards Pittsburgh or some other random municipality.

That's the thing they say in favor of lazy eyes. That the lucky bastard who has one can see in two directions at once. Seems like that would give you a migraine the size of a Sasquatch, but who knows? Maybe it was more like you always got to view the world in split-screen, like your own personal version of *24*. I always managed to follow whatever Jack Bauer was up to whenever there was more than one piece of video moving on my TV screen.

Of course, the eyes were just the appetizer of the three-course meal that was Barry Filer's face, the tuna tartare before the entrée. The main dish was the skin on said face. It looked a little like somebody tied this guy's ankles to the trailer hitch of an SUV and dragged him facedown over sandpaper for a few miles. It was probably the result of something a lot less dramatic – the kind of catastrophic teenage acne that could make a guy think he would never get laid, even if God had custom-fitted him with an ocular set-up tailor-made for a threesome.

That left dessert. Finishing off this dispiriting dinner, sitting on top like a rancid cherry on a vomit sundae, was a lump of jet black hair that looked like some kind of animal that had shot itself in the head after it caught a glimpse of itself in a polished silver hubcap in a parking lot. When I say lump, I mean lump. It didn't seem like a stray hair could ever escape from that hirsute brick.

We were in Midtown Manhattan, sitting in one of those sprawling endless hotel lobby bar areas that seemed like a waiting room for a corporate-sponsored Hell. Even though it was Saturday, there were still a lot of people wandering around uncomfortably dressed for business - especially the women. If you think sexism is dead, first of all, you're an idiot, second of all, you never notice how we make the female gender engage in foot torture on a daily basis by tagging high heels as "sexy."

Maybe we guys should tie colorful strings around our balls and attach them to our necks with enough tension to lift them merrily above our cocks. Maybe that should be "sexy."

Anyway, Mr. Barry Filer was certainly dressed for success. He had on the best suit Joseph A. Bank had to offer, as well as a classy maroon tie. You couldn't see a guy like this going casual – I even pictured him showering in a suit. Me, I went the other way with wardrobe. I was wearing my shittiest jeans and a black t-shirt, with my twenty-year-old leather jacket. I was pushing sixty and was increasingly at risk of looking ridiculous, as if Marlon Brando couldn't figure out how to get past *The Wild One* and played Don Corleone as a greaser, but it was how I dressed, so the hell with it.

We sat across from each other with a small cushioned almost-table between us. Like I said, it was Saturday, but I didn't care, I usually lost track of what day of the week it was anyway. After the perfunctory introductions and talk about the weather, I quickly realized this was not going to be a long meeting and I was grateful, because Mr. Barry Filer, who was probably in his late twenties, was nervous and just plain bad at human interaction. He stuttered and his voice was unpleasant. I don't mean he made it unpleasant just for my benefit, it was just indiscriminately unpleasant. If a duck could talk – a real duck, not one of those Donald-Daffy shitbirds – it would sound like Barry. Extrapolate one of their quacks into English and you'll get to what I mean. Better still, imagine Billy Corgan singing after a Drano margarita.

"So…M-m-mister Bowman."

"Max."

"Max. I-I work for…"

I stopped Barry in his tracks.

"Mr. Filer, you're from Washington. Do you really want me to know who you work for? Or would you rather be the only person I know about? You mentioned on the phone that extreme discretion would be involved here. So maybe whoever you're doing this for would like to remain a whoever."

"Whomever."

"Granted." Great, a grammar expert.

He put his cupped right hand to his mouth and almost burped. Holy shit. This poor fucker was also perpetually gassy. In addition to the horrible head and voice, God installed a defective gut on this boy. A lawsuit was in order.

'Well, y-y-you're probably right. He…I was told you could find out certain things." Pause. "You're older than I thought."

"I'm not doing the Ironman, Barry. And this isn't *The Bourne Identity*. I'm assuming I'm not going to have to jump through any windows or hang off the bottom of any helicopters. I'm just gathering information, correct?"

Hand cupped to mouth. Almost burp.

"Well, y-y-you were highly recommended by the Agency."

It was comical how that kept 'em coming twelve years later. I mean I had been in the CIA for a long time, starting way back when what was left of Reagan's brain was Commander-in-Chief, so I established myself well enough. After I went freelance, I kept getting a steady stream of customers. Most of it was shit work. Usually, the Agency had lost track of an ex-agent and a higher-up for some reason got in a sweat about what had happened to him. Did he defect to China? Worse yet, was he writing a tell-all that might make that higher-up look like a moron, which was probably about as difficult as breathing? They didn't have the time or the resources to go after all these lost sheep, so they hired me to do it, because I knew them and they knew me. And by the time I found the guy, they usually forgot they were looking for him.

This was different. This was Mr. Barry Filer.

Up until I met Barry, these jobs almost always started with a call from my old friend Howard Klein, who I started out with at Langley way back when. Howard was a good guy, but he was also a miserable man who married a miserable woman and was intent on having a miserable life – which, I guess, is why he stayed a government employee. That's why I had to be careful with Howard – misery was just as dangerous as ugly. In his case, it made him resent me for my freedom. I told him repeatedly that it wasn't all biscuits and gravy, that freedom didn't include dental, but it still pissed him off that I could binge watch old *Bonanza* episodes on Netflix on a Wednesday if I wanted to.

Anyway, I digress. Mr. Barry Filer obviously wasn't with the Agency or he would've let me know. But he acted like he represented somebody else more important than both of us put together. My hair was up, I wanted to know more and I was sorry I had stopped him from giving me the name. So I tried another way back in.

"Can I ask who recommended me?"

"Well, it was m-m-my…I mean, me. I recommended you to m-m-me."

He gave me a creepy smile, like he was proud he learned so fast not to mention anybody else's name – and even prouder that he had almost made a joke. There was no way for me to find out any more now. Since I had requested the lowering of the Cone of Silence, I couldn't ask for it to be retracted. So I kept my cakehole shut and he kept on talking.

"B-b-before I go on, I have to first m-m-make sure you'll be…well, as we discussed…discreet. I n-n-need to know you can be trusted."

Sigh.

"Barry, you had to already know I could be trusted before I walked into this lobby. Otherwise, you wouldn't have called me in the first place. Asking a guy if he's trustworthy is like asking him how big his dick is. You have no idea if he's lying until you pull his pants down."

That puzzled him. It puzzled me. I have no idea how my mind works sometimes.

"We…I checked you out," he nodded. "Y-y-you're right."

He pulled out an envelope. It was the envelope they leave in the hotel room with the chain's logo on the back flap, next to the small three-page notepad and the cheap pen that looks like a straw filled with ink. But there was nothing cheap about this envelope - it was, as they say, bulging. Bulging to the point where the glue on that back flap was straining to do its job.

Another creepy smile.

"This is a fifty percent deposit. Cash."

He handed it over. I don't usually look, but…

"Shit." I ripped open the back of the envelope and let my thumb travel over the top edges of the bounty of large denomination bills inside. I glanced back up at my new benefactor. Creepy smile was wider than ever. He knew how I'd react and wanted to be part of the excitement.

"I know i-i-it's a great deal more than your customary fee. But we…I want to m-m-make sure you come back for the second half. And that you understand how serious this particular thing is."

I hate high expectations as much as I hate Indian food.

"A *thing*," I said, almost in disgust. "I'm doing a *thing*."

Cupped hand, almost burp.

"I-I didn't mean to infer this was all that complicated. This is much like…what most clients approach you for."

"So I'm looking for somebody."

"K-k-kind of."

Kind of?

Barry pulled out a flash drive from his suit jacket pocket. I reached out but he wasn't ready to give it to me yet.

"Th-there's some basic information on here - for somebody you have to talk to first before you do anything else, in person. This is where discretion is v-v-vital. You don't email this information – or any information you find out along the way. You don't talk about any of it on the phone. You don't share any of it with anyone else, period. Ever."

A big pause. One of his eyes had me in a death grip. I didn't know if I was supposed to fold like a lawn chair or what.

"Okay, Barry, chill out. I'm not in third grade and you're not the principal. You already gave me the money, so let me go on my way and do what I do."

Wrong move to make. It was the first moment that I saw deep into his soul, and the only thing warm in there was the rage. It was from long ago, pre-pubic hair - kids beating him up about his eye, an asshole dad? Who knew. There's never a shortage of shit to drag into adulthood to make sure we repeatedly fuck things up, especially when you look like Mr. Barry Filer.

"I have to make sure it's done right," he shouted as loudly as he could without actually shouting. "As you'll learn, a l-l-lot is involved."

Cupped hand, almost burp.

I stuffed the envelope into my inside jacket pocket. It barely fit.

"Look, Barry, you don't need to worry. I'm old, but that means I've learned what *not* to do. As anybody who's worked with me will tell you, I get things done and nobody hears anything about it afterwards."

"I know that. I'm more worried about your b-b-bedside manner."

I smiled. He had a point.

"I'll be good. Promise."

His shoulders visibly slumped. I had said the right thing, without really even trying to. He stood and extended his hand, I did the same. We quickly shook on it.

Then he reached into his pocket.

"Almost forgot."

His hand came out holding a cheap cell phone. Obviously a burner.

"Use this to c-c-call me. Only this. The number is programmed in the phone. K-k-keep it on you at all times."

I took it - and the phone charger that he dug out of his pocket on the second try.

"This is necessary?" I asked.

He nodded.

"S-stay in touch."

"Count on it."

The Island

As I rode the F train back home, I thought about Mr. Barry Filer. He flew all the way to New York to talk to me for less than three minutes. I guessed the flash drive would give me some answers, but I wanted to know more right then and there.

I got off the subway and rode up the three endless escalators that delivered commuters up out of the bowels of Roosevelt Island. As I watched the tiled walls go by, I pulled out my iPhone, waiting for the service dots to appear in the upper left corner of the phone face. Yeah, I had an iPhone. I finally broke down and bought one about a year ago and now the thing was more in charge of my life than I was. You did good, Steve Jobs, even though your bedside manner wasn't reputed to be high quality either.

My service dots appeared. I hit the Howard button in my Contacts list as I headed for the subway station exit, walking past the tall-as-me sculpture of what seemed to be a glass gong, which made no goddamn sense at all in my artistic estimation.

The phone rang on the other end.

"Hey, man."

The greeting always made me flinch. Howard Klein was the kind of guy who always said, "Hey, man," because he thought it made him cool. Which wasn't going to happen.

"Howard. Just met up with somebody…"

He immediately cut me off.

"Are you on a secure line?"

I looked around as if I was wondering who the hell he was talking to, just to entertain myself.

"On a secure line? Howard, this is Max. Max Bowman. Yesterday, I looked at the pictures of your kid's wedding on Instagram. What…"

"You want to talk about shit, you need to be on a secure line."

"Since when?"

"Since I've been telling you for the last twelve years."

"It's never exactly been a sticking point before."

"Well, it's sticking now."

Oh, baby.

I was outside, a nice end-of-April day after a winter that caused me to repeatedly question God's existence, so I stopped by the retaining wall by the sidewalk that came up to my elbow, behind which was an elevated patch of grass and trees. I leaned back on the wall and allowed the rest of the subway riders to walk past me. I can walk and chew gum at the same time, but I needed to focus. I'm old enough to understand when things are rapidly getting fucked-up without me having to lift a finger.

"You know, Howard, this is the second time today someone's been very serious with me."

"You should try serious, it might look good on you."

"Howard, c'mon. I'm serious about what I do or you wouldn't keep throwing my name around, would you?"

"Look, something has changed. That's all I can say. And you have to take that change *seriously*."

I was back in the principal's office and, again, I had no idea why.

"Howard, how about you stop pretending everything didn't just get strange with this phone call? How about you admit that, up until now, you've been sending confidential information straight to my Yahoo! email account, the same account where I get spam about walk-in bathtubs, burial insurance and Russian brides, and that *now* all of a sudden it's all about the secure lines?"

A beat.

"Fine."

He kept wanting to assume we were done talking. But I was a dog with a bone.

"All I get is fine? Okay, then I guess I'll have to ask a series of questions to find out what this is all about. Like they used to do on *What's My Line?* Is this case bigger than a breadbox?"

"Max, update your fucking references. *What's My Line*, Jesus, didn't they give out buggy whips to the winners on that thing?"

"You're the same age as me, Howard."

"Yeah, but I try to exist in the current millennium. Another thing you might wanna try."

Another pause. I decided to try again. What the hell.

"So – this whole "something has changed" business. Does that have to do with my new client?"

"I don't know what you're talking about. And, by the way, you're still not on a secure line."

"Which means you do know what I'm talking about."

"Max. I don't have time for this."

"You don't *want* to have time for this."

"Gotta go, the other line's blinking."

"Color me perplexed."

"Color you disconnected."

Click.

I turned to see a squirrel running up a cherry tree followed by an angry beagle trying to climb up after it. It was too soon to tell which one of those I was about to be. At the very least, I received confirmation that shit was weird. Sometimes, it's enough to know that you're paranoid for a reason. But that big, fat envelope in my coat pocket was starting to feel like it weighed three tons.

Time to keep walking. Time to get home. On Roosevelt Island, that never takes too long.

Roosevelt Island is about two miles long and a tenth of one across. It's got parks on either end, the one at the top has an ancient lighthouse near a huge ancient hospital, the one at the bottom has a brand new giant cement statue of Franklin Delano Roosevelt's disembodied head. There are exactly three ways to get to Roosevelt Island unless you're a bird; the tram from the Manhattan side, the Roosevelt Island Bridge from the Queens side, and the subway from both sides. You can't walk or drive directly to the city itself from the Island – which is why most New Yorkers don't make the effort.

Why would they?

First of all, there's no place to eat. Yeah, there's a Subway, and mediocre-to-poor sushi, Chinese and pizza places, and a sports bar where you can get a decent burger, and a Starbucks, but that's about it. No great neighborhood places like in the rest of the five boroughs. And don't think about getting anything better brought to your door. You can only get delivery from Queens and only from the places desperate enough to want to send a delivery guy across the bridge on a bike. You call and ask a place if it delivers to Roosevelt Island, and you can time the pause with a stopwatch. They don't want to say no, but eventually they will.

Second of all, the population is half Chinese and the other half is disabled and/or elderly. Why so many Chinese? There must be some kind of flyer circulating around Beijing touting the wonders of Roosevelt Island, otherwise I can't explain it. As for those who are no longer able to walk, I guess it's appropriate that an island filled with people in wheelchairs should be named after Roosevelt. To me, they serve as a daily reminder that I don't need or want that my time is running out.

Third, there's the problematic history of this place. When it was called Welfare Island, it hosted a notorious overcrowded asylum, a workhouse populated by irredeemable convicts and a smallpox hospital you could enter any time you liked but never leave. In other words, if you're looking for Paradise, keep moving – this chunk of land has always been seen as a dumping ground for the exiled, the demented and the doomed.

I loved the fucking place.

Clearly, I had the personality of a demented and doomed exile, especially since the events of twelve years ago. Plus it was quiet in a way Manhattan never could be and it was manageable in a way Manhattan never wanted to be. Fifteen minutes away from La Guardia, twenty minutes from JFK and a great bodega at the bottom of my building that sold organic milk, so I wouldn't grow tits from synthetic cow hormones.

My building. It resembled the projects you'd see in the opening credits of that seventies TV show, *Good Times*. Most of the residents in my building had their rent subsidized by the government; old-timers, poor *Good Times* families and the like. I was one of the few people paying most of the freight on the place, which didn't bother me, it was still a good deal for this neck of the woods. I lived on the 13th floor, where else? At least the building still had the balls to call it the 13th floor, not like the other high-rises where they went right from the 12th to the 14th. They'd rather look like they flunked arithmetic than deny ancient superstitions, which was typical in a country that tried to ignore climate change while the seas rose, the forests burned and the reservoirs dried up.

Immediately next door to me lived neighbor Larry, around sixty-five years old, grey hair, grungy cap and stubble. I didn't know what was wrong with Larry and I didn't want to find out. He was barely able to walk due to oozing sores on his leg, but he managed to double his speed when he finally got a cane to work with. Because Leg Sore Larry wasn't all that mobile, he stayed at home covering every inch of the walls of his shitty little apartment with pictures ripped from whatever magazines they still actually churned out of a printing press. His ongoing sideways Sistine Chapel rip-and-tape mural extended to his front entrance, where he was in his Scarlett Period, Scarlett as in Scarlett Johansson, whose magnificent everything was the centerpiece of every photo on the door facing our common hallway. It added just the right touch of continental charm associated with every smelly college dorm hallway.

Lest you think I'm a cruel man who doesn't care about the disabled, you're entitled. From my side, Leg Sore Larry tried too hard to befriend me when I moved in and then turned surly when I didn't greet him with open arms. After that, he started stealing my *New York Times* on a regular basis. I suppose we had a lot in common - like me, his marriage was long over and his kids didn't talk to him. The difference was I didn't mind being alone and he did. But something about him made me think his problems began long before his legs started leaking.

On the other side of my door was Nancy with the Breathing Apparatus Face. That was my version of the Frank Sinatra classic love song, *Nancy with the Laughing Face*. True, my rewrite had a few too many syllables in the title, but my sick mind made them fit to the tune. Nancy was one of those confined to a wheelchair who also had, as my song title suggested, some sort of breathing tube attached to some sort of contraption in the back of the wheelchair that was required to be on twenty-four-seven. She wasn't a sight most people would enjoy, but I liked her. In contrast to Leg Sore Larry, Nancy always had a big smile and a nice greeting for you. She was clearly not going to have a lot of enjoyment during what was left of her life, but she was going to make the most of it anyway. I might have married Nancy if sex wasn't out of the question. Maybe I was just captivated by the knowledge that she was physically incapable of stealing my *Times*.

I unlocked the door and went inside my two bedroom apartment. I didn't really need that second bedroom anymore, it was where my daughters slept when they used to visit. Used to. I threw out the rest of their stuff last year.

"You're back already? What the fuck? You barely had enough time to ride the train and back."

Jules didn't wait to be in the same room with me before she started in. She would always begin abusing me as soon as I opened the door. She kept at it as I walked down the flight of stairs inside the front door that led down to the actual apartment. Despite what Mr. Barry Filer thought of me, I did have a semblance of a bedside manner. Jules', on the other hand, was removed at birth. Against my better judgment, I had given her a key three months ago. Now she thought she lived here.

"It was a short meeting," I told her.

"What, you just blew each other and left?"

That made me laugh until I actually pictured what she was describing.

If it wasn't for anti-depressants, Xanax and HGTV, Jules would've been very much at home in the island's old asylum. Right now, she was OD-ing on one of those half hours where a couple pretended to look for a house and invariably narrowed it down to three choices. The half-hour inevitably ended with one of them saying to the other, "Are you thinking what I'm thinking?" and then the show cut to whatever shitbox they decided to buy. This is what passes for a TV show now. Bring back the Lone Ranger.

I turned the corner into the living room, where Jules was sprawled out on my poor excuse for a couch in her panties and an *Anchorman* T-shirt she had nabbed at a Marshall's close-out for $2.99. It was purple and featured Will Ferrell sitting at a desk with no pants. She was overcharged.

The house show went to commercial so she was free to talk to me.

"So – what crap job do you get to do now?"

"I'm not sure. And when I am sure, I still can't tell you."

That got her attention. I always told her everything. I had nobody else to listen to my shit.

"What?"

"You heard me. Howard's suddenly talking about secure lines and everybody's acting like I'm the guy that's going to bring down the government."

She sat up and considered me.

"So you're doing something important. That should make you feel good, right?"

"I don't like important. Important means somebody's watching over your shoulder and sticking their fingers in your business."

"So why'd you take the job?"

That's when I removed the big, fat envelope from my pocket. Her eyes almost came out of her head.

"HOLY FUCK." Then, because she's Jules, "Those aren't all ones, are they?"

I shook my head slowly. "I gotta look at some files on the computer and see what this is all about."

"You're buying me a nice dinner tonight, right? OFF this godforsaken island, right?"

"Do I get sex?"

"Oh, when don't you, asshole?"

I shrugged with a smile. The commercial was over and she was back eyeing real estate, the kind neither of us would ever buy. We could never be suburban. Or stable, for that matter.

Jules was nice, but I didn't know if it would go much past where it was. She kept her hair blonde even though it was brown and her weight went up and down more than the stock market, but she was cute, if a little snarly. Then again, I liked unreasonable women, maybe because I needed somebody to shout in my ear to make me feel something. She had been a cabaret singer with some limited success, then her acute acid reflux did some damage to her vocal cords – which made her a singer who couldn't sing. However, yelling wasn't a problem.

Even though she had lost her singing voice, luckily she wasn't stupid and got a job as an assistant at a law firm. She hated it, but the medical plan covered her meds and the salary allowed her to save up for the operation that would restore her instrument. She was close to having enough money, but I wasn't sure why she was bothering. She was in her forties now and wasn't about to become a star, especially since her repertoire stopped at 1963 with Eydie Gorme and *Blame It on the Bossa Nova*. She claimed not to listen to any music that came afterwards, except for some Broadway shit. That's why we got along; I loved Sinatra and knew all the standards. But I also loved the Beatles, the Stones, Nirvana and even Kanye West, which drove her insane.

"After what that asshole did to Taylor Swift?" she'd shriek at me.

I'd reply, "Listen to their music side-by-side. You'll know who deserves to have an award taken away."

That was another problem - she lived in the past and wanted both of us to get a condo there together. Despite Howard's opinion of me, I still wanted to pretend maybe something new might work, but she wasn't budging. In her words, "The passage of time can kiss my ass."

Whenever she said something like that, my heart sort of melted. Nothing like misanthropes in love.

Even though it was only Saturday, I knew she'd be there all weekend. She was already making noises about giving up her place in Harlem and officially moving in with me. We'd both save money, right? I returned the noise with quiet. It was a good trick – Howard wasn't the only one who knew it.

I went to the second bedroom, which was what I used for an office even though there was still a queen bed taking up most of the room. I sat down at the IKEA desk, pulled out the flash drive Mr. Barry Filer had given me and shoved it into the USB slot. Of course, it shoved right back because I was holding the fucking thing upside down as usual. Unlike many things in life, with a USB you can only be wrong once, and after I flipped the thing, the screen came up on my computer with the contents.

More weirdness.

There was exactly one document on the flash drive. One. It was a massive 11.3 kilobytes. And when I opened up the document, it contained exactly one small piece of information – an address.

In other words, I still didn't know who or what I was after. To find that out, I had to go to Virginia.

I hated Virginia.

The Davidsons

The address was located in Virginia Beach, where a lot of D.C. elites settle down once they rape the taxpayers enough to afford the admission price. There were no instructions telling me to go there, but I didn't know what else I was supposed to do. I just wondered if I had to pay for this trip myself out of the cash I had been supplied with. But when I got around to emptying the hotel envelope to see just how much green was in there, I discovered that Mr. Barry Filer had thoughtfully included a credit card with my name already on it. Attached to the card was a Post-It Note with neatly handwritten instructions (I suspected Mr. Barry Filer's fine penmanship at work) to use the card for traveling expenses. I called the credit card company to check on the credit limit and was told there was none. I could charge however much I wanted. So I guess somebody trusted me.

Somebody with excellent credit.

I lived up to that trust - I didn't go put a Lamborghini on the card. Instead, I charged a flight down to Richmond, a lousy sandwich from an airport kiosk and a car rental. It was another hour-and-a-half drive to get to Virginia Beach, but that was okay with me. The longer it took the better.

Because I wasn't in good shape.

Even though the address came to me without a name attached, it wasn't very hard to find out who owned the property. And when I did find out, I started sweating and still hadn't stopped, even though it was only about fifty-five degrees out. A cold front had hit the Eastern seaboard and had cooled things off considerably for everybody but me - I was in the middle of my own personal heat wave. Why was I so nervous?

After a curt female voice at the intercom buzzed the gate open, I wheeled my rented Taurus through it and around the perfectly maintained circular driveway leading me to the foot of what was to all intents and purposes a big fucking mansion. Looking at this monstrosity with windows, I suddenly wasn't just sweaty, I was shaky too. And deep down, I knew why I was so nervous.

The truth was I had gotten lazy.

I had not only lost my edge, I couldn't remember what it was like to ever have had one. I didn't want to see it, but, over the years, the agency had been feeding me an increasing number of crap assignments, stuff a Boy Scout who knew how to use Google could have handled. The decline was obvious, but I ascribed it to Howard's trajectory, not mine. Yeah, he was in a senior position at Langley, but, at every opportunity, I knew they were shoving him further to the side of the real action, preparing him for his final severance package, which would be a nice bundle after all those years. That meant in turn that whatever jobs he threw my way weren't going to be anything earth-shaking. We were getting old and things were winding down, that was my excuse for allowing things to slide without a fight. The reality was I wanted shit to be easy. I didn't want drama. I had had enough of that in years gone by.

Unfortunately, when there's no drama, there's nothing to prevent you from going completely to hell.

I didn't stay in shape. I had too much Jack Daniels at night. I had too many burgers at the sports bar. And I watched too much HGTV with Jules, instead of checking out whatever quality television the internet was demanding I take in. Nor was I reading great literature or compelling nonfiction. No, I was only reading new compilations of old comics I bought when I was a kid. I told myself I was only doing it to laugh at how much sense they didn't make. How the hell did two-inch-long wings on the Sub-Mariner's ankles make it so that he could fly? How did the Thing, who was made of rocks, have a girlfriend? Wasn't intimacy an issue? All the lube in the world wasn't going to help the entrance of a cock made of rocks feel less than traumatic, right?

These kinds of inquires weren't the kind of thing a grown man should occupy his time with, but, as long as I made enough to get by, I felt okay about throwing my ambition into storage and filling my days with whatever didn't threaten me. But a dozen years of coasting was catching up to me – because I now had to deal with the guy who owned this monster mansion. Why the hell would someone hand me an assignment that involved him? And why were people already treating me like I fucked up before I had done a goddam thing?

Nothing made any sense, which made me sweat even harder.

As I got out of the car, I eyed the estate and the beautifully manicured lawn that went on until it met the beach and the ocean put it all to a stop. I mopped my brow with the back of my hand and climbed the steps up to the massive double front doors that had matching American Eagles on them. Then I hit what I guessed was the doorbell. It was a button in the middle of a beautifully sculpted American flag and I thought to myself that there must be a special doorbell store somewhere in a special rich people mall that only they knew about.

And then the door opened.

"You look pale," she said.

"Hello to you too," I replied.

She flinched as if she wasn't used to anybody talking back to her, which she probably wasn't if she was a part of this household. That meant I had to grope for my bedside manner fast.

"Sorry, I've been a little under the weather."

She still didn't know what to make of me, but then again, she was in her bathrobe and slippers and looked like she just rolled out of bed, even though it was close to three p.m. But she still looked good, kind of like Cate Blanchett if she ate a little. She was in her early forties but you could've realistically guessed five years younger. I already knew who she was, but I didn't want to give the game away.

Meanwhile, she gave me the onceover. I was wearing my usual T-shirt, leather jacket, jeans, with Converse black sneakers. I did accessorize for this special occasion by wearing a Mets cap. I loved a loser, if it wasn't obvious by now. Maybe I should've worn a coat and tie for this special occasion, but my Sunday-Go-To-Meeting clothes were all in a corner of my closet buried under five pounds of dust.

"Okay," she finally said, "get out from under the weather and tell me who the hell you are."

"I told you over the intercom at the gate. My name's Max Bowman. I was told to come here by Mr. Barry Filer."

"Who the hell is Mr. Barry Filer?"

"I wish I knew. The internet's never heard of him, as far as I can tell."

She blinked.

I said, "You don't seem to have any idea why I'm here. So why'd you let me through the gate?"

"Because nobody dares push that intercom button unless they really should be here."

"So – let me in."

Having been hoisted by her own petard, she threw open the door and waved me in. I walked into what seemed like a Four Seasons hotel lobby, only nicer and without a reception desk.

"I usually don't answer the front door, but the help's off today."

"Good for them," was my answer.

"So why are you here?" she finally demanded as I walked around enjoying the smell of the fresh flower arrangements.

"I don't know, I was sent to this address to talk to somebody who presumably needs a job done. That's about all I know."

"That's not a lot."

"I'm painfully aware."

A long pause, the kind of a pause a pizza place takes when you ask if they'll deliver to Roosevelt Island.

Finally, she said, "Hmmm," if you can actually say "Hmmm." She walked towards the entryway to another room. I assumed I was supposed to follow, so I did.

"You live here?" I asked. "Or just visiting?"

Her back provided some more information. "Living here. I just got divorced."

"He got the house? You must have had a shitty lawyer," I said and immediately regretted it. Jules always said that neither of us should be let out into public.

"No, I *chose* to move back here." She looked over her shoulder back at me. "Any other questions?"

"Give me a little time."

"I'd rather not."

I followed her through the lobby area into some sort of sitting room with the type of furniture you'd find in a funeral home and the kind of old art hanging on the walls that you'd find in a museum in Florence.

"Any of these valuable?" I said, eyeing the paintings.

"You don't recognize the artists?" she said.

"No."

"Surprising. You look old enough to have been around when they painted these."

I smiled at the jab. "You did just get divorced, didn't you?"

"Yes, a wounded animal is the most dangerous kind, don't you think?"

She motioned for me to sit down, and I did. She remained standing and stern.

"Do you want some water? Or something a little rougher?"

I looked at her and considered my options for a few moments too long.

"You're not answering, which means you really want a drink but you're afraid you'll look like an alcoholic since the sun is still up."

"Jack Daniels, all by itself with a couple of ice cubes."

"Good boy."

Then she was gone and stayed gone. It didn't take that long to pour a shot of Jack. I mentally shrugged and turned on my phone to distract my nervous system - and I found there was plenty of distraction to be had. Jules' dirty little secret was that she was a psychic – a goddamn witch, to be exact - with the very specific but very powerful gift to instantly know when I was in a room alone with a strange woman.

There were 50 texts from her, the highlights of which included:

> *THERE'S NO FUCKING FOOD IN YOUR REFRIGERATOR.*
>
> *BTW, the boring fat couple picked the ranch house with the shitty pond.*
>
> *You still buy PLAYBOY? WTF???*
>
> *I'm BORED. Come HOME.*
>
> *Just saw commercial for older women having dry painful intercrs & it made me horny. Is that wrong???*
>
> *COME HOME*

The texts went on like that for a while, then things took a somber turn:

> *Don't have to worry about your newspaper anymore*

Leg Sore Larry?

> *Went to get Starbucks,*
> *EMS was pulling him out of apt*
>
> *Sheet was over head.*
>
> *have you ever looked inside his rat nest?*
>
> *On the next episode of Hoarders...*

I stared at the phone with an expression of disbelief. Leg Sore Larry was gone. I couldn't be happy about it. Neither could Jules.

Kinda sad tbh

I looked up, almost having forgotten where I was, as my hostess returned. She was out of the bathrobe and wearing slacks and an expensive top that probably cost more than my rent. She also didn't have my drink, which I needed now more than ever. Not getting it pulled the rug out from under my brain.

"I found out why you're here," she said flatly. "And it would be best for everyone if you weren't."

Back in the principal's office.

I got up, feeling a little sick again. No Jack, dead Larry, and getting treated like shit all combined to create a minor explosion in my head. "Maybe I *should* go. Everyone associated with this thing is more interested in abusing me than getting it done."

She felt my pain and softened a little.

"You know who my father is."

"You're Angela Davidson."

"Yes."

"Then I know who your father is."

"Well, I'm very protective of him."

I was getting more than a little tired of being questioned. "Do you think I want to hurt a living legend? What, you think I'm going to sucker punch him? Make fun of his wrinkles? Force him to advertise reverse mortgages? What do you think I'm up to here? Give me a hint, because, again, *I don't know.*"

"No, no, no, I didn't mean…" She trailed off. "It's just…he…he's losing his mind."

She let out a big breath.

"What should I do? You tell me," I said a little too harshly.

She looked away and then turned back to me. In spite of the bullshit, I think she actually liked me.

"I'll take you to him. Everything's gone too far. You'll find that to be a recurring theme."

She walked, I followed.

After hiking about fifty miles through the house, we arrived at a big set of double doors that she opened for me. I walked inside and found myself at the back of a screening room with four rows of seats, seven across. In the front one, dead center, was a very old man watching a very old film about a cavalry outpost in the old West. Angela nodded her head down towards him and indicated I should go on and introduce myself. It kept being clear she wanted no part of whatever was going on and was desperately struggling not to take it out on me.

I carefully made my way down the darkened aisle as my eyes adjusted to the lack of light. On screen, an ancient Native American chief was telling John Wayne, playing older than he was at the time with grey hair and a moustache to match, that they were too old for war.

"Yes, we are too old for war," answered Wayne. "But old men should stop wars."

The old chief replied, "Your men die. My men die. No good."

That summed things up.

As I approached the front row, the movie suddenly stopped and the house lights came up. The old man got unsteadily to his feet and let out a little cough.

I was face-to-face with General "Devil-Eyes" Donald Davidson.

General Davidson was one of those war generals that the public glommed onto and built into a mythic status, another one of America's endless succession of John Waynes – Patton, MacArthur, you know the names. Davidson made his name during the first Iraq War, Operation Desert Storm, back in 1990, along with General "Stormin'" Norman Schwarzkopf.

But, while Schwarzkopf threw off the aura of a big friendly teddy bear, albeit a teddy bear who commanded 700,000 soldiers, Davidson was a fearsome figure whose nickname reflected the cold, hard stare he threw at anybody he thought was less than they should be. After that first Iraq War, Davidson wrote a couple of best-sellers (or, more likely, somebody wrote them for him) and he later became a highly-paid commentator on one of those 24-hour news networks. That last gig didn't last long, because he was too straight a dealer for that brand of phony outrage. Still, he had made plenty on the speaking circuit and obviously, from the looks of this place and his daughter, he had a few bucks in the bank.

I knew all this from reviewing his Wikipedia page. I didn't have a lot of time to do all the research I usually do before meeting up with somebody this high-profile – shit, he was the most high-profile guy I ever had to have a conversation with – but I found out enough to get a sense of him. He was retired now, and hadn't been seen in public in years. There were rumors of health problems – and the man standing before me in his solid black silk pajamas and matching bathrobe was in fact a shadow of what I remembered him looking like. He used to look like Clint Eastwood in his older Dirty Harry days – now he seemed closer to Barney Fife on Weight Watchers. He was bone thin and looked older than dirt.

He thrust out his hand, which demanded to be shook. I complied with orders.

"An honor to meet you, sir. I'm Max Bowman."

"You're older than I thought you would be," his sandpaper voice let me know.

"That's a common reaction these days, sir."

He didn't smile, but his eyes indicated he appreciated my comeback. He sat back in his chair, where I saw he had his own customized control panel for the room built into its arm. I had the feeling he spent a lot of time in here. He glanced back at the now-darkened screen.

"I love that movie."

"*She Wore a Yellow Ribbon*. The middle leg of John Ford's cavalry trilogy. And the only one in color."

This time he did smile. I was finally doing well in the principal's office.

"I love 'em all. Well, the first two, anyway."

"Ford only did the third one for the money, sir."

"Is that right?"

"*Rio Grande*. Yessir." I was winning at Trivia Night too.

"Explains a lot."

"My father worked with Ford, so I've seen them all. He saw to it when I was a kid."

"Your father worked in movies?"

"No, sir, he worked in the O.S.S. during the war – Ford did some documentaries with that group during the war."

"He did *The Battle of Midway*, correct?"

"Yes sir. My father said he was the greatest artist who ever lived. When he wasn't drunk."

Suddenly, he looked angry, but not at me. "Ford understood the military better than any other director. All of his service movies…they reflect military purity. Do you understand military purity, Mr. Bowman?"

"I think so, sir."

"Tell me what you consider it to be, Bowman." A command. I knew, because he was this close to throwing a "Private" in front of my last name and that almost made me chuckle, an impulse that quickly vanished once I realized I had been given an assignment by a beloved American hero.

I took a breath.

"Well…these are men entrusted with a sacred duty that forces them to take others' lives as well as put their own at risk. And that duty should not be compromised by political schemes, lies or a simple thirst for blood. The military should be entrusted with a mission, a justified and moral mission, and the military should be given the responsibility to carry it out according to its finest traditions."

Wait – did I really just say all that? I thought I must have – because, judging by the old man's face, I had just transformed into John Wayne myself.

"You think about things, don't you, Bowman?"

"Yessir. A lot more than I realized, apparently."

"Then you probably know this country hasn't experienced military purity since 1945. Korea, Vietnam, Iraq, Afghanistan…there wasn't much of a reason for any of that."

That explained why he didn't work out at Fox News.

"Sit down," he commanded again. "We have some things to go through."

I did as he requested and left a seat in between him and me. That's what guys alone in a theatre do unless they're looking for a dance partner. He stared straight ahead, I leaned towards him and eyed the side of his withered face.

"Do you have children, Bowman?"

"Yessir."

"Drop the 'sir.'"

"Yes…"

"Do you ever have misunderstandings with your children?"

"No. They don't talk to me so there's nothing to be misunderstood."

He turned to me. I was another step closer to being in his club, whatever it was all about.

"So you understand it. You saw for yourself how conflicts can develop. You know how a family can start out with the best intentions and lose its way."

"On both sides, General."

"Both sides?"

"My kids don't talk to me and my father disowned me."

He turned and stared straight ahead again.

"I see. That must have been very painful for you."

I said nothing. There was nothing to say without saying everything and that would take much longer than either of us had the patience for.

"But it says something about you. You won't be controlled, will you?"

I shrugged, but doubted he could see it.

"Anyway, you did a good job for me a few years ago. That's why you're in here."

My hair went up again. "I did a job for you?"

"Through the Agency. You found a couple of retired officers I was trying to track down. I needed to reach out to them on a private matter."

"I remember that. It was actually a very easy job, but thank you."

The door to the screening room opened and Angela entered carrying two drinks. She gave me a little of the stink eye, but it was fleeting. I wasn't bothered, especially since she was finally handing me my glass of Jack – and she was generous with the amount. She handed an equal amount in a glass to General Davidson and did a head cock towards me for his benefit.

"Daddy, he's a Jack man too."

That really warmed the General up. "You must be the son I never had," he said as I saw a shadow pass over Angela's face. He raised his glass in the toast position, I raised mine and we both took a large sip.

"It must be hard for you," I said carefully. "Your son."

With that remark, Angela turned on her heels and got out of the screening room as fast as she could without breaking into a full run. I watched her go, but the General did not.

"It was hard – and it continues to be hard."

"But you have to be proud he died a hero."

"I would be if he weren't still alive." He took another sip.

So that was it. That was why his daughter thought he was going senile.

Just over ten years ago, First Lieutenant Robert Davidson was killed in action in a firefight back in Afghanistan and was posthumously awarded the Silver Star and the Purple Heart. Tributes in his honor ran day and night on the news networks because of who his father was. Members of his unit told reporters in detail what a wonderful, brave guy he had been. I remember catching a few minutes of the funeral and seeing General Davidson cry like a baby. As they say, parents shouldn't outlive their children. Robert had been his only son. Now Angela was all he had.

"He's not dead."

The General was looking me straight in the eye, almost daring me to challenge him.

WTF? One of the most widely-reported deaths since Elvis Presley didn't happen? This was like saying Hitler was caught running a 7-11 in Queens. And just like that, the panic was back in my gut, because I sure believed that Robert Davidson was dead. Did I happen to mention there was a funeral? And that he was buried in Arlington Cemetery? I guess if it came down to it, the General and I could go over there at midnight and dig him up so we could both sleep easier.

Maybe this was why everyone was freaking out. If this ever got out, half of America would believe the legendary General Davidson had lost his shit, and the other half would believe the kid was alive and spin it into a new conspiracy theory that would be instantly promoted by Charlie Sheen in a YouTube video.

I had to stay cool. Discretion. Bedside manner. Discretion. Bedside manner.

"How can you be sure?"

"I have sources. That's all I can say."

"Sources. Do I have access to…"

"No. I don't want them involved."

My head was spinning.

"General, I at least need a place to start"

He turned to me.

"I don't have one."

For the first time, he looked vulnerable. The fire went out of his devil eyes, maybe because of a few tears lurking somewhere in the back of them.

"No one will take me seriously, but I'm not crazy, Bowman. I needed someone to help me with this, so I asked who found those officers for me. I looked at your records and saw you've been doing this kind of thing for a long time, you've done it well and without any posturing. The fact that you're outside the government now means a great deal to me, because I need someone in an independent position. You can operate on your own and not let anyone intimidate you out of doing your job."

"Who would want to intimidate me?"

I held his eyes for a moment. Then he looked away uncomfortably.

"I don't know. Maybe no one."

"If there's anything you know, any information you have, General, I really need you to share it with me now before…"

"There's nothing," he snapped. Then, more quietly, so quietly I had to lean in closer to hear, "I would only be guessing and that might prove…difficult for you. It's far better for you to find out what you can on your own, without being prejudiced by me or anyone else."

Military purity. He went on.

"You might not find anything. You might come back here after you're done and tell me that I am crazy, that my son is indeed dead. I'm not expecting miracles. I'm only expecting an effort and I expect you to make one."

Once he got all that out, he suddenly seemed tired. I finished my drink, stood up and said, "Don't worry, the effort will be made." Then I remembered something, something that had been left in the air.

"General, you started this by talking about parent-child misunderstandings."

"Yes. My son and I weren't speaking when he…disappeared. One of the great regrets of my life. And maybe the only regret I can still erase."

I nodded and we exchanged curt goodbyes. As I walked back up the aisle, the lights went down and the Duke came back to life.

I headed out of his one-man theatre feeling bad for the guy. He wasn't the American hero anymore, he was just another sad old man who screwed things up with his boy and wanted too much to fix them after it was too late. It didn't take a shrink to realize this was just about wish fulfillment – but he had to know on some level that not many wishes ever come true.

The Blue Toyota

After I had left the Davidson estate, I was, if anything, more of a candidate for Jules' myriad mental prescriptions than before I went in. How did I draw this card? The one that had the picture of the last remaining general-hero in America? Schwarzkopf was dead and Petraeus was caught diddling his biographer, so Don "Devil-Eyes" Davidson was it. And somehow, he was entrusting me with a mission that a lot of people, including his daughter, were nervous about being carried out.

And boy, was his daughter nervous.

On my way out, she had been waiting in the hallway, looking as tense as a closer with a one-run lead and the bases loaded in the bottom of the ninth.

"You know this is a ridiculous wild goose chase. You know my brother's dead."

"I haven't heard anything that indicates it's not. But…"

She grabbed my arm. Not lightly either.

"So just take the money. Just take the money, come back here in a few weeks and say you hit a dead end. I don't want the people of this country thinking of him as some kind of Alzheimer's-ridden freak show."

"To me, he seemed completely lucid. Maybe he's misguided. If he is, I'll put it all to rest and nobody will be the wiser."

I gave her one of the cards I had printed up through some internet company that only charged ten bucks. We lived in a golden age, all right.

"Feel free to call me if you need anything. Or even if you don't. I don't want you to be nervous about me."

It was a smart move, I thought. "Thank you," she said and in a genuine way.

As I got on the 1-64 headed back toward Richmond, I replayed the conversations again and again in my head. Nothing seemed to add up to much of anything. Angela didn't want the family embarrassed and the General didn't want his boy to be dead. On the other hand, I was getting paid a lot of money to do something.

I just had to figure out what.

Was it even possible Robert was still alive? How could a very public death on a very distant battlefield translate into a secret resurrection over a decade later?

I needed a little traveling music to calm down and create some thinking space, so I turned on the rental car's satellite radio. I paid extra for it — well, my new credit card did. I dialed up and down, past the Springsteen channel, past the Pearl Jam channel, even past the Elvis channel, until I settled on the Sixties' station for a few seconds. Then I realized it was playing *Hooray for Hazel,* a song I hadn't heard in forty years and never wanted to hear again; it always made me think of the TV maid on that sitcom I hadn't seen in forty years and never wanted to see again.

I searched a little more and found the Sinatra station – only, what the hell, it wasn't playing Sinatra, just some other song recorded by one of the endless legions of Frank wannabes that sang Frank's songs with Frank's arrangements without Frank's talent. Would they dare play Bon Jovi on the Springsteen station? No. And yet, here they were playing Tom "Dukes of Hazzard" Wopat's take on *That's Life*. Check it out for yourself and get back to me after if you make it all the way through without throwing yourself off the nearest balcony.

I moved on and, finally, at a loss, I stopped on a hip-hop channel, which was playing *We Dem Boyz* by something called Wiz Khalifa, according to the read-out on the radio screen. I stuck with it because it made me feel younger than a hundred and fourteen. It wasn't half bad either, it just wasn't half good. Still, I wasn't one of those guys who went around insisting music was better when he was a kid. *We Dem Boyz* beat *Hooray for Hazel* by a country mile. My dirty little secret was I liked a little hip-hop once in a while, and it had to be a secret or Jules would have applied a sledge hammer to the back of my head.

My brief musical journey must have loosened the rocks in my brain, because they suddenly gave way to reveal a bright, shining light bulb, like those that signify an idea in the cartoon world. It was actually pretty obvious. The General said he had a source. It seemed a good bet who that source might be – or at least I could narrow it down to two possibilities. After all, he had also mentioned the fact that my hunt for the two retired Army officers a couple of years before had been at his request – and he was cagey about the reason he wanted them found. All he would say was it was about a "private matter."

Nothing could be more private than this.

If one of those guys had told the General his son was still alive, he probably didn't want to be called on it by somebody like me. And if neither of them knew anything about this bizarre claim, then I couldn't let anything slip or the General and his daughter would have me shot at sunrise, if they even waited that long. So every move I made had to be a stealth move. I had to get information from people who had no idea what I was after. And I had to do it in person.

If I tried to do this over the phone, it wasn't gonna work. No, I had to go to where they lived and knock on their damn doors. I had to be able to see their faces.

As I drove toward Richmond mulling this over in my head, I couldn't help noticing a blue Toyota in my rear view mirror that seemed to be working very hard to stay exactly three cars behind me. It was as if the driver had read some secret stalking manual and was following its instructions to the letter. If he really was tailing me, he really sucked at it, because, otherwise, I never would have spotted him, because I hadn't been at all worried about anyone tagging along after me. I had gotten to the point in my life where it was laughable to think that someone would actually consider it worthwhile.

Yet, there the fucker was, hanging back those three cars – as he had been doing for the last forty miles or so.

Still, because he was so obvious about it, I dismissed his existence in my head. When you drive on an interstate, you constantly see the same vehicles over and over. Like that truck that didn't believe in abortion, according to the giant sticker on its back. It kept passing me going downhill and I kept passing it going uphill. So maybe the blue Toyota was using me as a pace car or something. Whatever, it wasn't worth taking seriously.

I had other things to worry about. For starters, I needed supplies. I searched the highway exits for one of big box store plazas - the kind that always has a mammoth Old Navy overpowering the scenery next to an equally mammoth, vacated Barnes & Noble. I spotted one too late to take the exit, so I took the next one a few miles up the road so I could backtrack.

That's when the blue Toyota reminded me it was still there.

In my rear view mirror, I saw that it was getting off where I was getting off. Then I saw it was backtracking along with me. Which meant I had to pay some attention.

But I also spotted a Banana Republic tucked away in the corner, which was exactly what I needed. Yeah, I would have to park a few football fields away – it was Sunday and the place was mobbed – but I was going to be gone a few more days and I needed some clothes. And not just some clothes, better clothes. I needed some shirts that had buttons and maybe a jacket that didn't look like a cast-off from Fonzie's closet. I was heading into the heartland and I needed to dress for success. Or, more accurately, dress like someone to be trusted.

But the hell with it, I was still going to wear my jeans and Chuck Taylors.

I finally found an open parking space, pulled my rental into it and got out of the car. I scanned the immediate area for my friend in the Blue Toyota, but saw no sign of it parking anywhere else or cruising around the lot. So I shrugged it off again and trotted over to Banana Republic. And began the godawful task of buying some clothes.

Like most men, I don't do clothes shopping happily or competently. This was no exception. The hardest part was finding a pair of black jeans that fit over all the takeout food I'd consumed since the last time I dragged myself into a clothing store. I ended up with a casual jacket, three shirts, two pairs of jeans, some socks and underwear. The one bright spot? It all went on my brand new credit card. Hell, these were travel expenses, especially since the clothes were crucial to the job at hand.

At least that's what I would tell Mr. Barry Filer.

Maybe the nice new silver watch I also bought wasn't all that necessary, but I was felt entitled to reward myself for all the unpleasantness swirling around me. And speaking of unpleasantness, there was some more to get out of the way. I had to call Jules to tell her I wouldn't be home that night.

It went about as I thought it would. Turned out I was an asshole cocksucking monkey fucker who raped his mother. I guessed I could live with that if I had to. When she was finally done enumerating my unusual, illegal and wholly fictitious sexual proclivities, she let me know she wasn't staying the night at my place.

"If I stay here, I'm just going to have nightmares about the ghost of Leg Sore Larry dripping ooze piss from his lesions. That doesn't make for a restful fucking night, now does it?"

"Can't deny that."

"Besides, it's a lot closer commute from my place to work than from your place. And I don't have to sit there on the F-is-for-FUCK train sandwiched like a sardine in the middle of all those smelly bastards from Queens."

"They can be smelly."

"Yeah, and…WHY ARE YOU AGREEING WITH ME SO MUCH, MR. DUMBASS?"

"I just appreciate every hair of your bogusly blonde hair."

Silence.

"And I need one small favor…"

"Oh SHIT, I did not see THAT coming."

Of course she did, we were at the point where we both saw pretty much everything coming. Luckily, what I was asking for wasn't that big a deal on her end. I just needed her to open up a couple of documents from my folder of case files on my computer and text me the information I needed – which was the addresses of those two retired Army officers Davidson had asked me to retrieve years ago.

"Sure. Sure, Max Bowman, I'll do that shit for you. Only now – I get TWO nice dinners when you get home. And one of them is gonna be at the Gotham goddamn Bar & Grill, what do you think about that?"

My wallet began to silently weep. When the President came to Manhattan, he ate at the Gotham goddamn Bar & Grill. When I went into Manhattan, I got a hot dog off the cart.

"Okay," I said, "but no appetizers."

"HAHAHAHA, you're a comedian! Guess what, asshole? Appetizers AND dessert. Not only that, but also – dessert *WINE*."

"Okay, okay, okay."

"And – I WANT US TO BUY A DOG."

What? A dog?

"I'll think about it."

But I wasn't going to. If giving her a key to my place had been the equivalent of digging my own grave, agreeing to co-parent a dog with her would be asking for the dirt to get shoveled over my face.

Not that I actually related that charming metaphor to her. I didn't want to hear more speculation on what other monstrosities my penis was capable of penetrating. Instead, I told her I missed her, said goodbye and put the phone back in my pocket, next to the burner given to me by Mr.

Barry Filer. And actually, a part of me did miss Jules. I had to admit that to myself. I didn't have much else in my life, and I kind of liked being around somebody who said "fuck" more than me. And she said it a fucking lot more.

It took the entire length of our conversation for me to make it from the Banana Republic to my parking spot in the far corner of the lot. At which point I realized I never should have written off the blue Toyota. It had left me a message that was far from a friendly one; all four of my tires were slashed, leaving my rental resting completely on its rims. I dropped my Banana Republic bags and just stood there for a few seconds, staring blankly at the car. The thought that immediately leapt to my mind was that I was glad I bought myself the watch.

According to that watch, it took about an hour forty-five to get a replacement car from the rental company. That kind of pissed me off, since I had checked every box and every insurance upgrade on the rental form – my new credit card could take the punishment, after all – so I expected some kind of superior service. But I forgot this was America and that ever since all of Mom and Pop's little businesses went under, the corporations were fine with screwing over one individual customer. There were a few million others out there on hold waiting to give them money, why give a shit?

At least I had things to do to pass the time while I was waiting. Jules had texted me the addresses, accurately and quickly as I expected – and she had even gone to the trouble of putting "fucking asshole" in between every other word. I liked the fact that she was willing to put that kind of time and effort into our relationship. The addresses were close to what I remembered – one in Kentucky and one in Missouri - which meant I could drive the whole trip and avoid any more cramped pain-in-the-ass flights. I liked a long drive – and it would give me time to think out my approach.

Then the rental company finally showed up with my new car. We all agreed it was some damn teenager who ripped apart my tires and we went on with our lives. I got back on I-64, then, when I got to Richmond, I took I-95 north towards D.C. It would be a couple more hours, but some things had to be addressed before I continued west.

10 miles outside our nation's capital, I spotted a Hilton Ramada Holiday Inn whatever-the-fuck generic hotel.

I pulled off I-95, parked in the lot and headed for the entrance.

I went in, power-walked through the lobby and came right back out the back door – all so I could walk back around the front to where I had originally parked.

And there in the parking lot, I saw, as I expected I would, a familiar blue Toyota cautiously coming to a stop a few spaces away from my new rental. I waited to see who was going to get out of it.

And holy shit if it wasn't a damn teenager.

The kid was wearing expensive ripped jeans and t-shirt, trying to look street for too much money. He was skinny, furtive and was holding a heavy-duty X-ACTO knife in his left hand as he approached my shiny new rental car. But I was able to get right behind him before he got too far. I knew this was an amateur because he never felt me coming.

"Hold it, Billy the Kid. You don't want me to use what's sticking in your back."

What was sticking in his back was the end of the tire wrench from the trunk of the rental. But he didn't know that.

He stopped immediately and put up his hands. Poor little bastard was shaking. Finally, someone else besides me was in the damn principal's office and I got to be the damn principal.

"Drop the knife," I barked like a tough guy. I'm up to it when there's no chance of me getting hurt.

He dropped the knife. I picked it up.

"Thanks," I said. "Sorry for the surprise, but I didn't feel like wasting another hour forty-five today, it's already starting to get dark. Now turn around."

He did. I showed him the tire wrench. His eyes went wide. I was suddenly a magical trickster. Maybe I would turn him into a frog.

"What's this all about?" I asked.

He looked glumly at the ground. But not before I noticed the family resemblance.

"Your mother's name Angela?"

No response. Which was a response.

"Well, go home and tell Mommy you didn't scare me off. And maybe have her give me a call."

He stood there not knowing what to do. I pointed the tire iron at him.

"Bang."

He skedaddled away, back to the blue Toyota, which he jumped into just as fast as he could, stumbling and almost falling on his face on the front seat. Then he drove off with a loud squeal, leaving a little of the tire tread behind in the parking space.

I had the feeling he was going to be up all night on Hulu watching old *Family Guy* episodes trying to calm himself down.

Five more miles up the interstate, I checked in under a phony name at a different Hilton Ramada Holiday Inn and took my luggage, by which I mean the Banana Republic shopping bags, up to my room, headed straight for the bathroom, and finally took the shit that had been trying to fight its way out of my ass for the past three hours.

I felt about twenty pounds lighter, and thought about maybe taking a shower and watching some garbage TV to relax. But who was I kidding - I knew I couldn't relax. So far, everybody I had been in contact with today was deeply unhappy - and I knew I needed to add one more name to this little anti-party.

An hour later, Howard threw open his front door. He was in his pajamas. I didn't figure him for a pajama guy, I figured him for a boxers and t-shirt guy. I'm usually right about these things, so I was momentarily taken off guard.

"What the fuck are you doing here?" he asked, logically enough.

"I figured if I wasn't going to sleep tonight, neither should you."

Howard and his lovely wife Janet lived in the Palisades, a nice neighborhood near the Potomac River and the Georgetown campus – another Washington elite community. They weren't in the nicest part of this nice neighborhood, but where they were didn't suck either.

I looked Howard over a moment, since I hadn't seen him in person in a few years. He had always had the face of a rat, now he had a shaved head on top of that, so that he resembled an albino lizard. All the old guys shaved their heads now, cutting their losses once their hairlines retreated to the back of their skulls. It almost made me miss my dad's comb-over. Me, I still had most of my hair, and it was still the same brown color as it was when I was a kid. The difference was it no longer matched up with the wrinkles in my face. It was starting to look like a wig or a dye job, proving that you got punished even for the things that went right.

"How the hell did you find out where I lived?" Howard asked.

"Do you have any idea what I do for a living?" I asked.

He frowned and ushered me in. I saw Janet's bathrobed back beating a hasty retreat into the kitchen. I knew she was still friends with my ex and I knew she wanted nothing to do with me.

"Do you know what time it is?" Howard asked with a whine as he plopped down on the sofa.

I pointed to my nice new silver watch and nodded. "Give me five minutes and a drink and I'll be out of your hair."

"I don't stock Jack."

"How about the closest thing?"

He disappeared again as my phone vibrated. My regular phone, not the Mr. Barry Filer phone, which, thankfully, had stayed silent ever since he gave it to me. I took my phone out, saw the caller ID and answered the phone.

"How's your boy?"

"How did you know?" Angela Davidson asked with some surprise.

"He has your nose."

She sighed.

"You didn't have to scare him like that."

"Don't worry, the tire wrench wasn't loaded."

She wasn't laughing at my jokes. Instead, she went on to tell me, with too many words and at too fast a speed, that it was her idea, she had just sent the kid to scare me off. I told her she shouldn't have put him in that situation if he didn't know how to pull it off, she could have gotten the boy killed if I was actually dangerous. She seemed to accept the fact that I wasn't dangerous a little too readily for my taste.

"Look," she said in almost a whisper as Howard returned with a glass of something, "Just take the money, give my father a good story about how you couldn't find anything, or better yet, say you found out my brother really is dead so he'll forget this whole mess."

"You're repeating yourself. And unless you know something I don't, I'm assuming that's exactly what will happen. Which makes me wonder, if there's nothing else to this, why would you send your son out to slash my tires?"

"I told you, I don't want my father to be embarrassed."

"Is that your only kid?"

"Jeremy. Yes. He's a good kid. Just turned eighteen."

Howard rattled the ice in my drink, indicating extreme impatience. I took it from him. Probably Jim Beam or some shit like that.

"Well, I should go. I'm with someone and they think this is rude."

"Who are you with?" she asked sharply.

"It's not another woman, so don't be jealous."

Sometimes I think I haven't done my job if the person isn't still talking when I hang up the phone. She was still talking, but I was done with Davidsons for the night.

I put away my phone, sipped the drink and sat down in a chair. Howard sat back down on the sofa and asked who had been on the phone.

"The General's daughter."

He paused a little too long. I wanted a tell and I might have gotten one.

"The General? What General?"

"So you don't know the particulars of my assignment?"

"Was I the one who gave it to you?"

"No, that was Mr. Barry Filer."

"Who the fuck is that?"

"I was hoping you'd know. Maybe this rings a bell - his eyes gravitate to different magnetic poles."

"Cross-eyed?"

"More at cross purposes. Anyway, I googled this guy's name and came up with nothing, except an accountant in Iowa and an insurance agent in Washington state."

"I have no clue who you're talking about."

"Then here's to the clueless."

I raised my glass to the toast position and then took a big long sip of whatever whiskey I had been supplied with, while Howard stared at me with a dismal expression.

"You're pathetic. You come storming over here in the middle of the night to blame me for everything and I had not one damn thing to do with whatever you're in the middle of. I don't know any General, I don't know Barry Miller…"

"Filer."

"I don't know anything, including why you're here and not in New York on that godforsaken island. I'm going to go get a damn drink myself."

He went into the kitchen, where Janet still was. There were a bunch of urgent whispered words that were as loud as they could be and still be considered whispers.

"Hi, Janet," I yelled merrily just to piss her off a little more.

She returned fire – and she was definitely packing more heat than me.

"Hel-LO, Max! While you're in town, you should stop by and visit Allison and Edgar. They're just two streets over. We see them all the time."

Allison my ex-wife and Edgar the guy she married after me. Both with the Agency. Thanks for bringing that up.

"Oh," she added, just to really mess with me, "And Lorie's still living with them, if you didn't know."

I recovered from that psychic punch to the gut and mumbled, "Last I checked, none of them were interested in talking to me." Then I took another big gulp of the brown stuff to further self-medicate. There were more words in the kitchen that I couldn't make out, not that I really wanted to, then Howard re-emerged, looking wounded and without a drink.

"Everything all right?"

"Peachy," came his answer. Then he gave me a deeper look. "What the hell are you doing with yourself? You're getting too old for this, you know. Then what? I don't imagine that you have anything saved up for your golden years."

"You and your wife can visit all the money I have. It's just two streets over, according to her."

Howard glanced nervously at the kitchen.

"Don't start anything," he said quietly.

"I didn't. Anyway, don't worry about me. Did you know half of all Americans don't have any money saved for their retirement? I saw it in the Times the other day."

"Great. You'll have people to talk to at the homeless shelter." He immediately felt bad. "I'm sorry, man."

I stared him down for a few moments.

"What?"

"You know something."

He blinked uncomfortably.

"Cut the shit, Max. I gave them your name is all. They came to me looking for the name of a guy who had done a job some time ago. I figured out it was you, I gave them your name and contact info, that's it. They said don't talk to anybody about this. Can I go to bed now?"

I sighed and looked away.

"I'm in over my head, Howard. You're right, I am too old for this shit."

"So maybe think about quitting this assignment."

"I've never done that."

"This would be a good time to start. Why not?"

My turn in the hot seat. Howard frowned.

"You need the money, don't you?"

"It's been pretty quiet this year," I offered. "And Mr. Barry Filer pays well."

"You gotta come up with a Plan B, my friend."

I took another sip, while Howard worked up the nerve to give me some more advice.

"Look, man," he said softly, "You should talk to Allison while you're here. At least clean that mess up."

"I didn't make that mess, despite the other opinions out there." I glared at the kitchen accusingly, then drained my glass. Then I stood up and handed it back to him. He seemed startled that I was actually going to let him go back to bed.

"Hey, you can hang out a couple minutes. It's cool."

I saw Janet lurking in the kitchen shadows and said, "I don't think it is, Howard."

He got to his feet. "How long you in town?"

"Leaving first thing tomorrow."

Things hung between us. We had known each other too long.

"You should have never left the Agency, man."

"You know I didn't really have a choice."

"Max, you're a good guy. It's time to move on and get a life. You still got time."

"You can counsel me on my future after I get done with this. I'll either end up famous or dead."

He looked like he was going to cry. He took my arm and walked me to the door.

"Look, you need anything, you know where I am."

Then he actually hugged me.

Dinner Date

Well, that was fun.

It was Monday morning, mid-morning actually, and I had spent more time drinking than sleeping the previous night. On my way home from Howard's, I had found a place on the D.C. side where I could procure a small bottle of Jack. I paid for that myself, because the drinking had nothing to do with the job, it had to do with the ghosts that always waited for me around these parts. The ghosts of my marriage, my kids, my parents and…well, the one ghost that nobody talked about, but nobody could forget.

I woke up with a splitting headache and a determination to stave off the spooks and get back on track with what I was supposed to be doing. Just because Howard's wife insisted on keeping the bad old days alive didn't mean I had to participate. I had spent a lot of years burying that shit in the basement of my subconscious and I wasn't about to get it out of storage at this point.

I had something to keep me busy so I worked at refocusing. That process began with calling the front desk and asking if I could keep the room another night. They were agreeable. I wouldn't be leaving today because, now that the General had actually told me what I was after, I needed to do the research I would have done before I left Roosevelt Island, had I had any clue what I needed to be researching. I never liked walking into situations blindfolded - and that's all I had been doing since I met up with Mr. Barry Filer.

I found a Best Buy nearby, where, on a Monday morning, there were a lot more blue-shirted salespeople than customers, not to mention about eight billion more DVDs than the American people were inclined to buy at this point in the digital revolution. I was pleased to see the entire run of *Mr. Ed* had finally earned its own boxed set, but I had to wonder when *Hazel* would have her day. Maybe there would be no hooray for her after all.

After a brief high-level consultation with an employee who looked like he had never been laid and maybe never would be, I bought an economy-priced Chromebook – well, my new credit card did, anyway. Then I came back to my room, which had the "Do Not Disturb" sign still hanging on the doorknob. It was still hanging there when I unlocked the door and went in. My experience has always been that the housekeeping people always show up just when you don't want them to. Besides, I'm neat for a guy my age. I don't really need cleaning up after.

I ordered up a club sandwich, no mayo, from room service and hooked up my new purchase to the hotel Wi-Fi. And I tried to find what I could about First Lieutenant Robert Davidson and his tragic death at the age of 32, half a world away.

Of course I knew going in that I would be looking at the "official" story. Back in 2005, most "war journalism" was a lot more like reprinted press releases than actual reporting. This was no exception. Robert Davidson was a patriot and a hero. This was a horrible tragedy for America and his father. He died for his country and we had to keep fighting idiotic wars to justify his sacrifice.

I read some more. About how Robbie signed up with the Army right out of high school and put himself in Ranger School, working towards Special Ops status, rather than going the straight officer route at West Point as his dad had. That decision maybe provided the contours of the tension between father and son that the General alluded to during our conversation; the son bought into Bush and Cheney's disastrous left turn into Iraq in 2004 and the father knew it was folly. Still, Robert Davidson had apparently served valiantly both in Iraq and then in Afghanistan, where he was killed.

Assuming he was.

Again, this was the "official" story. Back then, there were a lot of them. Jessica Lynch had been a scrappy little hero, Rambo with a menstrual cycle – until she blew the whistle on the military's myth-making bullshit. Then there was the really tragic tale of Specialist Pat Tillman in the Army Rangers. He gave up an NFL contract to go fight in Iraq and Afghanistan – which, to Americans, was like giving up heaven for hell. When he was killed in combat overseas, he was lionized as the ultimate warrior. Except it turned out he wasn't killed in combat – he was killed by his own unit's weapons and the evidence pointed to the possibility that the other guys offed him on purpose for God knows what-the-hell reason.

So I wasn't about to just accept the media coverage of Robert Davidson's demise. The more I read about what happened, the more questions popped up in my head.

First of all, everyone in his outfit all mouthed the right platitudes to the press about how wonderful Davidson was, how brave he was, how his father should be proud of how he died, the usual – but all their talk felt like the kind of generic blurbs you'd hear at a funeral from a priest who had never met the deceased in his life. They said nothing personal and nothing to indicate any of them had any sort of close bond with him. There was something missing – something that would have indicated they might have actually liked the guy or even had known him at all.

Second of all, and this was a big one, no one in his outfit *saw* him go down.

It was true. He was accompanied by no other military personnel when he suddenly took a couple of bullets from an Afghan rebel.

The only people he was with – were from Dark Sky.

Most people knew about Blackwater, the controversial American "private security" company that received about a billion in government contracts to help police Iraq and Afghanistan during the wars. They ended up being accused of negligence, racial discrimination, prostitution, wrongful death, murder of innocent civilians, and, on the fun side, the smuggling of weapons into Iraq in dog food containers. Of further interest was the fact that several family members of contractors who worked for Blackwater and ended up dead sued the company for details of those deaths – which Blackwater refused to provide. The company was finally kicked out of Iraq in 2009 by the new Obama administration and had all their military contracts with the U.S. cancelled. After that, with lawsuits swirling around their corporate heads, they changed their name in a last-ditch attempt to stay in business - because that's always a great solution to the problem of being a bunch of fucking murderous dicks.

But Dark Sky? Nobody knew what the hell they had been up to overseas. The overwhelming majority of Americans didn't even know they existed.

While Blackwater mostly protected State Department officials, Dark Sky's Middle East role was a lot more nebulous – and dubious. There were rumors they had close ties to America's favorite hit squad, Seal Team Six and other high-level clandestine Special Ops personnel. At the Agency, I heard rumblings that they were given license to do whatever they needed to get the job done, to the point where somebody high-up finally pulled the plug on their overseas ops around the same time Blackwater found itself flushed down the government toilet. I didn't know exactly what kinds of things they did wrong, but word was they made Blackwater's sins look positively forgivable. But they were buttoned-up tighter than Blackwater – there were no public scandals or lawsuits dragging their name into the media spotlight. As a matter of fact, the government was still funding their existence.

So - what was Robert Davidson doing with them?

The story was he went ahead alone with them to scout out some rebel territory, leaving his men behind - when the unexpected rebel attack happened. Again, he was the only casualty and no eyewitnesses ever came forward to say exactly what happened. There were no quotes from Dark Sky personnel in the newspapers about the incident, just an official statement from the company expressing their remorse. Their side, as always, was all buttoned up nice and tight.

The reporting was all perfectly believable – and because it was the General's son, there was an air of respectful restraint. So everybody expressed their sadness for a few moments and the world went on. This wouldn't be a Jessica Lynch or a Pat Tillman situation. No, this episode lacked any kind of family pushback or contradictory evidence – so it would be swallowed whole and digested without discomfort by all of America.

It made me realize why Davidson liked John Ford films. This was a movie director who was fond of ripping apart glorious national myth-making, even as he celebrated the preservation of the myths. In *The Man Who Shot Liberty Valance*, a character famously says, "When the legend becomes fact, print the legend," and that was Davidson's credo too. The General would never blow the whistle on his fellow soldiers – it was good for the country to perpetuate patriotic myths. No, he would only curse out the government privately because it wouldn't provide the troops with a "pure" mission.

And that's why he wanted to send me out to handle this situation quietly and under the radar. If his son was still alive, he wanted to understand the situation before he took any official action.

But if Robert Davidson was still alive – where was he and what was he doing? My thoughts were going around in circles. I still didn't know enough to even try and figure out that angle. So, to kill time, I checked out a few online gambling sites, wondering if I could get away with using my brand new credit card to win a million or two at virtual poker.

I was just recalling how bad a poker player I was when my iPhone started vibrating.

I picked it up off the desk where it lay beside the Chromebook, recognized the Caller ID again, and answered.

"Let me guess. You want to know where my car is, so your kid can come slash the tires again."

"I hope you're amused inside your own head, because those are the only laughs you're going to get."

Angela, as usual, wasn't in a joking mood.

"What can I do for you, Ms. Davidson?"

"Where are you? Are you still in town?"

"Not in your town. I'm up the road, near D.C."

Pause.

"Can I come see you?"

I checked my nice new silver watch. 4:30.

"Well…I hate to eat alone."

"Tell me where to meet you."

Was I crazy for inviting Angela Davidson to dinner after she sent her kid out to sabotage my rental? No. I needed all the information I could get and I knew there were probably a few details only she could provide. After all, this was her younger brother – she would know what he was all about.

I was still a little shaky from the bender the night before when I pulled my rental up to the D.C. hotspot where I asked her to meet me. I didn't want her anywhere near my hotel, because I didn't want to become the victim of any more of her family's mischief. I ended up getting to the place a couple of minutes late – and I don't think she was too ecstatic about my tardiness. She was actually looking pretty hot in a small black skirt and close-fitting top as she leaned on her Mercedes and glared at the boarded-up graffiti-ridden windows that bore the address I had given her.

Whoops.

I parked across the street and walked over to her.

"This must be a very exclusive place," she said, her eyes throwing a few poisoned daggers my way. "So exclusive it doesn't have windows. Must be some pretty important people in there. They *really* don't want to be seen."

I looked the façade up and down and sighed.

"Pancho's Tacos. The best bad Mexican food in town. What the hell."

"The best *bad* Mexican food?" she said in disbelief as she threw her head in Pancho's direction.

"Cheesy and greasy," I said, still staring at the outline of "Pancho's" left behind on the top of the front wall from where the letters were removed. "Guaranteed to clean out your system in an hour."

"Well, my system's fine, thank you. So let's go where I like to eat. Leave your car, I'll drive."

"Your kid going to come cut the brake lines this time?"

More daggers.

Where she liked to eat was, as expected, expensive and jam-packed with Washington movers and shakers – and sadly devoid of greasy tacos. This was a five-star restaurant that felt as if it needed a few extra in recognition of its super-elevated status – if you threw a bread roll in any direction, you were bound to hit a cable news pundit smack in the kisser.

My idea had been to stay as incognito as possible and here she was getting us a table at a place where everybody cared less about the food and more about the other people that were eating there. A Clinton or a Bush wouldn't have been out of place, which meant a Davidson was more than welcome without a reservation. We were a real Lady and the Tramp combo, since I was dressed for Pancho's and she was for whatever you still dressed for these days. Luckily, I was at least wearing my brand new Banana Republic jeans – and of course, my nice new silver watch, which quickly caught her eye.

"Nice watch," she said, looking over the top of her menu. "Did you just get that? I don't remember you wearing that when you were at the house."

"You're observant."

Her approval faded as she looked me in the eyes.

"You still look pale. Maybe you should see a doctor."

"No, I should've seen less whiskey last night."

"Hmmm," she said, "Again with the whiskey. Do you perhaps need to go to a meeting?"

"I'm not an alcoholic, but thanks for asking. No, last night was a special occasion. Call it a return to the scene of the crime."

A waiter stopped by. Angela ordered a wine that I could neither pronounce nor afford. The waiter was impressed by her selection, so I joined in the general excitement. When he was gone, she went back to her menu and continued the cross-examination.

"What kind of crime are we talking about?"

"My first marriage."

She peered over the top of the menu at me again.

"Who was the perpetrator?"

"I'll leave that to a jury of my peers."

She actually laughed and went back to the menu. "Well, that's a trial I hope gets televised. Mine didn't go so well either. And neither did the second one. And now at my advanced age, it's tough finding guys like you. The roast chicken looks good."

Wait, what did she say before the thing about the chicken?

"Guys like me?" I asked. Shit, did my voice just go up an octave?

"Guys who are just…guys. Straight-shooters, like my dad. No bullshit."

"You must have men lining up. You're in good shape. And aren't there a lot of big shots who'd just like to have the Davidson name attached?"

"Who the hell needs someone like that? They don't give a shit about me or anything about me. I've been through that too many times. The first husband married me for my money. The second for my name. I'm not optimistic about there being a third."

"So you're not seeing anyone right now, I take it?"

"No, you?"

"There's someone. A singer who can't sing. It's casual."

I felt my phone vibrate in my pocket. I didn't have to take it out and look at it, I knew it was Jules. As usual, her witch-like powers sensed a female encroaching on her territory.

"Does *she* know it's casual?"

I shrugged like a guy would. She seemed to find that attractive.

The wine came and, as the waiter poured, we both ordered the roast chicken. A little later, the food came and then another bottle of wine. We became almost as roasted as the chicken. During all that, we talked a little about baseball, movies, a few other safe subjects. Too much was hanging in the air, so I decided it was finally time to push things and do some business.

"So this is nice and everything. But why did you want to come all this way to talk to me?"

"I was interested in what you were going to do. How you were going to approach it."

"Well, I'm not anxious to share my plans with a tire assassin."

That flustered her and she didn't fluster easily.

"Look…I'm really sorry…really, really sorry…but you already seemed rattled and I thought…"

"You thought some unknown stalker taking out my tires would scare me off. And then you wouldn't have to worry about what I was going to turn up."

"I guess I underestimated you."

"People often do, even though I'm usually not up to much."

"Well, let me correct you on something. Again, I'm not scared of what you're going to turn up. I'm scared about my father's weird obsession getting out to the media."

She was starting to hit that line a little too hard. And suddenly, I no longer believed her.

But I did have to try and get at least get some information out of this dinner about the Davidson brood, because I sure as hell didn't get a lot of protein. The chicken was good but, as usual in these kinds of places, it was only enough to fill the belly of a small child, not a big doughy man who only had a club sandwich six hours ago and was expecting to devour Pancho's Combo #3, two tacos and a burrito with rice and beans on the side. Goddamn, I was going to give myself phantom diarrhea.

"Your mother – she passed away?"

"Three years ago. She would've been able to talk Dad out of this crazy shit."

"Tell me about your brother. Your only sibling, right?"

She looked away. This wouldn't be easy.

"Yes, and it doesn't really matter about Robbie now, does it?"

"Your father alluded to some…conflict with him."

"It makes no difference." Now she was getting pissed.

"Your father seemed to think it did. I thought it was interesting he went into the Rangers program instead of West Point. Seems like that might have disappointed your dad."

She finished her glass of wine. Her hand was shaking. She got up her nerve, pushed her head forward in my direction and made her pitch.

"Here's why I really called you. I'm assuming my father is paying you very well to do what you're doing. He's not a cheap man and this is important to him."

I didn't say anything. She pulled back a little, let all that sink in, and then moved forward again for the kill.

"Well, I have some money too. And I will double what he's paying you to just stop whatever you're thinking of doing. Give it up. Again, report back to him with some credible information that he'll buy. And then drop it. Forever."

So that was it. Intimidation failed, now it was going to be bribery. I wasn't anxious to find out what her third move would be, but I had no doubt it would be coming.

She went into her purse. It was a nice bag. Probably cost more than the payoff she was offering me.

"I can write you a check for a deposit of sorts, if that…"

My turn to move forward as I waved off her offer.

"Angela, I think you've again underestimated me. I don't do that kind of thing, ever. It's the reason I have any kind of reputation at all. If I can't be trusted, I don't get hired. And besides…well, it just ain't me."

She turned and signaled the waiter with an almost violent gesture to get his immediate attention. Lots of heads turned. Members of the Washington elite like Angela didn't spin their arms around in the air at a place like this. I got the hint.

"I guess it's time for the check. You want me to handle it?"

She shook her head furiously and dug into her purse for her wallet. Eye contact was no longer in her repertoire. When the waiter came over, she shoved an American Express card at him and asked him to expedite the check, she had somewhere to be, a destination which was anywhere I was not.

"I'm sorry to disappoint you," I went on, kind of wanting her to like me again. I knew that what she was doing now had nothing to do with me. I just wanted the same thing to be true for the first part of the meal. I wanted her to not just have been greasing the wheels for the pay-off when she acted like I had a shot with her.

"You didn't disappoint me. Life did."

Oh, boy. That's where we were.

We sat quietly for a minute or two, until the waiter returned with her AmEx card and the receipt for the meal. She scribbled on a generous tip and signed it. Then she got up and walked out, leaving me the poorest and most alone guy in the room.

That wouldn't have been the case if Pancho was still making tacos.

The poorest part, anyway.

Gas Leak

It was Tuesday morning.

I avoided the Jack – and the Jules – when I got back to the hotel the night before, and slept moderately well probably because I ducked both J's.

Although I did keep thinking about Angela during the night. I was a man, so of course I pictured her naked a few times, but mostly I thought about what she was hiding. She seemed to erupt like an overheated volcano every time I mentioned her brother - she wouldn't divulge even the most basic piece of information about him. She just wanted me gone and the whole thing forgotten. Not only that, she wanted it too badly, which meant there was a huge skeleton in some closet somewhere whose bones kept rattling in her ear to the point where it hurt.

Anyway, I was done with the dead ends around here. It was time to hit the road.

And suddenly, I felt all balanced and Zen again, like I could just focus on the case and ignore all the *Sturm und Drang* and other bullshit surrounding it. Because I was finally getting the hell out of D.C. and leaving all the pain from my past in a crappy midrange hotel room.

Plus, I was beginning to believe all the danger of the Davidson case lay in the pain of their past. Whatever they were all scared of, whatever they were worried I might stir up, it seemed to be all about things that had been, not things that were. If there was some scandal attached to Robert Davidson, it was old and moldy and there was no reason to drag it out into the light if I ever found out what it was. Frankly, I didn't care what it was and wasn't anxious to find out. I had a simple job, to prove the guy was dead, and that was my only obligation. If there was some nastiness lurking from days gone by, I'd leave it where it was.

But the idea of Robert Davidson still being alive? That was dumber than a dog barking at itself in the mirror.

So it was just a matter of what the ugly truth had been about the guy. Maybe Angela was just afraid if I uncovered it, I'd blackmail her or go right to the *National Enquirer*. In any event, the only real threat to me so far had been a teenager attacking my tires. I needed to relax about the whole thing, again, it was just another job despite the involvement of living legend General Donald Davidson.

All of that self-manufactured reassurance put me in such an almost good mood that I was heading towards giddy as I prepared to pack up, check out and hit the road. As I gathered my luggage - the Banana Republic shopping bags, that is - I called Jules. I had waited until the last possible second to make sure she'd be at work, where she couldn't scream obscenities at me.

But, then again, if Angela consistently underestimated me, I consistently underestimated Jules, who, when she answered, immediately said in a pleasant and professional voice that she would call me back in a minute. Then, as I saw it in my head, she quietly got up from her desk, took quick, purposeful strides towards the elevator, rode it forty floors down to the ground level, walked out of the high-rise where she worked and ducked into a back alley where she knew she could scream as many obscenities at me as she damn well pleased.

"Where the FUCK have you been, Fuckhead?"

Only two fucks? That was hardly worth going down forty floors.

"I got drunk night before last. I bought a laptop. I researched. Last night, I had dinner with someone connected with my case."

"Who is she?"

"Did I specify a gender?"

"Am I wrong?"

"Are you ever?"

A sigh.

"I just miss you."

I was getting tenderness?

"Jules, we never see each other that much during the week anyway."

"You're not in the greater metropolitan area. I don't like that."

"I'm not having sex with other women. I've mostly just been freaked out, okay?"

"What is it with this case?" She sounded worried for the first time.

"You don't want to know, but don't get concerned. I think everything's all right now."

As we talked, I used the television remote in the room to check out of the hotel – and, of course, kept it all on my new Mr. Barry Filer-issued credit card. Very easy. Thanks to technology, we would soon never have to converse with any other humans again. Then we could all just stay home and comfortably drown in our own filth.

"Are you coming back today?" Jules said with more than a little urgency.

"No…I'm going to be gone probably a few more days."

"FUCK WHAT FUCK FUCK FUCK???!!"

Okay, the alley was a good call.

"Look, I have shit to do. I don't get mad when you go to work."

"Goddammit. Where are you going?"

"I'm not on a secure line."

"Oh, Jesus, really? After all this time, you're going to pretend to be serious about what you're doing?"

"I can't talk about it."

"I'll blow you when you get home?"

"Still not talking."

A pause. This was a strange conversation and I was about to find out why.

"I have enough."

I stood still in the middle of the room.

"Enough? Enough what?"

She paused, then it all came out in a rush.

"Enough money, doofus. I made an appointment with the doctor, the one who does the vocal cord surgery. I think I can cover the deductible, the co-pay, whatever Obamacare is gonna make me cough up, and get the operation. I think…maybe I'll be able to sing again."

It sounded like those last two words made her cry a little.

Wow. No wonder she was so edgy.

She had been waiting for this day for years, ever since her singing voice went out in the middle of a gig. Back when she was 22 and just out of college, she left Kansas and came to New York to be a Broadway star, not to wait on dick lawyers who only saw her as a paperwork receptacle. Apparently, she had a genuine talent. Even had a write-up in *The New York Times* back in 2009 about her cabaret act. I wouldn't know. I only found her after she lost her singing voice. But I was curious what she really sounded like when digging into some Cole Porter.

"That's great news, Jules."

"Yeah. Except I won't be able to talk for two weeks after surgery. At ALL."

"That's more great news, baby."

"Ha ha, douchebag." Another pause, then in a small voice. "Will you help take care of me?"

"Uh…yeah, nursing isn't really in my skill-set, but you can crash at my place if you want."

"I'll do that thing you like me to do with my vagina."

"So many great offers. This isn't a Groupon, is it?

"Fuck off."

"When are you seeing the doctor?"

"In two days. Wish me some fucking luck."

"You got it. Now wish me some fucking luck."

"You got it. Don't get killed."

"What? How the hell would that happen?"

"I don't know. It just popped in my head."

An uncomfortable pause.

Jesus. I had to remember – she was a witch.

We acted like nothing had happened and said our goodbyes, then I made it out to the rental with my Banana Republic bags, feeling like Don

Draper on his last televised road trip, and took off west for Kentucky. It would be an all-day drive, which left me too much time to think.

As Jan took me where I needed to go – Jan was the name I gave the helpfully-efficient female voice of my phone GPS - I couldn't help but feel like a shit for allowing myself to get all hot and bothered by the rich hotness of Angela Davidson. When she casually indicated a guy like me was in her wheelhouse, it made me a little weak in the knees and almost hard between the balls. I knew now that she was most likely just warming me up for the bribe and I let my dick do the thinking instead of my head, as men sometimes do.

I had to get better about this shit. Jules was going to need me and I should be there for her. It didn't feel good being alone out here and she seemed more and more like a good deal I shouldn't pass up. I was suddenly more than ready to put her in my will, if I ever was fortunate enough to have anything to leave anybody.

Maybe we *should* get a goddam dog.

Enough with the Romantic Adventures of Max Bowman and on to where I was driving to – the residence of Colonel Curtis Allen, somewhere near beautiful Booneville, Kentucky, which, I had discovered when I looked it up, was named for Daniel Boone, noted frontiersman who, legend had it, had a run in with a bear at the tender age of three. Or - wait – that was Davy Crockett, wasn't it? Which one had a coonskin cap? Maybe both of them? Didn't the same guy play both of them on TV in the sixties?

Did I mention history wasn't my strong suit?

Anyway, Colonel Allen had literally put himself out to pasture, retiring with his wife to a modest home out in the middle of endless farmland, where I had managed to find him three years ago at the behest of (I now knew) General Davidson. Back then, I didn't have to leave Roosevelt Island to find the guy, I just worked the internet, got a number and gave a call. He answered and my job was done. I just had to hand off his contact information to Howard and that was the end of it, I thought. Those were the days. Now I was headed to a town where, according to the last census, a staggering total of eighty-one people lived. I was pretty sure that added up to fewer bodies than were currently occupying the bottom floor of my apartment building.

Back then, when I did reach Colonel Allen on the phone, I recalled that he was polite but not all that friendly. I believe I even got the distinct impression he didn't want to be found - which is why, I guess, they had to hire the likes of me to undertake the hunt. This time around, I dug a little harder but didn't find out much more about him. He abruptly retired from the service seven years ago, a couple years after Robert Davidson's death (or not-death, depending on what you believed). He had been Robert's commanding officer, but he wasn't in Afghanistan when whatever happened happened - he was in the midst of transferring from Kabul back to a desk job in the States. It wasn't clear if he wanted out or they wanted him out.

Anyway, if he knew something, then he was worth the extra driving. And even if he didn't know anything, he was at least on the way to Missouri, which was my next stop. That's where my second potential lead was – Colonel Allen's commanding officer, General John Kraemer, who I already didn't like because his last name was a whole lot harder to spell than it needed to be.

Wednesday morning.

I had spent the night in Lexington to the north of Booneville. I had stopped there because I wanted to be sure I could find a motel where the rooms had doors on them. I woke up feeling sore and a little tense. I had talked myself into staying calm yesterday, now I had to reboot that dialogue, because I didn't know what would happen when I actually started talking to my first lead.

It took about an hour and a half to get down to the Colonel's neck of the woods. I passed through the towns of Richmond, Irvine and Waco and wondered if Kentucky stole all their town names from other states. Finally, I was on State Route 28, coming into Booneville, which looked pretty much as I expected it to look. A few scattered mobile homes, a lot of pick-ups, a Quick Mart and many, many more trees than people. The only thing that was unexpected was a huge ancient black-and-white photo of a major league baseball player that was hung on the outside of the courthouse. I didn't recognize the guy, but I assumed he must have hailed from these parts. Either that or there was a judge in there who was a huge fan and had a lot of clout.

I had spent a lot of quality time with Jan, my GPS voice, over the past few days and I was starting to think we had the makings of a beautiful friendship. I found her calm efficiency sexy as hell. I kept imagining her making erotic suggestions to me in bed with the same flat emotionless tones she used when telling me when to stay to the right so I could take the next exit. At one point, I got so into it, I considered pulling over and jerking off, but thought better of it. I kept worrying about seeing a state cop's face peering at me through the car window as I was just merging into Jan's lane and didn't think that would reflect well on me.

So it would remain platonic with Jan, who was telling me how to navigate Booneville at that moment. I was to take a right off the main highway, which I did, and, as I drove up the narrow but newly-paved road, I saw a clump of older, larger "classic" wood frame homes. Jan went on to tell me that my destination was two thousand feet ahead on the left. Did I detect disappointment in her cold commanding voice that I hadn't yet consummated our relationship?

As Angela Davidson would say, "Hmmmm."

I switched off my twisted imagination as I approached the clump of homes and refocused my brain back on business, wondering how I would broach the subject of Robert Davidson if it didn't come up. Then I wondered which home was the Colonel's, whether it was the big one in the middle or not.

And then all hell broke loose.

They say you experience these kinds of extreme moments in slow motion. And whoever "they" are, they seemed to be right. A second suddenly seemed like a minute, and all the moments that made up each one of those seconds stuck to my memory like stills shot by someone taking a burst of photos, one after the other after the other.

They flipped by in order like a slide show...

The big house in the middle erupting into a giant ghastly fireball.

The sky filling up with giant toothpicks, which I quickly realized were all that was left of the house.

A rusty metal mailbox with an American Eagle on it landing on the hood of my car with a huge thud, leaving an equally huge dent.

A black SUV smashing savagely into the passenger side of my car like a heat-seeking missile.

A grinning nasty face, a face way too happy considering what was going on, behind the wheel of the SUV ramming into me. And a face that was oddly familiar.

My car flying around from the impact until it came to a stop facing the opposite direction of the way it had originally been going.

My airbag deploying as everything went black, my last conscious thought being that the grinning horrible face looked exactly like that of…Chuck Connors.

Chuck Connors?

In the words of Jules Nelson, "FUCK WHAT FUCK FUCK FUCK?"

I woke up in the ambulance, which was tearing down the state road with its siren blaring. I moved my hands and feet to make sure everything was still in one piece.

The EMT guy was looking at me in confusion.

"Chuck Connors?"

"You saw him too?" I asked.

"No, I didn't see no Chuck Connors. You woke up and said Chuck Connors. Who is Chuck Connors?"

"The Rifleman," I muttered. Wasn't it obvious?

"The what?"

"Didn't you ever watch *The Rifleman* as a kid? Lucas McCain?"

"No offense, mister, but I weren't no kid when you were a kid."

I still felt the heat from the explosion. "What happened to that house?"

"Only word I got is they think it was some kind of gas leak. Shame, old army guy and his wife both got killed."

That woke me up.

"You was just in the wrong place at the wrong time. But how'd your car get so banged up?"

"Nobody got the guy?"

"What guy?"

"Chuck Conn…never mind. Nobody else was around when you pulled me out?"

"No sir."

"Chuck Connors?"

The local Booneville lawman was probably as old as me and sported a long grey moustache over his craggy face. His gut hung over his belt to such an extent that I was pretty sure he had even less fun shopping for pants than I did.

"Yeah," I said, "The guy whose SUV hit me looked exactly like Chuck Connors."

"*The Rifleman?*" he said in disbelief. Thank God I was with someone from my generation. "He's gotta be dead by now, huh?"

'Yeah," I said, sitting up on the examination table. I was a little banged up but nothing serious, according to the very young doctor that had checked me out earlier. I pushed back at Doogie Howser and declared that surely I had a concussion from the car crash or the blast, but Doogie said no, I must have fainted, no head injuries. I guess, emotionally, I just was a delicate flower after all. Now the doctor was gone and the sheriff wanted to talk to me.

"So you're telling me a guy who looked the Rifleman deliberately banged into the side of your car just as the house blew up."

"That's what it felt like."

"That don't make sense. Why would this man do such a thing? Especially in the middle of that horrible explosion. Most likely he was panicked and lost control. Most likely."

He nodded to himself. He solved everything in his head and that was good enough for Booneville.

"But he took off."

"Well, he was probably as scared as you were."

"Who says I was scared?"

"Doc said you fainted."

I was leaking manliness every second I stayed there. Especially since I was wearing this stupid paper patient gown from which my ass could instantly detect which direction the air conditioning was blasting from.

"What were you doing down here, anyway?"

"Was going to visit Colonel Allen."

"Good man. That was just a damn shame. Moved back here a few years ago after serving his country. His family was from around here originally, y'know. Gas Company's got some explaining to do."

He sat down and I think he farted. Maybe he was focusing too much on gas.

"Well," he went on, "Thanks for talking to me. Just wanted to see if you noticed anything unusual while you were driving up there. Besides Chuck Connors."

He shook his head and smiled. And remained seated there, like he was waiting for someone to build a Waffle House around him and bring over a cup of coffee.

"I wanted to get dressed?" I eyed my pile of clothing over on a small table.

He got the message and got flustered. "Oh. Oh! I am sorry, I'll get out of your hair, Mr. Bowman."

"Before you do," I said as he struggled to get up and I walked over to my stuff, "I'd like you to let me know if you find anything out about exactly what happened with the house."

"Or if I see Chuck? Hey, you know they still show a whole bunch of those episodes on one of the cable channels, on the weekend, I believe. He was a big guy, huh? You know he played pro baseball and basketball before Hollywood?"

I yanked out a card from my wallet and gave it to him. "Yeah, I did."

He read the card. "Lost and Found. Max Bowman." He looked up. "You some kind of detective? Like Jim Rockford?"

"Sort of. I used to be with the CIA."

All that fainting stuff washed away with that disclosure. Now he was looking at me like I was some sort of ancient Babylonian God.

He leaned in with a whisper. "They didn't blow up the house, did they?"

"No, sir, I don't believe so. Please hang on to the card though, okay? In case you find out something?"

He nodded solemnly. And stood there staring at the card for a few centuries.

"I still need to get dressed."

"Oh! Yes, yes, of course, have a good day, Mr. Bowman."

He was gone and in another minute or two, so was I.

Lockdown

I was awake.

If I had been asleep for the past dozen years, well, the extended nap was over. My eyes were wide open and my brain was on fire. That's because the house blowing up and Chuck Connors ramming me from the side a few hours ago were far from the scariest parts of what was going on.

What was truly terrifying was realizing how closely someone had to be monitoring me for those two things to happen at the exact moment I arrived there.

Whoever was behind this obviously had to know where I was going the whole time. But that was something I hadn't told anyone, not Howard, not Angela, not the General, nobody. True, Jules had texted me the addresses out of my computer, but she didn't strike me as the "traitor within" type. Besides, again, whoever was tracking me had to have known *exactly what time* I would show up there. I don't think Chuck Connors was sitting there for days on end with his motor idling.

So how would someone know all those little details?

There were three ways and they all related back to Mr. Barry Filer. Which meant I had to destroy those three ways and do it quick.

First, the burner phone he gave me to call him. It probably had tracking spyware built into it so my location was always an open secret, even when I turned it off at night. That's how good that shit was these days. So, when the rental company delivered my newest replacement vehicle to me in Booneville, I placed the burner behind the back left tire of the car and backed up over it. Then I ran the car forward over it and then backed up over it one more time. I put the contents in a Ziploc bag, sealed it up and threw it in a dumpster outside the Quick Mart.

The second thing giving away my movements was my new and beloved endless benefactor, the credit card. It, of course, created an instant paper trail of where I had been and what I had been doing there. I drove north back to Lexington, where I stopped at the first big national bank branch that I could find, CitiChase Wells Fargo Bank of America. I parked, went in and withdrew as much cash as the card would allow. That turned out to be two grand. Then I left the bank, ripped my beloved new credit card in two, wiped a couple of tears and threw it into a sewer grating outside the bank.

Call it a shitty Viking Funeral.

The third and final thing was the flash drive. I called Jules at the office where, by this time, it was close to quitting time for her.

"It's me," I said.

"OHMIGODOHMIGODOHMIGOD!"

Pause on my end.

"It's still me."

"GET EXCITED, BOZO!"

"I think I'm excited enough after what I've been through."

"No, no, no, moron! Tuesday after next! There was an opening! I scheduled the surgery!"

Pause on my end.

"Is that okay?" she finally asked. "Please tell me it's okay, please, please, please."

"Well, I hope it is."

Pause on her end.

"HOPE??? Oh, FUCK me in the ass if we're down to hope!!!"

"We don't do anal, remember? Look, I need you to do something important for me and no, it doesn't mean you get a third nice dinner."

"Talk about a preemptive strike."

"You need to go to my apartment after you get off…"

"And how do I get off without you here?"

"You go to my place, you go into my office, you unplug the desktop computer and you pull out the flash drive that's sticking out of the front."

"Sounds real exciting so far."

"Then you take that flash drive and you physically destroy it. Use the hammer I have in that drawer in the kitchen, whatever, smash the thing…"

"I'll pretend it's your penis…"

"Then go out and throw the pieces in the East River."

"You know it's not a river."

Oh, here we go again.

"It's a saltwater tidal strait, everybody who ever made a map should be fucking ashamed of themselves, just watch the way the water moves, the way the direction completely CHANGES day-to-day, in no way, shape or form is THAT fucking slice of shit-ridden water…"

"Jules…I've heard this before and I don't have time to hear it again."

Pause on her end.

"Is it really this bad?"

"I gotta go – just promise me you'll take care of this."

"I take care of everything, cowboy."

"I know."

I said a fond goodbye and hung up.

The flash drive - that's what really got me. Boy, had I been a stupid son of a bitch. A whole flash drive with only one itsy-bitsy document on it, what did I think that was all about? No doubt it also contained more hidden spyware, which, when I shoved it into my USB slot, installed itself into my home computer and transmitted everything that I did with the PC over the internet back to whoever was watching me. Which meant they could see the document Jules had opened at my behest and see which two addresses I was planning to visit. By this point, they had also probably copied every single file on my desktop, not that there was anything all that exciting on it. It may have been like closing the barn after the horses got out, but I wanted the thing out of my computer because I didn't want to take any more chances. It was obvious I didn't have a real big margin for error moving forward. As a matter of fact, I needed to lower the odds against me and that would require some heavy-duty help.

With my new rental car, my third so far on this trip, I drove around the city until I found what very well could have been the last remaining pay phone in Lexington – outside a dilapidated 7-11. I used it to make a collect call to Howard's office on his direct line.

"Yeah?"

Thank Christ he was there.

"Howard. Me."

"A collect call? You can still make those? Where are you?"

"Are we on a secure line?"

"You're asking *me*? Remember where I work? I'm always on a secure line. What's going on?"

"A lot."

I didn't want to tell him about the explosion. With any luck, nobody knew about it yet, since Booneville wasn't exactly at the center of the media universe.

"Such as?"

"I don't want to say too much, but I need a big favor. Remember what we did for Jerry Mendelsohn back in 2002 or so?"

"Yeah."

"I need that done for me. Like yesterday."

A pause.

"Jesus, that's a big ask. I don't know. You're not…"

"Howard, this is serious in ways you can't imagine."

He sighed.

"Let me see what I can do."

"I need it in the morning."

"Jawohl, mein fuhrer. I'll send a courier."

"Perfect. Tell him to meet me…"

I looked down the street. I saw a familiar yellow and red sign.

"…at the Denny's on East High Street – Lexington, Kentucky. I don't know the address, but there's probably just one. Nine a.m. tomorrow. Can your courier make that?"

"Yeah. He'll make it."

"Nothing to anybody about talking to me or where I am. The courier shouldn't even know my name."

"What the hell is this about?"

"As usual, I wish I knew. But you have to do one more thing for me."

"Okayyyyy…" The "y" trailed down to the lowest possible note on Howard's scale. That meant he was worried about how deep *he* was getting into my shit.

"I'm not fucking around, Howard. You know me. I don't hit the panic button often."

"All right, all right, just tell me."

I told him.

When I was done, I went to a nearby CVS and bought a small pad of paper and a pen, along with a bottle of Coke Zero. I wrote down all the numbers that I might need that were stored in my iPhone, then I did to it what I had done to Mr. Barry Filer's burner, just in case they were somehow tracking my personal phone too. Losing that iPhone hurt worse than losing the credit card. I had three Words with Friends games going with Jules that would never get finished.

Oh well. That bitch always won anyway.

I returned the rental and took a cab to an Embassy Quality Express Whatever Suites near the Denny's I would be visiting tomorrow morning. I checked in with cash and a phony name. I unlocked the door to the room, entered with my Banana Republic shopping bags, sat down on the bed and exhaled. It had been a long day filled with unwelcome surprises, including the deaths of two people I never even got to meet. But it was just about over. The sun was going down and I had done everything I could do before the courier arrived tomorrow morning. Since my body was still aching from the crash, I took a few of the pain pills the doctor in Booneville had prescribed to me, washed them down with some Jack, laid down on the queen bed and watched half of a bad movie on HBO before I finally fell asleep.

Thursday morning.

I woke up at seven-thirty, shocked that it was that late and I had slept that long. I hadn't even had dinner. Clearly, my body was screaming for sleep and the pain pills had helped me get it. Now I had to get it together so I could get down to the Denny's well before the courier did at nine a.m. I pissed, showered, shaved, got dressed and went out the door.

The Denny's wasn't all that crowded when I arrived, so it was easy to get a booth with a good view of the door. I had to be ready for whoever walked through it, since there was always the chance Howard was a part of the problem, in which case it would be somebody a lot more hostile than a courier. I hated to think like that, but I had to. Of course, if they were sending some kind of assassin after me, I wouldn't be able to do much about it, since I was neither armed nor dangerous. But if I could see him coming, I would at least buy me a few moments to make a run for it. And I'd know where to run. I had checked out where the back door was.

I checked my nice new silver watch. It was only eight-twenty and I was starving, so I quickly got my order in and the waitress hustled back with my Coke Zero to kick things off.

I'm not a coffee person, maybe because my mother was a full-on addict. When I was a kid, I would find her half-finished cups of java all over the house. She would forget she was working on one cup and immediately pour another, just like a nicotine freak who lights one cigarette before the one he's smoking burns all the way down. Because of this, everything in our house smelled like stale coffee. When you made a call on our old-fashioned rotary phone, you got a contact high from the fumes left behind on the mouthpiece.

Anyway, that had been the least of her problems and, for that matter, mine.

My body still hurt like a son of a bitch from the shock of the crash. I was wishing I had taken another one or two of the magic pills when I woke up, but I couldn't chance being groggy with all that was happening. I plowed through my eggs and pancakes in about five minutes flat and waited. I remembered this was what people had to do before smartphones, just sit. And sit. And sit. All I could do was scope out the locals at the other tables and wonder what the hell was next for me.

Nine a.m. finally rolled around and the cavalry was nowhere in sight. General Davidson and John Wayne would not have approved. I tensed up. More and more I was sweating over who was coming to greet me, because I was growing increasingly worried about Howard's role in all this. He was acting very un-Howard-like, and if he wasn't on my side anymore, the ground would give beneath me very quickly. I just had to keep reminding myself that I had been deliberately kept alive so far for some reason. Hopefully, that would continue to be the official policy of Whatever-the-Fuck-This-Was-About Incorporated.

It took two more Coke Zeros and another half-hour before I saw the courier come in through the door. And holy shit - this was one scenario I definitely had not considered. He was an assassin, all right. But he didn't kill humans.

No, this little bastard killed tires.

I saw him before he saw me, and it was a good thing, otherwise I think he would have spun around and run all the way back home. I stood up, walked over, took Jeremy Davidson by the arm and marched him out of the Denny's. He looked at me, realized who I was and turned white. Good sign. That meant he had no idea he was meeting me either and he was just fulfilling a random assignment.

I led him around the corner of the Denny's to a side street with nothing much on it, except some vacant lots and a fire hydrant. We got about a block down that street, when I stopped and turned to him. We stared at each other a moment. He was too scared to say a word, so I frowned and grabbed the sealed, stuffed package that he was carrying under his arm. I began to tear it apart as he looked on.

"So – you're CIA now?" I said by way of making conversation.

"Summer job," he said breathlessly.

"Family connections, I take it?"

He looked away sheepishly. Meanwhile, I got the package open and inside was what I wanted to find. My new name was David Muhlfelder and I had the driver's license, passport, and credit card to prove it. There was also a new phone with encryption software included and another thousand dollars in cash. Thanks, Howard. I stuffed it all in my jacket pocket and threw the packaging in the trash. The kid was still standing there in his overpriced jeans and t-shirt, looking unsure of what to do.

"You can go," I said peremptorily.

He stood his ground, as they say in Florida after they shoot somebody they shouldn't have.

"Can I ask you something?"

I nodded.

"Are you out here to do the thing for my grandfather?" he asked tentatively.

I was a little surprised. He wanted to talk. Rare in the Davidson clan. And what he had to say could be important. This was an opportunity. Or as the Help Wanted ad in the Burger King window once said, a whopper-tunity.

"You eat breakfast yet?" I asked.

He ordered a Grand Slam and I ordered another. I felt entitled, since I still had a meal to make up for from last night. After the same waitress I had had before gave me some shit about my cholesterol, she left and Jeremy was again completely at a loss. He didn't seem to know what to do with himself, let alone me. But I knew. I wanted him to take the first turn of whatever conversational game we were going to play, so I waited. I was getting good at waiting. It's an art. You have to be like a Buddha, all-knowing and unmoving, my favorite position to assume, even though I was completely unqualified for it.

Finally, he turned to me.

"I'm sorry about the tires. It's just…my mom was upset. She didn't want you to do what you were doing."

"So she told you to come after me."

"No. I just went on my own."

That was a surprise. I guessed Angela was just protecting him by taking responsibility. Turned out she was a real mother and not just the kind of mother I had previously thought she was - the kind of mother that's half a word, as Sammy Davis Jr. used to say.

The waitress brought him a coffee and me my zillionth Coke Zero of the morning. I was starting to get that weird feeling I get after drinking too much of it, like bugs were dancing in my brain.

The kid kept on talking.

"I was studying some CIA tracking techniques and thought I'd try them. Maybe I could stop you without anybody knowing. Maybe my mom could relax about you making some kind of problem at least."

"She's been nervous lately?"

"Real nervous about Grandpa. He's had a bunch of small strokes."

I sized the kid up. "That was pretty ballsy, coming after me like that and not knowing anything about me."

"It's PMA," he blurted out.

?

"PMA," I repeated.

He continued to blurt, because he was nervous. "It's a discipline taught by this guy, this guy who was the Ultimate Fighting Champion, Andre Gibraltar, you probably heard of him. PMA is what he says he uses in fights and in life, to make things happen the way he wants them to happen. The 'P' stands for 'Power.' You have a powerful idea you want to accomplish, right? That's where it starts. Then you move into the 'M,' that stands for 'Mind.' You have to mentally have the will to put that power into action, everybody has ideas, not everybody has the will to go to the next step, and the next step is the 'A,' which stands for 'Action.' When you have the will in place, you translate that will into action and make things happen."

Oh sweet, sweet Jesus.

"You spend a lot of time by yourself, don't you?"

"I really want to join the CIA," he said too quickly. "If I put PMA to work in my life, I'm pretty sure I can become a great agent."

"Aren't you still in school?"

"Just got out of high school. Well, I graduate in June, but I got all my credits done last semester. I'm supposed to start college in the fall, but…"

He stopped. Then he began to study me with a little too much intensity.

"Is there egg on my face?" I asked.

"No, I just…you look kinda pale. I was wondering if you were okay."

"I've never had so many people concerned about my health."

"Sorry." He looked down, a little embarrassed, and not just about asking about my skin tone. I think he surmised that I was skeptical of the whole PMA thing.

"So you know your grandfather hired me."

He looked back up. "Um…yeah."

"You know why he hired me?"

"Um…yeah. My uncle, right?"

I sipped my Coke Zero. I was about to try and cross the Rubicon if this kid would hand me a paddle to help me do it.

"What do you think about it?"

"My uncle? Well…I don't know. He was always a little out there. I mean, I only saw him a couple of times when I was a kid. I was pretty young when he died, nine or ten maybe."

"What was he like?"

"He was really…I don't know…intense? Kinda…angry?"

"About what?"

"I don't know. He and Grandpa used to yell at each other about war stuff. Something about what my uncle was doing over in Afghanistan. I don't remember much. I do remember this one time, because it was really weird, when he came over with this guy…and Grandpa called the guy his 'girlfriend.'"

"What was this guy's name?"

"His first name was Herman. I remember that because I never met anybody named Herman before."

"I still haven't. What about Herman's last name?"

He shook his head and shrugged. "My grandpa acted like he knew him, but I don't know how."

"So you think your uncle was gay?"

Jeremy shrugged again, but no head shake this time. "I don't know. I didn't really understand what gay was back then."

Interesting. The first personal information I had about Robert Davidson was the fact that he had a girlfriend named Herman.

Meanwhile, Jeremy was starting to seem like a smart and earnest boy. I didn't really appreciate earnest as much as some others, but in this case, it seemed to fit. The PMA stuff was a phase, a way for him to try to become a man, which made me think the father wasn't much in the picture. I had to wonder - why was he telling me all this, when the rest of his family wouldn't?

"Are you with the CIA?" he asked.

"I used to be. Now they just hire me for jobs like this."

His eyes lit up. "You carry a gun?"

"It's been a couple of decades since I even fired one. Kid, the truth is I was a desk jockey the whole time at the Agency. They liked me for my brain, which was all I had to offer. I don't do Kung Fu and if I jumped through a window firing guns in both hands like they do in the movies, I'd probably end up falling on my face and accidentally shooting myself in the balls. So don't get it in your head that I'm any kind of superspy."

"I practice Kung Fu. Not Kung Fu strictly speaking, but MAU. Martial Arts Ultimate."

"Three letters again. Must be Andre's idea."

"Yeah, it puts together the best parts of Taekwon-Do, Danzan Ryū and Shootfighting."

That sounded painful. Our food came, which was a good thing, because it was time to get back to business.

"So why does your grandfather think your uncle is still alive?" I said casually as I poured syrup over my new set of pancakes.

"No idea."

"Where's your dad, if you don't mind?"

"He lives in Chicago."

That's all he said and I didn't go further. It was probably another long story I didn't want to deal with right now. I sent my fork in after the cakes, mentally assembling my next line of questioning. But then he changed the subject before I did.

"I…I really want to go with you."

My fork stopped in mid-air. I looked back at the kid. He was serious.

"I mean, before, I know….well, I know I tried to stop you, but…but things happen for a reason. Now I think I got sent to meet you on purpose. Maybe we should work together to find out the truth. It'll be good for Grandpa and maybe Mom too. And I think I can learn stuff from you."

"Your name's Jeremy, right?" He nodded. "Well, Jeremy, here's the thing. The reason I'm pale and sore today is because yesterday a black

SUV rammed me from the side while a few hundred feet away from me a house was in the process of blowing to smithereens. One smithereen even landed on my car hood."

His eyes widened.

"So I don't know what I'm in for here. I do know if I get you killed, many people would be angry at me – including me."

He ate a little, trying to come up with a response and finally found one. "But it wouldn't be like it was your fault or anything, it would be my choice, not yours – so my fault if anything did happen."

"That's not how everyone else would see it. Believe me, I've taken enough blame in my life."

"I just want my grandpa to be proud of me. He needs somebody to be proud of."

"So – join the Army. Wouldn't he want that more than anything?"

"I don't want to kill anybody, that's why I thought the CIA was good for me."

I laughed. "You don't think the CIA kills people?"

He shrugged. He was embarrassed again and I could see he felt stupid. I was a dick.

But at least now I knew why I liked the kid.

He was like me – he lacked the killer instinct. It was why my father didn't go far at the Agency and why I ultimately opted out. You either were okay with killing people – as a matter of fact, you saw it as the path to progress – or you couldn't get past the part where someone had to die for your ambitions, whether they be personal or political. Once someone at the Agency saw that sentimental streak in you, you wouldn't ever have a shot at rising to the upper echelon. Because they really didn't believe you belonged there at all.

"Okay, okay, kid, I know what you're saying, but…no. The other thing is, I'm going to be gone a while. You should get back to your job and your mom."

"That wouldn't be a big deal, I could just tell my supervisor I was helping you. And I could tell my mom they gave me a job that would keep me out of town for a while, she wouldn't know I was with you or anything."

I chewed my pancakes. He wouldn't stop and he still wasn't done. I was seeing PMA in action.

"I know what my uncle looks like. And I can talk to him, if he's still alive. He can't just blow me off, I'm family, right? I'm an asset here."

An asset? The kid was sharp. He made sense, but this was still ridiculous. The PMA inside him, however, wouldn't let up.

"And, look, I can tell you don't feel very good, you said so yourself. You're banged up and you could probably need some help, right? Just with running errands or something, getting food, whatever, I'm up for it."

Oh shit, I was starting to listen to him. What was next, a PowerPoint presentation to demonstrate through pie charts and animated graphs the enormous advantages of bringing Jeremy Davidson along for the ride? I wouldn't have been surprised the way he kept staring at me, trying to mentally will a positive ending to his proposal. PMA was winning the day.

"Look, kid, let's just finish the food. After we eat, we'll go back to my room."

He gave me a funny look.

"Don't worry, I'm not a pedophile."

A weird little smile crossed his face.

"Well, technically, I'm 18, so I'm legal."

We caught each other's eyes. He had a twinkle in his, so I laughed a little as I shoved the cakes in my mouth.

Inside my room, I packed up my Banana Republic shopping bags while he watched.

"So – I'm going with you, right?" he asked impatiently.

I finished up and looked over at him. I had just postponed the inevitable because I couldn't bring myself to say no. But now, I had to.

"Jeremy, it's not going to fly. There's no way I can justify bringing an inexperienced eighteen-year-old kid along on this trip. And don't be offended by the inexperienced part, hell, I'm too inexperienced to be doing this."

The kid suddenly turned angry. His eyes were set and looked just as scary as his grandfather's. This was the side of him that packed a box cutter, the side he fed with his PMA.

"If you say no, then I'll follow you again. I'll...I'll slash your tires again."

Whoa.

I half-smiled. "Really? You probably just took a cab to the Denny's from the airport, if I'm not mistaken. You gonna have the cabbie tail me across state lines? Or are you going to Uber my ass?"

"Well, you told me you have to get a new car. I'll get one too. And I'll follow you."

I used to have a terrier who weighed twenty-five pounds. When she planted all four paws on the ground, you couldn't move her with a hundred-foot-tall construction crane. This kid was reminding me of that dog. He was quiet in his resistance, not hysterical, but that made it all the more powerful.

"Look, PMA," I had decided right then and there that PMA was his new nickname. "All I have to do is call your mom...."

"You can't stop me. And she can't stop me," he said simply enough.

"What the hell are you trying to prove?"

"Nothing. This is just about my family."

"Family has its downside, you know. Trust me on that. You can end up realizing it's just a prison you have to break out of."

He got quiet again. I didn't want him to feel bad.

"Hey, I get it. You're fond of the old guy."

He nodded and shrugged at the same time. He shrugged a lot when, at the same time, he was agreeing or disagreeing with something. I suppose there was nothing teenagers loved better than to appear noncommittal about things they cared about the most.

"I am fond of him," he said. "He hasn't been happy. And he's been sick. I want to do something for him."

I walked up to him and stopped a couple inches from his face. I knew he and his PMA weren't kidding about following me. Maybe I could shake him on the road, but maybe I couldn't. And I really didn't want to be worried about what the circumstances would be when he might show up again. Maybe it was better to control the situation. I didn't know. My head was killing me and I knew I should take some more of those Jesus-sent pain pills. But that would mean I couldn't drive. The interstate isn't a good place to go ninety mph when you see three of everything. But he could drive for me. I'd get some rest and some strength back.

I was too weak. The PMA of it all overpowered me.

"Take out your phone."

He took out the phone.

I told him to text his mother and tell her that Langley was keeping him busy for a few days out in the field, like he suggested. Text her that he wouldn't be able to call, but he was okay, she shouldn't worry.

And after I told him all that, I saw the fire light up in his eyes.

He was going with me – and he knew it.

Branson

After PMA texted his mom, I also had him call his supervisor at the CIA and tell him I needed him for a few days. Not that the supervisor knew who I was, but you don't get to know everything when you work at the CIA, especially when you're only in charge of the couriers. After the kid made the call, I took his phone from him and told him he'd get it back when we split up again. Again, I was taking no chances.

We took a cab to another rental car place, where I'd be getting my fourth vehicle of the trip with my new phony David Muhlfelder credit card. In the cab, I told PMA how Mr. Barry Filer's flash drive had given away the addresses of the two people I wanted to meet up with and he instantly understood the problem.

"They're going to know we're coming."

PMA was right on the money, but it wasn't fun hearing it said out loud.

I tried to reassure him and probably myself. I told him about how I had asked Howard on the pay phone to act as the middleman with General John Kraemer, who had been the late Colonel Allen's commanding officer in Afghanistan and the second lead I had planned on talking to. Of course, with Colonel Allen's sudden demise, the General had now advanced to the first position, lucky him. Kraemer was also retired and lived on the outskirts of Springfield, Missouri. As I wanted to avoid seeing another old soldier blown sky-high, I asked Howard to contact him and set up a meeting with me some distance away from his home and in a very public location. Time and place could be the General's call and I wanted to do it Friday if possible. That would be tomorrow.

I also told PMA he was going to have to drive today.

"How do I know where to go?"

"Jan will tell you."

"Who's Jan?"

"My sexy GPS dominatrix."

I was surprised that explanation didn't prompt a few more questions from him.

When we got to the rental place, both my new phony-name credit card and my new phony-name driver's license worked like gangbusters and I rented a full-sized coupe. Soon the Banana Republic bags were in the coupe's trunk and PMA was behind the wheel. I relieved to just be riding shotgun, as I was goofy on pain pills. It would be another all-day drive today as we headed west toward beautiful Springfield, Missouri.

As the kid took the wheel, I made the other call I needed to take care of before I lost the cell phone signal out in the boonies on the interstate.

"Who?" Jules said on the phone.

"David Muhlfelder. I was referred to by a friend."

Pause.

"Quit fucking with me, will ya? I need this like I need another twat."

"I assure you, I'm not…"

"What phone number are you calling from? It's not…"

"I'm David Muhlfelder and I have an important case to discuss with your firm."

Jules sighed wearily.

"If things are this weird, I'm seriously going to swallow eight Xanax tonight and take a Whitney Houston bath."

"I'll call some other time."

"No, no, no, NO, I am sorry, SIR…I must have mistaken you for someone else I used to know."

"Well, before we go any further, I need a firm that excels at cyber security."

"Oh my goodness," she said. "That is SO us! For example, there was a situation yesterday with a flash drive that infects computers? I smashed that sucker under my heel and shut off the computer in question immediately. Then I threw the pieces into a nearby saltwater tidal strait!"

"I see. That's the kind of attitude I'm looking for. I'm going to be out of town for another week or so…then I'll call back and set up an appointment with you."

"A WEEK? YOU BETTER BE FUCKING BACK FOR MY OPERATION!"

And she had been doing so well up until then.

"I'm not sure what you're referring to, but I will be arriving in New York in a week."

"Wait…what was the name again?"

"David Muhlfelder. M-U-H-L…"

"…Felder, got it. And the number?"

"I'll be in touch."

I hung up. I swear, even though we were disconnected, I could still hear her screaming at David Muhlfelder with everything she had - even though there were four states between us.

Luckily, pain pills take the edge off of those kinds of disagreements, so I found the button that made my seat recline and got ready to take a nice little nap. But then my new CIA-gifted phone buzzed due to a text coming in from Howard. General Kraemer had decided our meet-up would be at 3552 West 76 Country Boulevard, Branson, Missouri – at eleven a.m. tomorrow morning.

Branson? Really?

Well, I asked for a public location and, in the Springfield area, you couldn't get much more public than Branson. I viewed the town as the brain-damaged cousin of Las Vegas, a country-fried strip of corny tourist attractions including a Haunted House, a Dinosaur Museum and a Hollywood Wax Museum. But the real attraction in Branson was the old-timey-by-design theatres owned by entertainers who had long ago diminished into vague memories elsewhere in America. People like Andy "Moon River" Williams, Tony "Tie a Yellow Ribbon" Orlando and Yakov "In Russia, party comes to you" Smirnoff, among many others, had all owned venues here, because Branson was where entertainment went to die – and sometimes even death didn't get in the way of ticket sales. Williams, for example, had been gone for at least three years, but his theatre still had an ongoing tribute act in heavy rotation. Which I could not believe. I mean, how the hell many Andy Williams fans were left? I barely remembered the guy at this point and, as people kept telling me, I was pretty old. I just remembered he had had a variety show in the sixties that featured a guy in a bear suit. Hollywood was brilliant sometimes.

I had driven through Branson exactly once many years before on a family trip, back when I had a family, just to see what all the hype was all about. I'm still wondering. The tourist area, as I recalled, was start-to-finish ugly and tacky with all of its attractions on either side of the same aging two-lane state road. Traffic in and out of the area was bumper-to-bumper, forcing drivers to crawl past such high-profile attractions as Hannah's Maze of Mirrors and the Celebrity Car Museum. We didn't stop in Branson then.

Tomorrow, I would have to.

As PMA quietly drove us onward on the interstate, I drifted in and out of sleep, my mind replaying the exploding house and the SUV slamming my car over and over, as if they were YouTube clips on an endless playlist loop. Haunting those images was a ghostly overlay of the face of the guy who looked like Chuck Connors, grinning his nasty grin, his sadistic eyes dancing with pleasure.

It didn't make for a restful drive. Especially since I didn't know if I if I was heading straight into another nightmare – and dragging an 18-year-old kid with me.

Why I was even continuing on with this job? It was obvious that Mr. Barry Filer had set me up for trouble, so who knew if the second half of my fee would even be forthcoming? And who exactly was Filer working for? The General farmed this out to somebody who had hired Mr. Barry Filer to employ me. It must have been someone the General trusted, and clearly, that trust was misplaced. Whoever he was, he didn't want the truth to come out – and was sabotaging my efforts in the most violent and intimidating ways possible.

And, oh yeah, he was also murdering people.

I tried to sleep some more while Jeremy fiddled with the satellite radio. He favored music that was a little more recent than *Hooray for Hazel* - from groups with names like Vampire Weekend, Cage the Elephant and some group that decided to spell "Churches" with a "V" instead of a "U." Yeah, band names were stupid when I was a kid – anybody remember the Human Beinz? - but at least they were pronounceable.

As we approached Springfield, we hit another big box store plaza, where we bought some more clothes and shit like toothpaste and a razor for PMA. As a bonus, we now had more shopping bags to use for luggage. At the same exit was a reasonable Ramada Radisson Wyndham Omni Whatever Hotel where we had no trouble getting a room - two queen beds and a little fridge. Perfect.

I stuck to room service for our dinner as I didn't want us to be too visible. But, as I had also procured another bottle of Jack at the plaza, we could still enjoy a few drinks. Missouri was an interesting state. It not only had the most bible colleges of any state in the country, it also had the most permissive liquor laws.

PMA never had Jack before and I thought the first slug might kill him. After he was through coughing, I threw in a little water and some more ice into his glass, and it went down a whole easier.

We talked a little after we ate. And drank a little more. The kid obviously needed to unwind and this was helping. I took a chance and asked about his father.

Turned out PMA's father was an artist of sorts. Angela rebelled against the military purity of her family and ran off to marry him in Vegas a couple years after she graduated college with a bullshit degree. It was the kind of relationship where romance soon gave way to reality and she suddenly realized she hadn't married an artist, she had married someone who *said* he was an artist – which is, unfortunately, very different. He could paint some okay shit, but nobody was going to line up and pay money for it. So he taught some art classes for spare change, but that hardly held up his end of the checkbook.

Angela stuck with the marriage for about ten years, mostly because PMA was in the picture, and only kicked the guy's ass out after she caught him using a young female student's naked body for a canvas. As PMA described it, Pops was painting a bowl of fruit right under the student's breasts. He then had the genius to incorporate said breasts into the artwork by transforming them into succulent, 3D apples that that perched perkily on top of the painted bananas in the painted bowl.

In other words, the guy was a fruitcake.

A.J. Longetti — the kid still shared the last name - tried to claim it was an artistic experiment. Maybe it was, but then Angela spied paint smeared on his dick - paint that was the exact same color as the base of the fruit bowl. General Davidson happily financed the divorce and her lawyer made sure the degenerate Dali didn't get a dime.

Angela moved on and married some snarky Wall Street guy who made millions in his thirties and retired young. She thought a self-made millionaire wouldn't need to use her, but she forgot about the biggest asset she brought to the party — her father. Turned out he wanted to run for political office with Angela's last name in his back pocket. Angela just wanted to run, and did so a little over a year ago.

The guy never gave PMA the time of day. He just wanted the kid to shut up and stay in his room, which he gladly did.

That's when Angela officially gave up on men, took the boy and moved back in with the General. She didn't know where else to go and besides, her father needed her. Her mother had passed away from pancreatic cancer a couple years back and the General was more than a little lost without his wife of fifty-two years to run the house for him. Angela was more lost than he was, so it turned out they both needed each other. Then the strokes began hitting the General and suddenly, the house became an even darker place than it was before Angela moved in.

As PMA told me all this unfortunate history, I thought about the father figures he'd been dealt over his eighteen years of existence. A broke "artist" for a father. A conniving rich prick for a stepfather. And an intimidating legend for a grandfather.

No wonder he was so into Andre Gibraltar and whatever guides to life the muscle-bound guru churned out.

We were both getting blotto on the booze by this point, which is why I guess the kid got up the guts to ask me some questions, as the Mets quietly lost on the hotel room TV.

"Y'got kids?"

I nodded. "Two girls. They don't talk to me."

"How come?"

"Uh...I broke up the marriage and they blamed me. That kind of shit."

That was only half-true, but I didn't want to get into it. It was still too soon and I didn't know where PMA and I would end up.

"Marriages break up. I'd still talk to my dad. If he wasn't a fucking ASSHOLE."

He drained his glass, then he stared off into space. I stared at the TV. The Mets were done, so I grabbed the remote and started going up and down the channels.

"WHOA STOP!"

PMA found a channel he liked and I quickly saw why. It was some kind of infomercial featuring Andre Gibraltar himself, in all his overblown vein-popping muscled glory, touting his MAU instructional videos.

"You know," I said, "This guy's probably an asshole too."

"Sometimes, ya gotta be an asshole," the kid mumbled.

"Who taught you that?"

"Nobody had to. You just watch things. That's all."

"Something tells me you're not good at being an asshole."

"Gotta learn how. Gotta learn how to DOMINATE."

I put my empty glass down and my head back on the pillow of my bed. Pain pills were happily swimming through my bloodstream and I was ready to join them for a pool party.

"Kid, it ain't like that," I mumbled.

The last words I heard before everything went to black were from this hulking brute of a man who was screaming from the television, "DO YOU WANT TO DOMINATE IN LIFE? DO YOU WANT TO

PROTECT YOURSELF AND THOSE YOU LOVE? DO YOU WANT TO BE THE ULTIMATE LIKE ME?"

"The ultimate." I heard the kid murmur to himself. "The ultimate."

The ultimate what? That was what I wondered as I dozed off.

Friday morning.

I woke up with a start after a nightmare in which Chuck Connors was strangling me – he had giant gnarled hands that seemed to have the power of steel gloves. It was as vivid as dream shit gets and I woke up feeling like I couldn't breathe.

Bad sign.

It was light outside and PMA was already up. He was naked and practicing his Martial Arts Ultimate moves by the window. From what I could see, he hadn't quite achieved the Ultimate, he was only getting close to the Passable. But I'd keep that to myself.

I really had to take a piss. At my age, you get up once or twice a night because your prostate says you will, but, due to the pain pills, I had slept all the way through to morning. I hurried past PMA, right in the middle of a flying kick, and broke his concentration. I heard him hit the floor with a yelp as I closed the bathroom door behind me.

After I took care of business, I eyed myself in the bathroom mirror. Was I still pale? Hard to tell. Most people looked pale in a hotel bathroom. I moved my arms a little. My body wasn't as sore, but I noticed some bruises from the SUV had appeared in various places on my torso. I suddenly felt cold and began shivering, still asking myself why I was going on with this job. But something else told me that if I gave up on it, that would mean I was giving up on everything. Now I was awake and I wanted to stay awake. Like Captain Willard in *Apocalypse Now*, I needed a mission and for my sins, they gave me one.

If I stopped now, I didn't know what I would be anymore.

When I stopped shivering, I came out of the bathroom. PMA was still moaning in pain on the floor.

"You okay?"

"Yeah. I just messed up the kick. Fell right on my tailbone."

He got to his feet to prove he was all right, with his dick swinging between his legs like an upside-down metronome. I told him I was going to order breakfast, so maybe he should put on some pants in the near future.

It would be about an hour to get to Branson, so we got in the car at around nine-fifty.

"What's our plan?" PMA asked as he started up the car.

"My plan," I said with a heavy emphasis on the "my," "is you leave me off a few addresses before the one I'm going to. I walk the rest of the way to the place and go in solo. You drive past, do a U-turn down the road a little, then come back and pull into the parking lot, where you keep the motor running until I come back out again. That means we should fill up the tank on the way in."

"What? Why are we doing all that? So I don't look like I'm with you?"

"Exactly. It's going to be hot today, so keep the air running in the car. When I'm done, I'll come find you."

Pause.

"What if you don't come?"

"Don't get melodramatic."

Of course, that's all he wanted to get. I wasn't the only guy in the car who needed a mission.

We arrived in Branson an hour later, only stopping for gas, and then we hit the horrendous traffic I had remembered from years gone by. We crawled down the road for a few minutes until I decided we were close enough. I told PMA to pull over and let me out and he did.

It was the first of May and the sun was celebrating by broiling the asphalt under my feet. The kid had left me out in front of what was billed as the World's Largest Toy Museum. I briefly wondered if the museum itself was the part that was the largest or were the toys themselves ten times normal size? Was there a Barbie the size of a Buick in there? A Frisbee you could bathe in? A big-screen 60-inch Etch-A-Sketch? These were the kinds of moronic thoughts I was distracting myself with as I continued walking towards the address and starting to sweat under the still-low morning sun.

After passing an elevated wooden Go-Kart track and a Hillbilly Diner, it seemed like the next building would be the one I was looking for. It was, in my opinion, a strange choice on General Kraemer's part. The huge sign that towered above the highway read "Willie Wilson's Wild West Theatre," and the building beneath it resembled a super-sized, Disney-ized old Western saloon.

I remembered that Willie Wilson was a country singer whose biggest hit had been "Alamo Jack," back in 1962 – it had crossed over on the pop charts, which is the only reason I knew it. The song was a ballad with a relentless Johnny Cash guitar lick underneath it about a Texan who was at the Alamo, but took some time to ride out to say goodbye to his sweetheart who was elsewhere. As I recall, the chorus of the song was the sweetheart's plaintive cry…

"Alamo Jack, don't you go back…

Alamo Jack, don't you go back…

Alamo Jack, don't you go back…

Or you'll get kilt for sure."

It was catchy when you were six years old.

As I approached the Wild West Theatre, I saw PMA pull into the parking lot, which was located on the right side of the building. There were only three other vehicles in the lot, but they all appeared to be part of the same convoy – a trio of souped up SUVs. That meant it wouldn't be hard to find PMA after the meeting. But it also made the whole thing seem not a little ominous. The SUVs were all black and shiny – just like the one Chuck Connors had driven into me in Booneville.

I started shivering again.

Ahead of me, I saw the entrance to the theatre, which, appropriately enough, was made up of two double-sized swinging saloon doors. That also seemed ominous, like I was walking into a gunfight. I was beginning to feel more than a little silly having thoughts like that, I was the one who had told the kid not to be melodramatic. But it was hard to feel otherwise when you were walking into a full-scale parody of a Western saloon.

What the hell. I swung open the double doors like only a gunslinger without a gun would – very tentatively.

There before me was a tourist-friendly version of the ubiquitous saloon set from countless TV and movie Westerns. There were the small round tables where the locals would play poker or just drink themselves into a stupor. There was a large stage that filled up the entire wall to the left, where presumably the saloon girls would perform, and maybe old Willie Wilson himself when he was still above ground. There was a massive, old-timey bar stretching along the entire length of the back wall, showcasing rows and rows of liquor bottles on the shelves behind it and about twenty barstools sitting in front of it. And on the wall to the right, there was a wide assortment of comical wanted posters, as well as antique bar signs featuring amusingly homespun sayings like, "Leave Your Horse Outside," "20 Beautiful Showgirls and 1 Ugly One," and "No Shooting Unless You're Aiming at My Wife." Charming.

The bartender looked up at me. He was a handsome young guy, well built, who looked like he might've aced a Chippendale's audition.

"Anywhere you like," he yelled across the room. He had to yell, the place was that big.

I started to look around when I heard somebody say, "Bowman?"

I turned and saw General Kraemer to the right, sitting in a dark corner of the bar by himself. He was dressed a lot like George Burns when he first shows up in *Oh, God!* -wearing a flannel shirt, khakis, and one of those fishing hats that had the netting over the top portion that covered his skull. He was in his early sixties but he already looked like he was in his seventies. And he looked tense as fuck. Nothing about this whole thing felt good.

I walked over, introduced myself, shook his hand and sat down. He was working on a coffee.

"I appreciate you coming down here, General."

He nodded curtly.

"Everything all right?" I asked

"I just want to know what this is all about."

I looked around the room. Just the hunky bartender, prepping the bar. I turned back to the General. Might as well get right to the point, because I didn't know how much time I had.

"Well, sir, there's been an inquiry…into the death of General Davidson's son, Robert."

"An inquiry."

"Some say there were some…irregularities, I guess you might say. I just dropped by Colonel Allen's home…"

"Allen? He doesn't know anything. He likes to pretend he does. He's got Retired Colonel Syndrome if you ask me."

"Retired Colonel Syndrome?"

"Yeah, Colonels who never make General. They get bitter and quit. Always ready to gripe."

"Well, I never got to talk to the Colonel. He's dead."

The General turned as pale as I apparently and frequently was.

"Dead?"

"His wife too. I was driving towards their house…and it just blew up. They said it was a gas leak."

I saw him glance at the bartender, who returned it with a cold, hard look. And then I remembered. The only vehicles I saw in the parking lot were the lookalike SUVs – no vehicle that presumably belonged to the General. So how did he get here? I couldn't see him grabbing a Greyhound.

"Look, Bowman, Robert Davidson died on the battlefield. Pretty black-and-white situation. I processed the papers myself out of respect for General Davidson."

Wow. He jumped right past that house explosion.

He kept talking, or rather, spewing. But at the same time, I felt his hand poking at my thigh under the table. I was pretty sure he wasn't trying to come on to me, so what was the point of the groping? Meanwhile, the words kept coming.

"…so I don't know what you mean by irregularities, Robert was under my command and I did everything by the book."

I put my hand under the table. He was pushing a scrap of paper at me. I took it and shoved it in my pants pocket, both playing like nothing was happening. That meant the bartender was bad news. But I already had guessed that.

"Sir, I'm certainly not questioning your integrity. There was an inquiry and I was simply asked to follow up on it. I did want to ask you about Dark Sky's involvement…"

The second I let the words "Dark Sky" out of my mouth, the show started without warning.

The lights on the stage across the room came to life. A triumphant Western theme blared over the sound system. I turned to the General, who was trying to tell me something with his eyes - something else I had already guessed. He was in some sort of hostage situation.

The music was the final clue.

It was the theme from *The Rifleman*. Which meant my nightmare was about to come to life.

Yes, my old friend, Not-Quite Chuck Connors, burst through the curtains to take center stage. He was wearing a cowboy hat, riding gloves, jeans and the same weird shirt the actual Rifleman wore on the old show, that corduroy shirt that looked like it had root beer barrels for buttons. It was scary how much he looked like the real thing.

Especially since he was holding in his hand – *The Rifleman* rifle.

Who the hell was this freak who was assuming the role of a TV hero from sixty years ago? And where the hell did he get the rifle? It wasn't just something you picked up at a nearby Walmart. *The Rifleman* rifle was a special one, a Winchester .44-40 with a larger loop than normal for the lever action located underneath the gun. That allowed Lucas McCain, the role Connors played, to flip the rifle all the way around in a circle. He would do this to cock the weapon as well as demonstrate to a potential enemy how bad-ass he was.

There was one other interesting element to the rifle, and that was the screw that jutted inside the loop – positioned so that all McCain had to do was slam the lever down and the screw would automatically push back the trigger and fire the gun. That meant he could shoot repeatedly with the rifle in a fast and deadly way – because it had been jimmy-rigged into becoming one of the world's first automatic weapons.

Not-Quite Connors did the Lucas McCain rifle flip in our direction, swooping the barrel around in a 360-degree circle, as he stared at us with unrestrained evil glee. I turned to the General, who was staring at Not-Quite Connors with unrestrained loathing. There wasn't much I could do but watch.

"The Willie Wilson Wild West Theatre is proud to present The Rifleman!" yelled the bartender, who quickly ran to the side of the bar.

With good reason, because Not-Quite Connors crouched down, aimed and began shooting the liquor bottles on the shelves behind the bar. Twelve shots, twelve bottles. The liquid poured down to the ground as Not-Quite Connors flipped his rifle around one more time.

He was using live ammunition. You could smell the gunpowder in the air.

He reached into his shirt pocket and began reloading.

I got up. I couldn't just sit there. The General grabbed my arm.

"Don't…" he whispered.

Not-Quite Connors crouched – and shot the General straight in the chest. Right through the heart. Another eleven shots that whizzed right by my waist.

The General slumped over. He was dead.

I froze and looked him over. His chest looked like ground meat from the force of the shots. And behind his shredded bloody shirt, I saw the wire.

They were, of course, listening to everything we said. Luckily, the General hadn't said much and neither had I.

Now there was the little matter of how this was going to end for me.

Not-Quite Connors jumped off the stage and his long legs made quick work of the distance between him and me. I didn't move a muscle.

"Want a shot?" he asked when he was close enough.

I looked at him in confusion. And that's when he turned the rifle sideways, holding it horizontally in front of his chest, and threw it right at me with both arms. I couldn't avoid catching it or it would have slammed into my chin.

As I reflexively grabbed onto the still-hot weapon, Not-Quite Connors rushed me and punched me in the head, knocking me to the floor and taking the rifle back from me as I went down. I hit the floor hard.

That's when PMA rushed into the saloon and jumped on Not-Quite Connors' back.

The idiot.

As I tried to get back on my feet, the bartender came running across the room and efficiently peeled the kid off Not-Quite Connors - and threw him a few feet across the room into a nearby table, where PMA and the furniture both fell all over the floor.

"Leave the kid alone," I said as I leaned on a table for support.

Then I noticed three other guys emerging from a backroom. All three were wearing blood-red jumpsuits and were packing nine millimeter pistols, all of which were aimed in our general direction.

Not-Quite Connors glared at me and flipped the rifle around again. "Get out of here," he snarled. "And remember whose prints are on this gun."

I glanced at what was left of the General. Turned out old soldiers really did die and there wasn't a lot I could do about it now - my responsibility was to get the kid out of there alive. I grabbed PMA's arm, pulled him up off the floor and yanked him in the direction of the double saloon doors so we could get the hell out of Dodge.

"You keep chasing this thing," bellowed Not-Quite Connors, "And you answer to me. I don't care where or when or how, you answer to me."

I didn't stop to respond. I didn't think a snappy comeback would serve my interests.

A couple minutes later, I was driving and the kid was breathing heavy.

"What the fuck. What the fuck. What the FUCK."

I checked the rear view mirror to make sure the SUV squad wasn't following us. It wasn't.

"WHAT THE FUCK!!!!" he screamed, much to the amusement of the kids in the back seat of the car next to us, waiting for the red light to turn green. The parents in the front seat had other feelings about it.

"That was the guy who rammed me at the Colonel's house," I told him in between gasping for air. He wasn't the only one breathing heavy.

"He looked exactly like the guy on that old show! The one they show Saturday mornings!"

"I'm aware."

"WHAT THE FUCK!"

I drove on. To where, I wasn't sure.

"We gotta go to the police!"

I shook my head.

"Why not?"

"After he shot the General, he threw me the rifle. He was wearing gloves. I wasn't."

As I said that, something else clicked. I suddenly understood why Not-Quite Connors had rammed me after the Colonel's house had gone up in smoke. It had thrown my car around in the opposite direction – so it looked like I was driving away from the house, not towards it. That's what the Booneville cop would remember.

They were setting me up. They made it look like I killed the Colonel and the General. Of course, the physical evidence might prove me innocent. Might.

I turned off the main drag of Branson as soon as I was able so I could get the car above twenty mph and put some miles between us and Willie Wilson's Wild West Theatre.

"I should've used a MAU move on that guy," the kid said as I clamped down on the gas pedal. "I just lost my focus."

"You shouldn't have come in there," I said angrily. "I told you to stay in the car."

"I was worried. I noticed in the parking lot…all three SUVs that looked the same. They all had Montana license plates. And one of them had a bashed-in front fender – and I remembered you said an SUV had hit you back in Kentucky, right? I mean, shit, I thought I better see what was going on, then I heard the shots. FUCK."

"Montana?" I said.

"Did they just buy that place to do that to you? I don't understand. Where do we go now? FUCK." He rubbed his temples and closed his eyes.

The paper.

I almost forgot the scrap of paper the General had slipped me under the table.

I quickly dug into my pocket until I found it.

"What's that?" he asked as I pulled it out.

"The General snuck this to me in the saloon." I handed it to him. "What's it say?"

"Michael Winters."

A name I had never heard before.

I hooked up with I-44 west and took it to the Springfield airport. I returned the rental to the company I had gotten it from, then walked over to the next kiosk over and rented a new one, my fifth rental.

But it was obvious that the Rifleman gang didn't want to kill me. They wanted me to do the same thing Angela wanted me to do, which was go back to General Davidson and tell him a fairy tale about how his son was dead and there was nothing unusual about it. Nothing to see here, nothing to see here. To make sure I did that, they killed the Colonel and the General and made it look like I did it, so they could intimidate me into backing down. They were also probably scared that the two retired officers knew something about Robert Davidson. But who were these freaks working for? It had to be someone in power, someone who in an official capacity who could blackmail me about the murders, someone who had sent out the mysterious Mr. Barry Filer to employ me.

I turned and looked at PMA, who was pacing like a maniac on the sidewalk next to me while we waited for our brand new rental car. He was too young for all this, I was too old and we were both way too amped from what had just happened.

"What the hell do we do next?" he murmured.

"That depends on who Michael Winters is," I answered.

That was when the guy brought my new rental around. A blue Toyota.

Huh.

Debrief

Houses actually blew up from gas leaks on a fairly regular basis, I remembered one happened in my neighborhood when I was a kid. So the death of an Army Colonel in Booneville wasn't a big headline-generator. It was just a random accident. Nothing to see, nothing to see.

However, an Army General getting his chest shredded with twelve rifle shots in one of the biggest tourist destinations in the country?

Not much random about that.

Which is why the kid and me were watching CNN go wall-to-wall with the story, latching onto the shooting as if it were a missing Malaysian airliner. Sending the tabloid attraction-factor of the story through the roof was the rifle left behind at the Wild West Theatre by Not-Quite Connors. Everybody my age and over knew instantly what the left-behind Winchester was modelled after, as well as some younger peeps who couldn't avoid the constant reruns. It was already being called "The Rifleman Massacre" – CNN's cue to show a lot of violent clips from *The Rifleman* that had been uploaded to YouTube.

Boy, they loved themselves some crazy news shit.

But there were some other facts buried under all the hyperbole - such as the fact that they had been holding the General at gunpoint the day before. That explained why the meeting had ended up at the abandoned Wild West Theatre – Not-Quite Connors and his gang had determined the location of our rendezvous, not the General.

PMA and I had driven on to St. Louis and found a low-cost, low profile Super Comfort Days 8 Whatever Motel, where we checked in around four p.m. I was back to using cash and a phony name, because I didn't know what shoe was going to drop next. Now we were listening to CNN's nonstop repetition of the one minute's worth of information that the network actually had about the shooting. But the kid and I did learn a few things we didn't know – like that Willie Wilson had died a year ago and his Wild West Theatre had closed its doors six months ago. I couldn't be sure how Not-Quite Connors and his buddies had gotten into the place, but I was pretty sure it wasn't legally and so was CNN. Since the Wild West Theatre had gone bust, however, all security video systems in the theatre or its parking lot had been shut down, leaving the cops almost nothing to go on – except the Rifleman rifle replica found in the saloon, the murder weapon according to the ballistics.

The murder weapon with my prints on it.

The CIA had my fingerprints on file, but, as a policy, didn't release those of any of its past or present personnel into the general law enforcement database. The Agency really didn't want any of its agents getting caught being up to no good without it knowing about it first. That meant the cops or the FBI couldn't make a match with me. First, someone would have to suspect me – and nobody knew who I was or where I was.

Well, I had to amend that. One person knew I was almost certainly at the scene of the crime. A person I was calling right now as I paced around the room.

"Yeah?" said the voice on the other end.

"David Muhlfelder here."

One of those pauses you could drive a truck through.

"I…will have to call you back, David. I'm in the middle of a few things."

"Okay, thanks."

I was disconnected. I looked at the CIA-gifted phone Howard had provided me in my new identity package and wondered if I should go introduce it to the back tire of my new rental, like I had the others. But, just then, it rang again.

"Hello?" I said.

"Great. Now you've got me using burners," he said very quietly.

Turned out Howard was worried about *his* phone, not mine. But that hardly made me feel better about things.

"Where are you?" I asked.

"In the stairwell, like I'm in a bad deleted scene from *24*. What the *fuck* is happening?"

"The time has come, Howard. I'll show you mine if you show me yours."

"Show you what?" he exploded. "I got nothing to show! You're the one who sets up meetings with generals who get brutally murdered by old TV western stars! Say, was Chuck Connors ever the Mystery Guest on *What's My Line?* I'm looking for a way to tie this all together!"

"Howard, you've been acting weird since I took this job. You know something and you haven't been square with me about it. Now I'm in the shit and I have a guest along for the ride who shouldn't be here."

The kid was staring at me. He was shaking his head like it was full of hot lava.

"Guest? What? Who's with you?"

"You start, Howard."

A pause you could fly an Airbus through.

"Look, it's not much. It's just…when they originally came asking for you, you know, to hire you for this job. It was…*who* was asking for you."

"And who was asking for me, Howard?"

"You're still on the safe phone, right?"

"Yeah. It's still safe, right?"

"Who the hell knows." Pause. Then very quietly, "You ever hear of the Underneath Secretary of Intelligence Oversight?"

"Yeah, Pentagon, right? One of the bullshit positions they put in after 9/11?"

"Bullshit, my ass. That guy has eighty billion to play with and a field squad of about one hundred twenty-five. Mostly overseas."

"What's the guy's name?"

"Andrew Wright. He was a Green Beret and used to work for the Agency. He was involved in shit in Honduras, Nicaragua, Beirut, he even smuggled arms to the Afghans when they were battling the Russians. He's still involved over there, but even we don't know what the hell he does and he's not telling."

"So what's the point?"

"The point is this high-up jerk-off doesn't personally call people like me looking for low-level people like you!"

"Is that a slam?"

"That's a reality, we're both low-level compared to this guy. He's the government's direct liaison to Dark Sky, you've heard of them?"

Another pause, this time on my end.

"Yeah. Yeah, I have. The DOD is still hiring that outfit?"

"Well, he is."

"Anything else?"

"Yeah."

His turn to pause. This was the longest one yet.

"It's this. After I gave him your information, he asked if you were…expendable."

"Expendable???"

For some reason, my underwear suddenly felt too tight.

"I asked him what he meant by that…he said he just wanted to make sure you weren't critical to any other operations. And then he hung up."

I had been standing, but I felt a little dizzy, so I sat back down.

"Expendable."

"Just tell me what he's gotten you into."

I told him the whole thing, starting with the General Davidson revelation and ending with the Not-Quite Connors confrontation. It was one of those stories that felt even weirder when you had to tell it somebody else. After I was done with the whole thing, I pictured Howard eyeing the empty stairwell, wondering if there was any way in the world anybody was listening in on him.

"Jesus. Jesus. Okay, you have to get back here."

"I'm not feeling like that's a good idea right now. I want to follow up on this name that Kraemer slipped me."

"Are you crazy? That's not a possibility. If they ever track down the fact that I gave you the new identity pack and…"

"Who's 'they,' Howard?"

"Shit, I don't even know anymore," he said with an exhausted mumble. "But look. The General's kid can't be alive, that's just ridiculous. If these people want you to quit, believe me, you should quit. Everybody wants you to quit, including me, so quit."

"I'm kind of tired of quitting, Howard. I did it twelve years ago and I don't think it's been good for me."

"Wait, you said you had company. Who's with you?"

"General Davidson's grandson."

PMA shook his head again, even more violently than before.

"Turns out he was the courier your people sent. He's working for the Agency. Summer job. Nice kid."

"General Davidson's grandson? And you're dragging me into all this? Holy shit, holy shit. Listen to me, Max, listen to every fucking word I'm saying. This isn't just your life on the line, this is mine. I've got over thirty years invested in this place and a nice fat pension waiting for me when I retire in a few years. You have no moves, Max. You're almost sixty, you're out of shape and you're in no way equipped to deal with this shitstorm. I'm not saying all that to hurt your feelings…"

"You're not. I give myself the same speech every morning."

"Then you know I'm right and you need to come back here, tell the General what you're supposed to tell him, get the kid back to his mother before she starts raising holy hell, then go back to Roosevelt Island and fuck that singer of yours."

"Have I ever told you to go home and fuck Janet?"

"No, because I'd laugh in your face, I don't want to fuck Janet, who does?"

"Don't look at me."

"Get back here, I'll protect you and get Support to Mission on this."

"I don't mean to hurt *your* feelings, Howard, but I don't think you can protect me. I also have the feeling that Support to Mission won't do anything about this. Plus there's the fact that I've been set up as a double murderer."

"I'll vouch for you."

"I don't know if I can take that check to the bank, Howard. This is serious shit. A general and a colonel were brutally murdered. Right in front of me."

"I get that."

"Then get this – I'm going to at least track down Michael Winters. If I don't get some idea of what's going on, who knows what's going to come back and bite us all in the ass? And here's the most relevant issue to me personally. Even if I talk General Davidson into letting go of this – how can I be sure they're not going to kill me afterwards? What would stop them then? They don't know how much I know."

"Jesus. Shit. Okay. Just…just do me one favor."

"What?"

"Don't do anything for a couple of days. Nothing. Don't go looking for anyone, don't poke any bears. Let shit cool off for a while. It's Friday, right? Take the weekend off. You could probably use it."

"What good will that do?"

"Maybe nothing, maybe something. I mean, I might find out something. If you've gone AWOL on the guy who hired you…"

"Mr. Barry Filer."

"…then Mr. Barry Filer might come back to me, right? And he'll have to at least have some kind of bullshit story to tell me. Maybe I can see what kind of room we have to maneuver here."

"Well, at least I know who he's working for now."

"That's not a good thing. Andrew Wright is the biggest spook there is. He's the king of the spooks."

I let out a blast of air. Going dark for the weekend wasn't a bad idea, even if it was Howard's.

"So, we good?" he asked.

"We're something. I'm not sure 'good' is the word."

I hung up.

"I can't believe you told him."

Now the kid was mad at me.

"Howard's the only guy I have I can trust, I have to tell him everything."

The kid threw a few furtive glances around the room and then finally accepted the situation.

"Let me ask you something," I said. "Did a man named Andrew Wright ever come to see your grandfather since you've lived there?"

"Andrew? You mean Andy? The old guy?"

A few chills went through me.

"Probably."

"He's got a limp – right leg, I think. Always in a suit. Came over a couple of times. Told me he and my grandpa started out together on some overseas stuff. I spent hardly any time with the dude, just talked to him on his way in and out."

That cinched that connection. Meanwhile, the kid was freaking.

"So what do we do? Are they going to send in a team to help us?"

"No. We're in no immediate danger. We're going to stay quiet until Monday."

He blinked.

"What – *here*?"

"You don't like outer St. Louis? We got here just in time for the beginning of the humidity season."

He turned back to the TV screen and the hysterical news anchors with the giant rifle graphic behind their heads. He was getting as hysterical as they were.

"We need guns! They're going to come for us!"

He turned back to me with burning eyes. PMA was turning his Power to be terrified into a Mental idea that he would have to shoot first and ask questions later, and that meant he wanted to commit the Action of buying some serious hardware.

"How often have you shot a gun?" I asked.

"A couple of times," he mumbled.

"Me too," I said. "We'll just end up shooting each other instead of anybody who counts. No guns."

"What the hell are we going to do?"

This was going to be the hard part.

"You should go home."

"A soldier never leaves his unit. My grandfather taught me that much."

I kept my eye roll on the inside of my skull.

"Look, Jeremy." I used his real name, the way my father used my first and middle names together when I was in trouble. "We've just entered a brand new and very horrible world. One that you shouldn't be anywhere near. We're getting you on a flight tomorrow morning…"

PMA pulled out his wallet.

"Why?" I asked.

I soon got my answer. He took out his ID, his driver's license, and he ran into the bathroom. I heard the toilet flush. This time, I allowed my eye roll its moment in the sun as he proudly came strolling out with a smirk firmly in place.

"You can't put me on a flight, I don't have ID. You can't put me in a rental either. I'm sticking with you and on Monday, we're going to track down that Michael Winters cocksucker."

"That's a premature assessment, we don't know if he actually sucks cocks or not."

"Ha ha."

"I can tell you're not really laughing."

Was it dinner time yet? I was hungry and desperate to stop this goddamn conversation. I grabbed the empty ice bucket. It was at least time to start drinking.

"Anyway," he continued, "I'm not going anywhere."

"Yeah," I said as I headed for the room door. "I figured that out. That's why I'm going to get ice."

When I came back with a full bucket, I found him practicing his MAU moves again. At least he kept his pants on this time. I poured myself the first drink and took one of the pain pills. My jaw hurt like a son of a bitch from the punch I had received in the saloon and the rest of my body ached anew from my collision with the floor. Things hurt bad enough just from getting old, I didn't need all this on top of it.

But I did need to try and find out who Michael Winters was.

I fired up the Chromebook and took a sip of Jack, feeling thankful that General Kraemer had found a way to get that name on paper before Not-Quite Connors used his chest for target practice.

The first Michael Winters that came up on Google was an actor who had been on the TV show *Gilmore Girls*. I wouldn't mind a weekend with Lauren Graham, but that had little to do with the fact that this wasn't the guy I was looking for. Nor did I believe the Michael Winters who was an orthodontist in Seattle had any relevance to the many, many, *many* issues at hand here.

The third Michael Winters I found was the one.

Michael Winters had been in the Army Rangers, just like Robert Davidson. He was in Afghanistan and served under General Kraemer and Colonel Allen, just like Robert Davidson. And unlike Robert Davidson, I knew where he was.

Corporal Michael Winters was discharged in 2007, according to army records. A medical discharge. A search on his full name, Michael Malcolm Winters, put him in Milwaukee, Wisconsin. I paid the fee to the creepy online service that tells you where everybody including your grandma is and got the address. We'd have to do a little backtracking, but luckily, it would only take five or six hours of driving to get up there. Hopefully, he would actually be there – and not already dead like the other two guys I tried to talk to. In any event, I'd find out on Monday.

For now, nobody knew where I was, not even Howard - and there was no real way for anyone to track me down, thanks to my new David Muhlfelder identity. So I let myself relax a little. It had been a long day and I was just starting to realize how tight every muscle in my body had been for the last few days. The kid was still practicing his moves, but I thought he deserved an update.

"Monday, we go to Milwaukee."

"That's where this guy is? What's his deal?" he asked in between pants.

"He served with your uncle in Afghanistan. Your uncle was his commanding officer, if I'm reading things right."

"He must know some shit."

I agreed. "He must know some shit."

We didn't really have a handle on what shit he must know, so we let it go after that.

After I finished my drink, I started to feel human and wanted to continue the trend. So I decided there was no harm in stepping out a little here on the outskirts of St. Louis - I thought the kid and I needed some outside time after what we went through in Branson, some touch of normalcy to maybe relax us a little. I knew I did. I was tired of drinking with a sweaty eighteen-year-old in anonymous hotel rooms.

We found a place where we could eat at the bar, a barbeque place that was pretty good. We ate our ribs, used some wet naps to wipe the sauce off our faces and had some more Jack. I just kept ordering drink after drink and, when the bartender was looking the other way, I would slip some to the kid. Feeling anonymous in a dark restaurant packed with locals made us feel like everything was a little bit better – or at least far removed from everything we'd been through the last few days.

"So," the kid said, a little tipsy. "We just gonna hang out here in the sticks?"

"You got any other ideas?"

"No."

He took another drink. He seemed irritated.

"Everything all right, PMA?"

"Yeah." He wasn't very convincing.

"What's the deal? C'mon."

"You think I'm a joke."

"No. What makes you say that?"

"You call me PMA. Like everything I'm trying to do is stupid. At least I'm tryin', dude."

"I'm sorry, kid, I'm just not much for self-help programs based around acronyms."

"You think the martial arts stuff is dumb too."

"I think Andre Gibraltar is kind of dumb, okay? Anybody who screams his sentences has emotional problems or Tourette's Syndrome." Of course, as soon as I said that, I remembered the woman I was involved with fit that particular description, but the realization amused more than disturbed me.

The bartender strolled over, wanting to crash our party.

"Andre Gibraltar? That guy's bad ass, you see his fight last month against Leonardo DiGrime?"

"Shit!" yelled PMA. "That was sick!"

The two of them actually high-fived.

Yeah, when I was a kid, I thrilled to the wrestling exploits of Bruno Sammartino, Gorilla Monsoon and Chief Jay Strongbow. But I figured out it was all fake by the time I was thirteen. Maybe this UFC stuff was for real, but to me, it was the old shit wrapped up in a new tattooed, shaved-head package.

The bartender moved on to a new customer, leaving PMA glaring at me.

"*He* thinks Andre's pretty cool."

"He's a bartender, kid, and you're better than that."

"You're not my dad." He took a big swallow and almost coughed it up.

Dad. Ah-ha.

"Hey – isn't he in Chicago?"

"Northern suburbs."

"You know, Chicago's kind of on the way to Milwaukee."

"I know."

"How long since you've seen him?"

"Five, maybe six years."

The cloud around his head was growing darker and darker. I knew the cloud well. My theory about most men is that to understand them, you have to understand how they were with their dads. It's called modeling – as you're growing up, you look to the closest thing around you with a dick and you pattern yourself accordingly. And you do it unconsciously, so that when you start to display that person's worst qualities, you have no idea where they're coming from. And that's when you start to get real angry.

I was no different.

Every kid expects his parents to be perfect and every kid gets angry when they find out they're not. Yeah, parents deserve some blame for their kids' shit, but they also deserve some praise for what went right. It really depends on which way the scales tip, when all's said and done. And some sins are easier to forgive than others - in my case, and probably in PMA's too.

He went on about the last father-son reunion.

"It was this one time when he came to see my Mom to get some money out of her. He pretended it was about seeing me. But it wasn't. It was about the money."

"Did you like your dad?"

He paused, like he wasn't used to being given permission to answer the question honestly. Probably nobody even ever even asked.

"Yeah, I did," he finally said. "When he was around, he was funny. He loosened things up, which my mom needed, trust me on that shit. You remind me of that part of him, kind of."

Okay, I had obviously had too much to drink, otherwise the next words that came out of my mouth would never have made it past the thinking phase.

"Let's go see him. It's right on the way and it'll kill some time."

His eyes widened. "Nah, dude, he doesn't want to see me. That's crazy."

"You think Chuck Connors shooting at us wasn't crazy?"

I didn't want to torture the guy, but I wanted to give him a choice. If he was going to see his dad, I thought it might be good for him to have an emotional Sherpa with him who could help him safely ascend the peak of parental disappointment - and provide the necessary back-up if he should fall along the way. Boy-to-man was a tricky transition and if the right person wasn't in the mix, it could end in disaster. And, okay, maybe it was the Jack talking again, but I felt like I was right for the job, even if I had never had a son of my own.

Of course, maybe I wanted one of my own.

Maybe I was desperate for a different outcome than the one I had with my own kids. Maybe that's why I was volunteering for this assignment.

"Let me think about it," he said. Then he looked at me as if he just discovered something about me he didn't know until this moment.

"You have kids, right?"

"Two daughters."

"And they don't talk to you."

"Yeah."

"I don't get that. You're not that big of an asshole."

That was the nicest thing anyone had said about my parenting skills in a dozen or so years. But since it was said by someone who had never seen those skills in action, it was hard to get on board with his assessment.

The kid drank from my glass again – just as the bartender turned and saw him do it.

"Hey, hey, enough already. You want me to lose my license?"

The kid gave him a look – then took another gulp from the glass. He was in a mood. And suddenly our happy friendly bartender was too.

"Did you hear me? Put the damn glass down."

I put an arm on the kid to stop him from perpetuating his idiocy, but the kid pulled it away and drained the glass dry. And that meant all the male bonding between PMA and the bartender was quickly torn asunder.

"Get the fuck out of my place – NOW," said the bartender said.

"No!" the kid yelled. "I – am – going – to – DOMINATE!"

The bartender pulled out a big flat wooden stick for some counter-domination.

"What the hell is that?" the kid laughed. "I can kick that stick right out of your hand – Gibraltar-style!"

"Is that so?" The bartender smiled and moved down to the part of the bar where there weren't any bottles behind him. Then he held up the stick and extended it out from his body to make it easy.

"Okay, tough guy. Give it a try."

"Hey, PMA, time to go…" I said, throwing my CIA credit card on the bar. I turned to the barkeep. "Cash us out here, huh?"

He smiled and shook his head. He wanted a show. I turned and saw the kid had backed up to the back wall. He was actually going to try this.

"Jeremy, NO!" I yelled like he was a dog and I caught him in the petunias.

Too late. He made a running start into his leaping kick.

He flew through the air – and got about halfway over the bar. And that's where he ran out of momentum.

He basically landed on his dick. A few glasses that sitting on top of the bar flew onto the floor with a crash.

"AWWWWWW SHIT! SHIT SHIT!" the kid shrieked, as he tried to remove himself from the top of the bar, where he was doing the most painful split I had seen in a while.

I turned to the bartender again and tapped on the credit card. "Like I said, cash me out. Put the glassware on the bill if you want."

But he was laughing too hard to hear me.

The Gallery

Saturday morning.

There was a noise outside the door to our room – loud enough to wake me up.

It was still dark outside and darker inside. I looked around the room. Everything was quiet and still. I decided to try and get back to sleep.

That's when Not-Quite Connors kicked open the door with his cowboy boot, jumped into the room and landed in a shooting crouch.

The kid got up from his bed, to do what, I didn't know, but Not-Quite Connors let twelve shots fly and they all went into the kid's heart, shredding his chest much like General Kraemer's.

PMA fell backwards onto the floor as the blood poured out of his chest and onto the faded hotel room rug around him, where it formed a rapidly-spreading scarlet stain. I sat up in bed as Not-Quite Connors reloaded and grinned maliciously at me.

But something was different about him this time.

Before, he had been clean-shaven, but now he had some kind of moustache-beard sideburn thing going on. I wondered if I had a move left to make as he finished reloading the rifle. But then, when he was done, he simply lowered the rifle, holding it in one hand at his side.

"He's all yours," he said as he quietly turned and left the room.

That's when I woke up.

The worst nightmares are the ones that start with you waking up in your bed. When it starts in what you know to be real, you're tricked into believing more deeply whatever insanity that follows. And I believed, Lord, I believed.

I let my head snap back to reality and then turned to see, happily, that the kid was alive and well and sitting in his bed.

But I still heard shooting.

I glanced toward the television. PMA was watching *The Rifleman*.

It was Saturday morning, the time when, every week, one of the cable channels showed four hours or so of old episodes, episodes where the Rifleman would shoot five or six bad guys, then go home and teach valuable moral lessons to his forever-traumatized son, who had already seen more killing at the age of ten than Genghis Khan had after the Mongol invasions. I silently groaned. Not the best way to start our day. The episode cut to commercial as I went into the bathroom for my morning penis draining – and also to rub a cold wet washcloth over my forehead. That nightmare had been a real bastard and it took me a while to shake it.

When I finally came out, the kid turned to me. He was just in his boxers, but sweaty. Apparently I slept through Kung Fu time.

"I thought you might want to skip practice after last night."

"If I hadn't been drunk…" he said with a scowl.

"Yeah. Anyway, can we change the channel? I think I've had enough of Chuck Connors."

He stared at the TV a moment.

"It's so weird watching this show. That maniac in Branson looked just like the real thing. His face was kind of different, but, shit, he was as tall as Lucas McCain," he said in such a way that I couldn't help but think that he had a nightmare too. And Lucas McCain, which was The Rifleman's real name, was indeed tall. Real Chuck Connors was around six foot five, six foot six, if I remembered right. He had at least four inches on me – and so did Not-Quite Connors.

Anxious to change the conversation, especially after my twisted sleep visions, I asked the kid if he wanted to get some breakfast. He was quiet a moment. Then he had a question of his own.

"You really think we should go see my dad?"

In the words of his mother Angela, "Hmmm."

"Look, kid, my opinion doesn't count. I know almost nothing about this guy. But maybe seeing him after all this time might help you settle any lingering questions you have about him. Plus I'll be there - so if he is an asshole, I'll be available to pin his arms behind his back while you punch him in the stomach."

That made him laugh. I didn't make him laugh often, but when I did, it was golden. Yeah, I thought he should go, but I felt a little guilty for it, only because I had realized somewhere in the middle of the night that his dad probably knew a little bit about Robert Davidson – after all, he used to be his brother-in-law. Since any information about the guy was scarcer than a temperature below eighty degrees during a Miami August, I wanted to talk to anybody who could maybe fill in a few blanks. I hoped I wasn't encouraging PMA to have a reunion with Dear old Dad just for that. It was hard to sort shit out when everything was all mixed up in a ball.

"We should go," he said, nodding to himself.

"It's your call. One question - do we know where the hell he is?"

"Yeah, I Googled him on your laptop." Pause. "He's got a gallery. In the Chicago Arts District."

A gallery? Really?

The show came back on the TV. The Rifleman was confronting some shady-looking dude in a bar. And then he said the magic words…

"If anything happens to the sheriff, you answer to me. I don't care where or when or how, you answer to me."

The kid looked at me like lightning was parting his hair. Except for the part about the sheriff, that's exactly what Not-Quite Connors had said to me in Branson. It was an easy guess that the psychopath was a big fan of the show – now we knew just *how* big of a fan.

I grabbed the remote and turned off the set. There were enough bad vibes in the air.

It was about a four-hour drive to Chi-Town, so we grabbed some breakfast at a nearby Denny's for old time's sake and hit the road. I was at the wheel, since, at the moment, the kid's license was working its way through the St. Louis sewer system. I felt a little better, so I only popped one pain pill instead of two that morning. My jaw was still really sore, but I could deal with that. Besides, I wasn't expecting any surprises for the time being. If I could get Not-Quite Connors and his newly-acquired facial hair out of my subconscious, I might even be able to feel good.

I thought about calling Jules, who was probably bouncing off the walls at either her place or mine this weekend. I had told her I'd be gone a day and it was rapidly turning into a week - plus I suddenly had a new name and no way for her to get ahold of me. Her surgery was still more than a week away, so I had to figure this would all be resolved one way or another by then.

PMA was quiet for a long time. Then, he started talking.

"I remember him teaching me how to paint."

"Your dad."

"Yeah. I was really young, six or seven. He showed me how he mixed the oils and everything. But I didn't have the talent for it. I couldn't draw a straight line. He didn't pay a lot of attention to me after that."

"That was about him, not you. Trust me. Everything my brothers and I did disappointed my dad, because everything in general disappointed my dad. He looked for disappointment the same way a cat looks for tuna. Your mom treat you okay?"

"Yeah. But she's always pissed off about something."

"I can see that."

We drove on a little bit.

"You're divorced, right? Did you ever get remarried or anything?"

"No, but I have a….a friend. A singer who can't sing."

"Why not?"

"Her vocal cords got screwed up. She's having surgery Tuesday after next. I'm supposed to get back home and nurse her back to health."

He stared straight ahead at the endless interstate.

"Maybe she'll have to nurse you back to health." He wasn't joking.

"10-4, good buddy," I replied because I sometimes said very idiotic things when I wanted to cover up the fact that I was shitless.

The Chicago Arts District was a collection of lofts, studios and galleries near the lower west side of Chicago. A hundred years ago or so, an immigrant family ran a dairy in this neighborhood. When the area fell victim to urban decay, one of the offspring began installing galleries as a way to turn things around. The whole thing had worked out so well that entire blocks were now devoted to artistic pursuits. Not the kind that I could pursue, because I'm worse than the kid. I not only can't draw a straight line, I can barely draw a crooked one. When I was a boy, I tried to copy Beetle Bailey cartoons until my fingers hurt, but sometimes pain does not beget great art - or competent Beetle Bailey knock-offs.

Of course, from what I heard from the kid, his dad was hardly Rembrandt either – which is why it was hard to believe he had his own gallery. To me, he seemed the type who would have conned some heiress into marrying him and whisking him off to a sleepy Caribbean beach town. But maybe we had all underestimated the talent of A.J. Longetti, father of Jeremy and ex-husband of Angela. Maybe he had found his groove.

We parked on Halstead, the street where the gallery was located, and walked up the sidewalk looking for his address. It was a charming neighborhood, filled with renovated brownstones and young hipsters swarming coffee shops. I felt out of place – but the funny thing was, so did PMA, who seemed somehow both younger and older than his peers. On the younger side, he didn't quite know how to connect with his peers, probably because he was an only child and never had siblings around to shake him out of his own head. On the older side, he carried too much of the burden of his lineage with him.

"This is it," said the kid. And he was right. We were at what was labelled The A.J. Longetti Gallery, a very small space in a building filled with tiny start-up galleries. Longetti's storefront was different from his neighbors', however. Like the late, great Pancho's Tacos back in Washington D.C., this gallery had its windows covered so you couldn't see inside from the street. It didn't take long to find out why – just the length of time it took to open the door and have a quick look.

Incredibly and ironically, the very type of art that had caused the demise of A.J. and Angela's marriage was now the source of A.J.'s success. Yes, the walls were covered with large framed photos of naked women with painted torsos. There was one on her side with her back to the viewer – she had the Chicago River flowing down through her ass. There was a version of the one PMA had described to me, with the fruit bowl on her stomach and her breasts as the apples – looked like McIntoshes. There was another model bent over, with the elephant mascot from the Republican Party on the right side of her ass and the donkey mascot of the Democrats on the left. And then there was the one cosmic cutie who had the Crab Nebula expanding out of her vagina.

I was surrounded by below-average art attached to above-average female bodies.

So far my favorite was the one featuring two female butts side-by-side illustrating the four stages of the butterfly's life cycle, one stage per cheek. Now there was a pupa I could get into.

The kid and I exchanged a bewildered glance that was interrupted by angry shouting from the back corner of the gallery. A small brown-haired and immaculately groomed woman who could've passed for Helen Gurley Brown's younger, thinner (yes, I said thinner) sister was loudly abusing a bald and spectacled forty-year-old man in black slacks and white shirt whose posture seemed to be trying to project authority.

"This is ART. Who the HELL are YOU to say it's PORN?"

The posture wasn't getting the job done.

"Do you KNOW how much MONEY I have? Do you KNOW how long I can keep you in COURT?" she continued as he backed up against the wall.

I turned to the kid. "I think your dad has a new girlfriend." He nodded as if he had already figured that out.

The bald four-eyed man hurried past us on his way out the door, while the woman glared at us as if we were working for him.

"An artist MUST be ALLOWED to SHOW HIS WORK!"

"I'm not arguing," I offered.

She approached me and softly put a hand on my arm. I looked at her face up close and tried not to shudder. Maybe I was wrong on that younger part - her face looked like an ancient chimpanzee's with skin so overloaded with Botox that it resembled the kind of plastic they used to make Barbie's skin.

"I am sorry. That gentleman is the landlord of this gallery. First he made us paper over the windows, now he is saying this sort of work doesn't belong in an environment that's devoted to serious art." She wound her anger back up and let it fly. "And WHO is HE to determine what is SERIOUS art???"

That's when the artist himself, A.J. Longetti, stepped in from the back room. He was small and squirrely, with a shaved head and olive-colored skin, wearing a NO FEAR t-shirt, cargo shorts and sandals.

Oh, and lest I forget to mention, weird facial hair. The kind I had seen in my nightmare. It wasn't a good omen that it was on his face instead of Not-Quite Connors'.

"Wanda! Wanda, Wanda, Wanda! You are a WARRIOR PRINCESS!"

A.J. hurried over to the woman's side, bent her back over and shoved his tongue down her mouth. She giggled as though she were seventeen and just got asked to the prom. He released her, then she straightened up and smoothed back her hair, which hadn't been disturbed in the least due to the ten pounds of hair spray holding it in place. Then she turned to us.

"A.J., these two…"

A.J. cut her off. He was at least a good enough dad to recognize his son.

"Jeremy?"

He gave the boy a giant hug.

"The prodigal son has returned home! Hallelujah!"

From what I heard, the prodigal label should have been applied to the father, but who was I to judge? Absolutely no-fucking-body.

A.J. stepped back and did a little soul handshake move that Jeremy matched reluctantly and not very well. Meanwhile, the woman's eyes widened with delight at PMA.

"A.J., is this your boy? Oh, he's soooo handsome!"

"Hey, look who he's got for a daddy, am I right?" he said, then he pointed to the woman. "Jeremy, this is Wanda…" And then he said her last name. It was the same last name of the second richest person in America, which meant she was either a sister or an ex. "She finally recognized my talent, son — and put her money where her mouth was. Maybe not her mouth…"

She gave him a lascivious smile - either that or her Botox was giving out. A.J. gave me a curious look, then turned to PMA.

"This your new stepdad or something? Doesn't seem like Angela's type. Isn't he past his expiration date?" He turned back to me. "No offense."

"Some taken," I said, shaking his hand. "I'm Max Bowman, your boy's just helping me out on something." Then I thought I'd impress him. "He's training with the CIA."

"The CIA," he said with distaste. "You gonna turn my son into a straight-up spook?"

"Well," I answered, suddenly not giving a shit. "Strangers things have happened. Like this gallery."

A.J. tried to stare me down, but then broke down laughing. Wanda started laughing along with him. That left us as the only two in the room who were still relatively stone-faced. After a little more small talk, Wanda invited us all out for a late lunch at one of Chicago's finest restaurants so we could all get to know each other a little better. But the only other thing I really wanted to know about Wanda was who she voted for in 1932, Roosevelt or Hoover.

At the expensive eatery, A.J. talked about his art until the main course had come and gone. He told us about how the human body was the greatest canvas of all – except, apparently, the ones with penises, since he never painted on a man's body, from what I saw – and how he was selling tons of prints of these things on the internet.

Yeah, I could see that. They were probably filling up the wall space in single guys' apartment where the Nagel prints used to hang.

He told us he had asked Wanda to help him establish the gallery, so he could raise the profile of body-painting in the art community. I replied that Goldie Hawn had already done that in 1967 on *Laugh-In*. Too bad Howard wasn't there to see them react blankly to my ancient reference.

Anyway, Wanda took it from there, angrily shouting about how the area's bourgeois Babbits couldn't deal with a nipple staring them in the face. That prompted A.J. to make out with her for a few minutes, right there at the restaurant table, causing me to consider whether the grilled salmon I had just ate would spring back to life, swim upstream and back out of my mouth. This was the second time in one week I had been embarrassed at an extremely classy restaurant.

Also the second time in eight years I had eaten at one.

Wanda, however, was not embarrassed. No, she was glowing with sexual energy.

"I did not even know what an orgasm was until A.J. went to work on me," she asserted with authority.

"Man, ain't that the truth," said A.J. "Little dusty down there when I first took a look, know what I mean?"

"We do, we do," I replied, signaling for him to stop because I feared for PMA's mental health, as well as my own.

It was a good move, because it reminded A.J. that we existed. He ended the make out session and actually asked what we were up to. The kid, being smart, let me take the lead on that.

"I was hired by your former father-in-law…"

The kid looked surprised that I was going there. But it was the only way I would find out anything worthwhile at this lovely family reunion.

"The General?" laughed A.J. "Now, there was a fun dude. So happy to welcome me into the family."

"Well, I could see where you two might not hit it off. Anyway, there are some questions about the death of his son, Robert…"

A.J. laughed even harder. "The Nazi? I knew that motherfucker was too mean to die…"

"Nazi?" I asked.

"Oh yeah, Robert was Hitler's number one fan. He had a whole record album full of Hitler speeches and storm trooper songs, you believe that shit?"

"He did?" Even PMA was shocked. A.J. turned to him.

"Yeah, Robbie swore your mom to secrecy about all the Nazi shit he had stashed away, he got it from some private collector when he was in his early teens. But what did the General expect, huh? The kid was sent to military school as soon as he got out of diapers. They went ahead and made that poor bastard into a killing machine."

A.J. mimed shooting an automatic weapon to make sure we got the idea.

"So who was this Herman he used to hang out with?" I asked.

"Herman?" A bigger roar of laughter. Whatever diners were still enjoying a late lunch threw a few annoyed looks our way, but A.J. didn't care and neither did Wanda. And I soon found out why. I was sitting too far back from the table and happened to notice that, underneath it, she was vigorously massaging A.J.'s groin. Inside my stomach, my salmon starting making noises again.

"Herman was Robbie's 'close companion,'" A.J. said with a raised eyebrow. "Those two were *tight*."

"Are you implying something?" I asked.

"Duh," he replied.

"You know Herman's last name?"

"I never asked, I just wanted to stay far away from that freak of the week."

"So he was in the military too?"

A.J. slowly shook his head.

"No?"

"Well, he was. He and Robbie signed up together. But I guess Herman was a little too psycho even for the army. He got out and ended up with one of those private army companies, you know, the ones who make the *real* money out of our international blood sport."

"Like Dark Sky?"

A.J. shrugged and I could tell he didn't know and didn't give a shit. I was lucky he remembered that much. Anyway, he had already moved back onto his favorite subject, himself. He still hadn't really asked PMA anything about his life. Wanda at least had the manners to do that, so, when A.J. stopped to breathe, she jumped in.

"Jeremy, are you still in high school?"

"Graduating next month."

"Then off to college?"

"I got into George Washington."

"From what I read, so did Jefferson," chuckled A.J.

"Anyway, I don't really want to go to school. I'd rather just start working."

That prompted Wanda to go on for about a half-hour about how education was important, like a very special episode of *Full House* or something. The kid's eyes glazed over.

"How tall was Herman?" I asked out of nowhere in the middle of the lecture.

A.J. didn't hesitate. "Tall dude." He turned to PMA. "You met Herman that one Christmas? What, maybe six five?"

PMA looked at me and knew what I was thinking. "I don't know, I was seven, everybody seemed tall."

I was suddenly glad to be having this lunch, despite Wanda's attempts to give A.J. dessert in his pants.

We went back to the gallery, where I was more than anxious to say my goodbyes. Then Wanda, again trying to promote normal familial relationships, came out with an unexpected invitation. We could stay the night at her condo. I begged off, saying I had to do some research that night, but Jeremy was welcome to go. PMA looked at me uncertainly, but then A.J. seemed to actually put some effort into getting him to accept and that made the kid say yes. I told them I would be holed up in a hotel for the night, but I would let them know where I was staying.

Then I walked back down to Halstead to my car, checking out a couple other small galleries along the way. Nobody else was painting real-life naked women, so A.J. seemed to have the market cornered on that particular niche. Maybe Wanda was just making a sound business investment? I had a hunch the partnership would probably sour after he took an ill-advised trip into the Crab Nebula and Wanda caught him with space-colored paint on his dick. Whatever. She was getting in one last thrill before it all ended - so what if A.J. was the Max Bialystock of the art world? Was anybody really getting hurt?

Well, one person might be about to.

I hoped the kid would still be in one emotional piece come the morning. Unfortunately, he had to learn. We all did.

I drove off in search of a quiet place to stay.

Sleepover

Sunday morning.

It was one a.m. and someone was banging the hell out of my door.

After I left the kid with A.J. and Wanda, I got depressed about spending the night in another random hotel room box. So I remembered that one thousand dollars Howard had sent me and went in search of a luxury W. Ritz Four Seasons Carlton Whatever suite with an amazing view of Lake Michigan. If I was going to be dead in a few days, I wanted more than my nice new silver watch from Banana Republic to show for it.

After a little wandering around, I found just the thing – an Experience Suite they called it, and I negotiated them down to a mere $899.99 for the night. I was probably the only guy that night who would experience the Experience Suite with only shopping bags for luggage, but the clerk was more concerned about the cash than my resemblance to a homeless person.

When I unlocked the door to the room and switched on the lights, I saw this was indeed an Experience. At nine hundred and fifty square feet, the suite was bigger than my apartment and infinitely more tricked out. The sitting area had a huge curved sectional couch with a fifty-two inch LCD television, a vintage record player with a selection of vinyl, and a wet bar stocked with booze. In the bedroom, the king bed had a mirrored headboard and goose down pillows – plus, of course, another fifty-two inch TV. They even threw in a Waffle Spa Bathrobe, whatever the hell that was, so I could lounge around in style.

After I called the number Wanda had given me and told her where I was staying (she approved), I took a bath in the whirlpool Jacuzzi tub, covered myself in waffles and poured myself some Jack. I went out to the sitting area to take in the view of the lake, which was magnificent. Lake Michigan was, of course, a Great Lake, but, to me, it looked like an ocean with no end in sight from my view on the eighteenth floor.

That's when I slowly realized there was nothing more depressing than experiencing an Experience Suite by yourself. And also, that if I ever told Jules about that I did this without her, she would rip my intestines out of my stomach and strangle me with them.

I took a brief nap while watching the Mets lose to the Nationals, one to zip. Right now, those boys couldn't hit their way out of a wet paper bag. What the hell. I woke up to a new Saturday Night Live and the musical guest was Wiz Khalifa, so I finally got to see what exactly what a Wiz Khalifa was. Turned out it was a guy with more tattoos than skin. I somehow made it to the end of the show and got up still covered in waffles. I planned to throw two more pain pills into my mouth and sleep the big sleep, as a great man once wrote…

…when someone started banging the hell out of my door.

In the words of Dorothy Parker, what fresh hell was this?

I assumed it wasn't Not-Quite Connors or he would have already shot his way through the door. Maybe it was just a drunk who came back to the wrong room. Whoever it was, I didn't really care. It had been a long day – a long week, for that matter – and I was ready to call the downstairs and sic security on whoever the hell it was, but I decided I'd better take a peek through the peephole.

Huh.

I made sure my robe was tied all the way shut and opened the door.

And that's when Angela Davidson started slapping the shit out of my face.

"What the hell were you thinking? WHAT THE HELL WERE YOU THINKING?"

She could hit. Damn, was she watching those Andre Gibraltar videos?

I backed up from the door and held up my hands on either side of my face to block her spinning hands of death. My robe was flying every which way, so I couldn't be sure she wasn't getting an exclusive show, but I was too busy protecting my jaw from more damage to inspect whether my modesty was intact.

I heard the room door slam shut behind us as I kept retreating from her assault until I fell back over the sectional couch and onto the handsome charcoal-grey area rug. Luckily, my head missed the glass coffee table by a few inches. I had gotten knocked to the floor more times this week than I had in the past fifty years – in other words, ever, since I outgrew the playground.

I looked up at her towering imperious figure. Goddamn if she didn't look hot.

"It's a little late for a visit, isn't it?" I offered.

"What have you been doing with my son?" she demanded.

"Mostly trying to get rid of him," I said as I self-consciously held my robe shut and awkwardly got to my feet. "What happened? Did A.J. drop a dime on my ass?"

"He called me and I appreciated it. He was very upset that you were indoctrinating him into the CIA."

"He's got a strong moral compass, that one."

"Why would you take him along on your little adventures? Who does this with an eighteen-year-old kid?"

I smoothed back my hair, walked over to the wet bar and offered her a drink. She opted for Jack, same as me, so she couldn't have been *that* mad. I told her to sit down and we'd talk this out. She sat on one end of the sectional couch and, after I handed her the drink, I sat down somewhere near the middle, which represented our positions pretty perfectly.

Then she just plain started crying. Oh Jesus, take me now. I mean, seriously.

"I've been so worried…I had no idea where he was. Thank God that creep called me. I jumped on the first plane out of D.C.," she said between sobs.

"Your boy doesn't take no for an answer. You should know that."

"Could you maybe get me a damn Kleenex?" she asked as the tears streamed down her face. I had once again forgotten my gentlemanly manners. I got the box of tissues from the bathroom and handed it to her, then stood there looking like the useless idiot I was.

"I made him text you, but that's all I could do. Believe me, things have been a little stressful out here in the field."

"Well, he's coming home with me."

I indicated my complete agreement with that idea, then I sat back down on the sofa. A little closer this time. She calmed down as her tsunami of tears passed.

"Why'd you come to Chicago? Did Jeremy actually want to see his sad excuses for a father?" she asked.

"No, the dad was just on the way."

"On the way to what?"

"Probably nothing good, considering all the people who have been killed so far. Which brings me to a few follow-up questions about your brother. I understand he had an interesting record collection, which apparently included some Nazi storm trooper tunes. Guess he skipped over that whole grunge music craze and went right to the Horst Wessel song."

No answer. Her mouth was still hanging open from my disclosure about the dead folks.

"Your charming ex-husband, who I hope was at least good in bed because he doesn't appear good for much else, filled me in on Robbie's hobbies and his sparkling personality. I'm also interesting in knowing more about Herman."

"None of this has anything to do with…"

"All of it has something to do with this," I interrupted. The hell with gentlemanly manners, I was tired of her bullshit, she was evading more than a Republican talking about race relations. "Ask your son what we've been through. The more I know, the more I have a chance of actually surviving this. So you need to lower the walls and let me in."

Did that sound too sexual? She swallowed most of the Jack in her glass.

"I'm so exhausted, I haven't had one good night's sleep since Jeremy left."

"And you're not going to have another one until you tell me what I need to know."

She looked away. "I don't know who to trust."

"You can be more specific. You don't know if you can trust *me*. Ask your boy. I think he'll tell you that you can."

"I don't want to bother him. He's finally getting some time with his father."

"And Wanda," I added as I got up to refill her glass and mine.

"Who's Wanda?"

"Well, I'd say she's old enough to be your ex-husband's mother, but I'm not sure she's young enough to even make that cut."

"He's with an old woman?"

"She's pleased with her orgasms, he's pleased with her money. Sound familiar?"

"You're a little cruel."

"Sorry. I'm a little on edge."

"I did think I loved him, you know. You were married young, weren't you? Didn't you think you loved her?"

"I wasn't totally convinced."

I handed her back her glass and sat down even closer to her as she finally noticed her lavish surroundings.

"Speaking of money, what did this place cost?"

"Forty-five bucks through Trivago.com. Now. Your brother."

"Sounds like you already know everything."

"If I did, I wouldn't be asking you."

She took a too-big sip from her glass. She was already worn out and I doubted if she had had anything to eat, so I knew, sooner rather than later, the booze would hit her hard. But I also knew I needed her to get past her inhibitions and tell me the truth about her brother.

A delicate balance. I *was* a little cruel.

She sat quietly a moment, then finally nodded. "Okay. Okay. What the hell, let's get this over with."

She told me everything. At least it sounded like everything.

Robert Davidson, her younger brother, was a shy and sensitive kid with an artistic bent. General Davidson, on those few days he was home, didn't like that. Military purity. He had his wife, who always followed orders even when she knew they would lead to disaster, ship the kid out to military school after he finished sixth grade.

That's when the trouble began. Robert came home for the holidays and summers a different kid. Something had broken, and what was constructed in its place wasn't pretty. That's when he started collecting Nazi memorabilia from rogue online sellers and begging sister Angela not to tell General Dad. That's when his eyes grew cold, that's when he stopped smiling, that's when he became obsessed with weaponry of all kinds.

At first, the General was pleased with the turn in Robert's personality, but then he began to sense just how far a turn it was. The General wanted his son to follow in his oversized footsteps at West Point, but Robert had other plans. He didn't like all the pomp and circumstance involved with the officers' training, nor was he particularly interested in rules and regulations. He was interested in becoming Special Ops, training for the Army Rangers and participating in whatever cool and brutal clandestine missions he could.

Like the kid, he wanted to dominate. I didn't like to think about the duplication of that pattern.

All Angela knew about Herman was that he was a higher level Ranger whose spell Robert fell under. Hence all the jokes about Robert being his "girlfriend." No one had any idea about Robert's sexuality, if it mattered. He was gone most of the time and he never mentioned a woman – or a man in that context, for that matter. There was no question, however, that Herman was his BFF – and also that nobody in the Davidson family liked Herman, especially the General, who sensed that Herman was feeding Robert's darkest impulses and causing him to drift farther and farther away from the family. Angela wasn't sure what her father thought Robert was up to – he kept all of that to himself. But at some point, about two years before Robert's death, the father-son relationship was severed forever. She hadn't heard from her brother since then.

So what was she worried about?

Quite simply, she was worried about everything she didn't know, an affliction I also suffered from. She had seen the growing madness in Robert's eyes and she knew whatever he was doing overseas wasn't going to make for a pretty bedtime story. She was relieved when the reporting on his death finally vanished from the airwaves without any unseemly dirt attached. But her heart was broken and so was her father's, because they both remembered the four-year-old boy who loved Cookies N' Cream ice cream, Inspector Gadget cartoons, and Hot Wheels.

As she told me all this, she let slip a few pertinent facts about herself. Even though she was the first child by a couple of years, the General had pretty much ignored her because she wasn't a boy and her mother had followed suit. She did everything right as a child to try and win their attention, if not their love, and it never really worked out. That's why she did the absolute wrong thing and married A.J., more of a disaster for her obviously than her parents. But she was happy she got Jeremy out of the deal, even though she worried about him too. She could see her brother in him…

And with that, she started to droop. I had to act fast and ask the biggest question I needed answered before I lost her for good.

"What do you know about Andrew Wright and your father?"

She looked at me with such squinty eyes that I felt that I had physically become out of focus.

"Andy?"

Andy. The nickname made him seem so…cuddly.

She somehow bolted up off the couch and onto her feet.

"I have to go…"

"Where exactly?" I asked as I got up. "Tell me about Andy."

"Can't…"

She turned and fell into my arms.

"I'm a little loopy."

She looked into my eyes. Oh shit. She kissed me. And I let her. It went on for a little bit.

I'm not the best-looking guy in the world, but I wasn't the worst either. I knew there was something happening between us, but I kept telling myself I was nowhere in her league, that I was imagining things.

But apparently I wasn't. In the D.C. restaurant, I guess she was serious about me being in her wheelhouse. Normally she'd have an open invitation to mine, but this wasn't the time or the place – I was already more involved than I should be with the Davidson clan. Plus, I was also in too deep with Jules, who I'm sure, if she were here and realized I had just now gotten to her name in my internal deliberations, would be slapping me so much harder than Angela had that my head would fly off my neck and into a nearby wall.

Which would save her the trouble of strangling me with my own intestines.

When the kiss was over, Angela looked up at me and asked, "I shouldn't like you, should I?"

She felt good in my arms, but no.

"Let me put you in the bed, Angela."

I walked her towards the bedroom.

"What are we going to do there?" she wondered aloud.

"Not that. I already have a girl."

"A singer that doesn't sing, right?"

"Yeah, but that's about to change."

"Is she pretty?"

"She'll do."

I gently guided her to a landing position on the bed.

"Am I pretty?" she asked, half-out.

"Too pretty for me. And maybe too young. I'm going to be sixty in a year and a half, you know."

"So will I…in eighteen…"

Her eyes were already closing. I took off her heels and put some covers over her. She was already gone. She had to have been most of the way there when she kissed me.

It was after two. I found a spare goose down pillow and a blanket in the closet and headed over to the sectional couch for what wouldn't be a very restful sleep. For one thing, there was this pesky erection I was lugging around with me. I could make that go away, but what I couldn't stop was the sadness I felt for the lonely woman sleeping by herself in my bed.

I was getting way too involved with this family. Maybe because I hadn't had one of my own in too long a time.

Family Time

"Does Andrew Wright have a limp? Right leg?"

Angela was still in the bedroom and I assumed she was still asleep. Meanwhile, Howard had taken it upon himself to give me a call from his new burner to make sure I hadn't gotten into any more trouble. He was oddly cheerful.

"I don't know, but I'll check it out," answered the new, suddenly-helpful Howard. "I also looked into Montana. You said all those SUVs had plates from there? Well, Dark Sky's corporate headquarters is here in D.C. But they have a training facility in Montana named Black Sun…"

"…in Montana."

"A couple hours north of Missoula."

"We used to track a lot of crazies up in that area, didn't we?"

"Still do."

"Black Sun," I wondered. "What's that all about?"

"Don't know."

Pause.

"So nobody's come after you to try and come after me?"

"Very, very quiet."

"Thanks for not saying 'Too quiet."

"You're welcome. So – you're going to Milwaukee tomorrow?"

"That's the plan. You going to talk me out of it?"

"Not yet."

How did our talks get so congenial? We wrapped things up and got off the phone.

My Waffle Spa bathrobe and I couldn't do much until Angela woke up, so I checked out the vintage record player. I had been reading about how all the cool kids loved vinyl these days - me, I just remember the giant scratch that fucked up *Come Together* every time I played Side 1 of *Abbey Road*, rendering an already-incoherent song off-the-charts nonsensical. I really couldn't fathom what the hipsters were thinking going back to this stone-age technology. Maybe they should give hand-crank phones another whirl while they were at it.

I went through the albums and found one lone Sinatra, one of his last on Capitol, *Nice 'N' Easy* – it was towards the end of his magnificent run with arranger Nelson Riddle and featured mostly remakes of old ballads from the Columbia days, but it still went down okay, even though Frank's voice had lost most of its syrup by then. I put it on and the title track, the only original song, started playing its gentle intro. I started thinking that might make a good song for Jules when she got her pipes back in shape. Which sent a huge wave of guilt crashing over my insides.

I grabbed my special Howard-sent phone and dialed. And of course, I woke her up. It was Sunday and it was before noon.

"Haah?" she said sleepily. Did I mention she wasn't a morning person?

"It's me."

A beat.

"David…Mal…Mil…Melfinger?"

"Close enough."

"You're going to give me a heart attack…where are you? Let me guess…you can't fucking tell me."

She wasn't awake enough to really build up a good head of angry steam. Hopefully that wouldn't happen until this call was over because, God knows, I had provided her with enough coal to fire up that particular furnace.

"No, I can't. But I just wanted to let you know I was okay…"

"Wonderful. By the way, did you want to know if I was fucking okay? Because I'm fucking not. Because my boyfriend is God knows where doing God knows what. Jesus, Max."

"When I can tell you more, I will. I don't know who's listening to what."

"Well, here's a question that should be safe. Have you had any more romantic dinners lately?

That's when Angela decided to come out of the bedroom in the suite's other provided Waffle Spa Bathrobe and say, in loud clear tones so I could hear her across the room, "I'm going to take a bath!"

I quickly nodded to Angela that she could do anything she wanted, but I was kidding myself if Jules wasn't going to notice that line of dialogue being shouted at me in a female voice.

"A BATH? Who, pray tell, is taking a GODDAM BATH? MUST BE A DIRTY WHORE WHO NEEDS TO GET CLEANED UP!"

"Jules, c'mon, it's not…"

Call disconnected.

I'd have to fix the damage another day, I couldn't tell her enough to calm her down, if that was even a possibility. Besides, I had a new distraction to attend to. There was someone else now banging on the hotel room door. Which was just what I didn't need, another surprise visitor.

I got up and went over to the door, where I again peered through the peephole.

Huh.

I opened the door and PMA hurried in. He looked as mad as Jules sounded.

"I'm done. Done with him."

Muttering to himself, he walked in a crazed circle around me as I shut the door. Then he stopped and noticed the room.

"Holy shit - how much did this place cost?"

"What happened with your dad?"

Suddenly in a good mood, he heard Sinatra and looked over at the record player.

"Vinyl? Cool!"

I thought about offering the counter-argument involving my old *Abbey Road* album, but let it go. "What happened with your dad?" I asked again.

The kid got angry again. He sat down like a bowling ball falling into foam and laid his head against the back of the couch. After a moment, he told me how yesterday, after I had left, his dad had screamed about all the CIA atrocities committed over the last five decades and how they had basically fucked up the life of everybody in the world. A.J. had a point - the only lives he fucked up were the ones in the immediate area. Anyway, A.J. then made him watch every CIA conspiracy video on the internet and accused the kid of being a tool of the military-industrial complex like his grandfather.

Wanda finally told A.J. to leave Jeremy alone and just spend some quality time with him. But the kid had had it. He went to the guest room after dinner and stayed there. When he woke up in the morning, A.J. was still pissed off. He told the kid that he was his only son and no son of his was going to be a stooge of an imperialist, fascist and several other ists government. The kid ran out of the house and took a cab over here with the few dollars he had left in his wallet.

"Sorry about all that," I finally said.

"What the hell," he answered. "You were with the CIA. You don't seem like such a bad guy."

I frowned. "I was glad to get out, Jeremy. To tell you the truth, I was glad to get out. My dad was CIA. He was in at the very beginning, he got into the OSS during World War II. Worked under 'Wild' Bill Donovan. I was raised to be an Agency man, so I became one, and I couldn't have been more of a world-class idiot. When you build your life based on somebody else's idea of what it should be, sooner or later it all goes wrong. In my experience anyway."

"So you're telling me I'm a world-class idiot."

"I'm not. I'm just telling you what happened with me, okay?"

He took a deep breath and let it go for the moment, as Sinatra asked the musical question, *How Deep is the Ocean?*

"Can we get some breakfast? Wanda served some vegetarian crap last night and I'm starving."

I sat down on the couch near the hotel phone. "Yeah, I'll order some up. But you should go ask your mom what she wants."

He gave me a weird look. "My mom?"

Oh. He didn't know.

I told him about what happened. The mad was back with a vengeance.

"That douchebag called her? He told her where we were?"

He got up and marched over to the bedroom door and opened it.

"Kid, wait, she's…"

He went inside and a moment later, there was a surprised lady scream. Then there were some words, some very intense words from which I got the mood, but not the substance. The kid came out again after a couple of minutes.

"She just wants some granola and yogurt, with a coffee."

"I just want you to know nothing happened between me and your mom."

His only response to that was, "She wants skim milk for the coffee if they have it."

A half hour or so later, after Angela was done bathing and I was done showering and shaving, we were all dressed and sitting around the lovely round dining table in the elevated portion of the room, enjoying a wonderfully expensive breakfast. Actually, it was more of a tennis match than a meal, as I sat with Angela and PMA on either side of me. They were facing each other across the table, lobbing quick strokes back and forth as they argued in the style of the old Monty Python Argument Clinic sketch.

"No, I'm not."

"Yes, you are."

"No, I'm *not*."

"Yes, you *are*."

"No, I'm *not*."

"Yes, you *ARE*."

And on and on.

Angela was demanding the kid come home with her. The kid was insisting he was staying with me. Clearly, it was up to me, New Improved Dad, to be the tie-breaker of our newly-formed dysfunctional family.

"Personally," I began very carefully, looking at Angela, "I think Jeremy should go home with you. The problem is, he flushed his ID down the toilet, so I'm not sure he can even get on a plane."

"You don't know anything, do you?" she asked me in a bitter tone. "All he has to do is fill out a form and provide his address and the last four numbers of his social. TSA will verify his identify and let him through."

Well, I did know some things, but I didn't know that.

The kid looked down at the expensively-tiled floor. He had gotten through about half of his steak and eggs and then quit. He knew he was beaten and there was no way to make him feel good about it.

"I can't believe my fucking father ratted me out."

"That's probably the best thing he's ever done for you, believe me," Angela quickly responded.

I knew this needed to be over. I was going to miss the kid, but I would be a horrible New Improved Dad if I let him continue on with me.

"You need to go home, kid. Let me deal with this shit alone."

"Thank you," Angela said to me without a smile.

"You're welcome," I answered with one.

We said our goodbyes outside the hotel as the doorman flagged down a cab for Angela and the kid. Angela and I exchanged a few looks that indicated last night happened, but nothing more. As the cab drove off, I had mixed feelings about it all. I was glad I wouldn't have to worry about PMA's butt anymore, but I liked having the company. There weren't many people I could say that about in the world, because I usually preferred being alone to dealing with others' ideas of where I should be and what I should be doing. But we worked together well. We were like the poor man's Batman and Robin, united in a battle for justice against the forces of evil.

We had military purity.

Yeah, I was jumbling up a lot of metaphors, but that was water under the bridge and the fair was about to move on. I went to the valet and gave him the ticket for my car, then dug a five out of my wallet to tip him when he came back with it.

It was time to go to Milwaukee.

Milwaukee

It was a couple hours drive from Chicago to Milwaukee. Even though I told Howard I wouldn't pay a call on Michael Winters until tomorrow, I wanted to get the bulk of the driving out of the way today. I wasn't going to pay for the privilege of another experience in the Experience Suite anyway, so I figured I might as well change cities while I was changing hotels.

Heading north on I-94, I committed the unpardonable modern sin of answering a call on my cell phone while I was driving - luckily, I managed to avoid swerving into any nearby billboards. It was Howard. He was calling because he dug out a hard copy of an old CIA one-sheet biography of Andrew Wright, King of the Spooks. There was a throwaway line in the middle of the bio saying Wright had injured his right leg during "contingency operations towards the Sandinista regime in Nicaragua." Whatever the hell that meant. It also meant General Davidson's pal "Andy" was definitely Andrew Wright - the same lovely gent who asked Howard if I was "expendable."

I thought about Michael Winters and wondered if he was still alive. A man died in the act of handing his name to me, so I hoped Winters was still a secret to everybody else but me. If he was holding on to something important about Robert Davidson though, he might be more than a little reluctant to share it with me, since he didn't know me from Adam. That was not the worst problem I could face – after all, Not-Quite Connors and his SUV crew might be waiting for me at his place, who knew? But at least it would be me and only me in danger - PMA was on his way back to Washington D.C.

Except now I felt so bad about the poor kid getting dragged back home by his mother that I suddenly felt guilty about constantly calling him PMA. Yeah, I could be a sarcastic douche at the drop of a hat, or even without any headwear being involved. If I ever saw the kid again, I would call him by his real name. He was only eighteen and I knew just how stupid you could be at that age, because I was also anxious to join up with the Agency.

My father assumed all three of his sons would follow in his footsteps at the CIA. But my two older brothers bolted, leaving only me left to fulfill the old man's ambitions for his progeny. At first, I thought that was a good idea. My dad had started with the Agency at the very beginning, when it still seemed like a small and sexy cloak-and-dagger operation with clear-cut missions, and he still talked about it as though it had a moral imperative. But after we licked the Nazis and the Japanese, America became the primary world power and the responsibility rattled the country to the core. We grew over-the-top paranoid, primed to destroy a threat even when there wasn't one – and that's when the CIA was expected to utilize secretive, elaborate and occasionally insane covert operations to do all the dirty work.

One typical early Agency effort occurred in 1954, two years before I was born, when the CIA pulled off one of its first coups in Guatemala. What was the justification?

Fruit.

Jacobo Arbenz, democratically elected leader of the country, had decided to make the nation more self-sufficient and less dependent on U.S companies. Arbenz made plans to give some government land back to its citizens, and that's where the trouble started. Some of that prime property was filled with fruit farms that were run by the huge multinational corporation, the United Fruit Company, which had such close ties to the Eisenhower administration that it was the only business that had a code name within the CIA. That meant it had more than enough clout to be taken seriously when it ran to the government in horror and claimed Guatemala was falling to the Commies.

Next thing everybody knew, Jacobo Arbenz was out of time and out of power, and Guatemalan military strongman Colonel Carlos Castillo Armas was in charge. It all went so well that the U.S. suddenly saw just how much a coup could do. So our government made it the default solution to whatever was going on that it didn't like. As everyone looked away, the Agency tried to topple regimes in Iran, Iraq, Syria, Tibet, Indonesia, Cuba, Chile, Brazil, the Dominican Republic and on and on and on. Not all the efforts were successful, but enough got results that the U.S. never lost the will to try, try again.

The higher I rose in the ranks, the more I rejected the patriotic bullshit getting thrown around when these operations were being planned. We weren't the good guys, we were just a runaway arm of what Dwight Eisenhower (and, to be fair, A.J. Longetti) had pegged as the military-industrial complex. I saw everyone around me just following directives without giving a thought to morality or respect for other populations. It didn't matter what other countries wanted. It only mattered what America wanted and it didn't have much to do with freedom or democracy. It had to do with money and power.

That's when I started to want out. That's when I really began to feel trapped.

My old man, however, was not going to take it lying down if I left the CIA to become…well, anything else. That was my other problem. I didn't have a Plan B as far as a career went. Besides – I had a family to support.

Allison had worked at the CIA too. After we started seeing each other, she wound up pregnant, even though she told me she was on the pill. She pointed out the statistics that said the pill didn't always work. Okay. Even though it was already 1980, I observed the ancient protocol I was brought up with and married her, despite the fact that I didn't really know her all that well - I had spent most of the relationship up until then stationed in Europe and only saw her for a couple days every few months. We didn't spend any consistent time together until I requested a reassignment back at Langley a few months before the baby was due, and we moved in together.

A week in, I remember standing in the shower with the steam swirling around me, realizing how I had fucked up the rest of my life. About the only thing we had in common was the baby growing inside her. But, like the CIA, I saw myself as the good guy. I wouldn't walk on a wife and a baby. I was making a habit of doing the right thing for the wrong reasons, or vice-versa, I couldn't quite sort it out.

The baby came, it was a girl and we named her Grace. Three years went by and there was another girl, Lorie. I loved the kids, but hated the atmosphere. I was screwed up in the head about everything, but I made the best of it - but, in this case, the best didn't represent anything all that good. That was a pill my father had been willing to swallow, but I had seen what it had done to his disposition.

By the time eight more years had passed, by the time I had lived with Allison for eleven years, I knew I was done and I knew she knew. That's when she turned up pregnant again. I was in the room when it happened, so it wasn't as if I was blameless. But I knew if that kid was brought into this world, it wouldn't be good for anybody, including the baby. I told her to have an abortion. In the end, because she knew I would be going one way or the other, Allison did what I asked to keep the peace. It had been a boy, she insisted on telling me.

When we finally split up, that was when my father really turned on me, just as he had turned on my second-oldest brother when his marriage blew up. According to his belief system, you didn't leave your family, you just didn't do that. My father had spent his life in a loveless marriage, never straying, and that was what was everyone was supposed to do. It was how my brothers and I were raised, which is why our first marriages were all disasters. My oldest brother was lucky – his wife cheated on him, so my dad turned on her and not him, even though he was a complete asshole to her.

As for me, after the divorce, Allison and my father became engaged in a contest to see who could make my life the most miserable. I had my freedom, but it had a huge price tag attached - my sanity. I wasn't able to totally break with their judgments about me and I went a more than a little crazy.

And then there was Lorie.

I didn't want to think about that.

Besides, I was close to Milwaukee, the home of Harley-Davidson, Miller (the King of Beers), and Laverne and Shirley. I had other things to think about, the biggest of them being Black Sun. I checked into another hotel room that belied my real economic status, cheap and anonymous, and started scouring my Chromebook for any meaning that might be attached to the name of the Dark Sky facility in Montana. And it wasn't hard to find.

The Black Sun was the name of a symbol popular with today's crème de la crème of hate groups, German Neo-Nazis, who used it as a replacement for the notorious - and outlawed in Germany - swastika. There was some bizarre mythology attached to it that claimed that two suns duked it out over three hundred thousand years ago and, apparently, the black one had taken the title. Heinrich Himmler had commissioned this particular emblem too close to the end of World War II, so it apparently never really got its day in the (black) sun. However, no good

Nazi relic ever really goes out of fashion, so here was the Black Sun, back and blacker than ever before, perhaps.

Of course, maybe the fine Dark Sky organization was unaware of this connection. Maybe they just thought Black Sun was a cool name. Yeah, that was it.

Monday morning.

I was heading for Metcalfe Park, where Winters lived on North 37th Street. Metcalfe Park was one of the poorest and most crime-ridden neighborhoods in the city of Milwaukee and as I drove through it, I could see the urban decay at work. I passed by many older homes with peeling paint, placed along cracked sidewalks which bordered pothole-ridden streets. I also saw that I was one of the few white faces in the area, if not the only one. That didn't bother me and I hoped it didn't bother anybody else.

I parked in front of what I thought was Winters' house and stared out the car window at the front door for a few minutes, hoping the place wouldn't blow up or Not-Quite Connors wouldn't jump out of the bushes. Yeah, I was shaking. My other house calls hadn't gone very well so far and this one felt like the most significant one of all.

So I waited. And nothing happened. No explosions, no gunshots, no 6'5" faux TV cowboy. So I went ahead and got out of the car, walked up the rotting boards of the stairs leading up to the front porch, and when I reached the top, rang the doorbell. Somebody yelled, "JUST A

MINUTE," and a few minutes later, a black woman in her mid-thirties opened the door. She was big, wearing a giant red t-shirt and shorts, and she didn't look like she took any shit.

"Is this where Michael Winters lives?"

She tilted her head a little and looked me over.

"You from the government?"

"Not exactly. Can I talk to him?"

"What about?"

"I just wanted to ask him a few questions about his service overseas. He served in Afghanistan, right?"

She didn't like that question.

"Oh yeah, and he was in Iraq too, and both of them fucked him up GOOD. He don't like to talk about it and I don't like him to talk about it, okay?"

"You his wife?"

"His sister. Don't think there's a woman out there that would deal with this shit if they wasn't related to him."

"My name's Max…"

"And I'm Beyoncé, and Jay Z and I have agreed that you still ain't talking to him."

"I'm really a nice person."

"Sir, I don't care if you was the Pope, you got to go…"

She stopped, looked over my right shoulder and down the street. I turned to see what she was looking at.

It was a skinny black guy in his mid-thirties, slowly walking towards the house, wearing a battered Brewers baseball cap, a black sleeveless t-shirt and old jeans that were too big for him, like maybe they used to fit but then he stopped eating. As he approached, he was staring at the sidewalk, fidgeting and muttering to himself. I had the distinct impression that this was Michael Winters. If so, his sister hadn't misrepresented him – he seemed like something had definitely fucked him up good.

Suddenly, he looked up and saw me on the porch. And he also saw Beyoncé looking back at him and shaking her head, as if warning him off.

Then he turned and took off like a bat out of hell.

I hurried after him. But me hurrying was a lot different than him hurrying. I probably looked younger than I was, but I definitely ran older. So it wasn't a few seconds before the person I assumed was Michael Winters was already a block or so ahead of me.

But then somebody flew past me and after Winters - and he was faster than both of us.

It was PMA – and, holy shit, the kid had wheels!

Up ahead of me, PMA was closing the gap between him and Winters – when both men approached a porch where a bald man whose body was shaped like a cannonball was sitting and enjoying his morning coffee. When he saw Winters fly by – and then PMA in pursuit - he rushed down from his front porch.

"HEY!" Angry Cannonball boomed at the kid. "What you doin' with Michael?"

The kid kept running after Michael. And Angry Cannonball went running after him, yelling at all the houses he passed, "HEY! SOME WHITE BOY IS AFTER MICHAEL!"

They started pouring out of their houses, in pursuit of the kid, forming an irate posse protecting one of their own. It looked like a photo negative of the usual lynch mob scene.

Finally, near the end of a block, the kid caught up to Michael and grabbed him by the arm. As those two stopped, the neighbors caught up to them. I huffed and puffed my way up to the gathering as quickly as I could because shit was about to happen.

The kid held onto Winters' arm as Angry Cannonball lit into him. PMA stood his ground and told Angry Cannonball we just wanted to talk to him. I finally made it and said the same thing.

"Who sent you?" Angry Cannonball wanted to know. The crowd made some noises that I couldn't decipher, but they weren't pleasant. On Roosevelt Island, there were Canada Geese by the score and, in the spring, they would gather around their baby goslings and honk and hiss at anybody who came within spitting distance. This group's sounds had the same aggressive intent.

"Look," I said through what little breath I had left, "we don't want to hurt him. We might even be helping him."

Michael Winters just looked at us all arguing with each other as if it didn't have much to do with him.

Angry Cannonball turned to him. "Hey, Michael, you want to talk to these people?"

Michael Winters shuddered, shook, shrugged. "Don't know, don't know, don't know."

Angry Cannonball turned back to us. "You see how he is? He don't need this!"

I went with my last resort – the truth.

"Michael," I said to Winters in as soothing tones as I could summon, "this is General Davidson's grandson." I pointed to PMA, who nodded quickly in agreement, because he saw we needed to close this deal fast.

Michael Winters' eyes widened.

"Yeah, that's right," PMA went on. "My grandfather thought you might know something about his son's – my uncle's - death."

Michael Winters turned to the kid and looked him in the eye.

"He ain't dead."

Angry Cannonball was puzzled. "What's this all about?"

Michael looked down again and put his hand on Angry Cannonball's shoulder.

"S'all right, Tommy, everybody, everybody, everybody. Let me talk to these guys. Let me talk, let me talk."

Angry Cannonball gave me and the kid the onceover and asked Michael if he wanted him and the others to come along, in case we weren't legit. Michael said no, this was something he could handle, he could handle, he could handle. The group started dispersing, giving us the evil eye as they went their separate ways. It was clear they were just taking care of Michael, because Michael was just someone who needed taking care of.

I turned to PMA. "How the hell did you get here?"

"I ducked my mom at the airport. I ran out of the terminal and hitched a couple rides up here. I've been waiting around here all night."

"Good on you, sonny boy. You saved my ass."

"Yeah," he said with a surprised and delighted smile. "Yeah, I did."

It was PMA at its finest. Shit, I wasn't taking away that nickname now – this kid knew how to put a principle to work.

We walked back to Michael's house, where we once again had to get past his sister the gatekeeper. She grilled Michael and offered to kick our asses all the way to Cleveland if he wanted her to, but, thankfully, our asses were given a pass when he put her off and said he needed to talk to us. He took us into the backyard, where there were a few lawn chairs and a cracked table on the patio.

We sat down. He didn't. He looked down at PMA.

"You really the grandson?"

PMA nodded.

"How'd you find out about me?"

I answered that one. "General Kraemer."

Michael began pacing, not looking at us.

"General's dead. He's dead. Way dead. You see the news? Scary shit. I didn't sleep, didn't sleep at all."

"Colonel Allen's dead too," I said

Michael turned to me and then started looking around the yard, as if spies might be hiding behind the crabgrass.

"I don't know what's going on. Nobody would believe me, nobody, nobody."

"Who's nobody?" I asked.

"Kraemer and Allen, they didn't. I wrote them both long letters and no answer. No answer at all. Then I wrote one more letter." He looked directly at PMA. "To your grandpa."

"What did it say?" the kid asked.

"I just told him what I saw. He was a father and a father needs to know if his son ain't dead."

Michael stopped pacing and looked off into the clouds.

"He was alive. The fucker was alive."

And then he told us what he saw.

Michael had served under First Lieutenant Robert Davidson in Afghanistan. He remembered how, in 2005, he was told to stay behind with all the other men in the outfit while Davidson went on Recon with the guys from Dark Sky.

I asked if he knew who any of the Dark Sky people were. He told me nobody was allowed to mingle with Dark Sky. Some tall dude named Herman, wearing the Dark Sky uniform, would come to where they were bivouacked and talk with Davidson and Davidson alone. And on this particular night, Davidson went off with Herman and never came back. Later, they received word First Lieutenant Robert Davidson, son of General whatever-his-name-was Davidson, had been killed by an I.E.D.

I told Michael the story on the news was different – they said Davidson was killed by an Afghan rebel in a firefight. Michael remembered the official story changing. He thought that was "fucking strange, fucking strange, fucking strange."

Anyway, it was a few years later, 2008, and he was doing his fourth tour in Afghanistan. He could feel himself slipping, could feel his mental state shredding from the constant fighting and the constant terror. They were in the green zone, in the notorious Helmand district, scene of the most brutal fighting of the conflict.

I remembered the time well, because it was when the Pentagon had not only unleashed the dogs of war in Afghanistan, but also injected them with rabies. The Iraq surge, a sudden influx of troops into that beleaguered country, had seemed to turn the tide and the Pentagon had a hard-on to apply the same model to Afghanistan. The code word was

COIN, short for counterinsurgency, a line of thinking which advocated overcoming a native rebellion with sheer military numbers. It rarely worked. Even in Iraq, the surge had only ended up as a temporary fix that was actually enabled by underlying political shifts.

Still, in 2008, it was seen as a success, a success that could be replicated in Afghanistan if the strategy was duplicated. With that in mind, more troops were sent in by NATO and America. But, unlike the Iraq surge, more boots on the ground didn't put out the fire. Instead, they made it burn out of control as the violence continued to escalate.

The Pentagon's next move was to send in not just more troops, but also more mercenaries, private killing companies like Dark Sky which employed plenty of what they called "snake-eaters," the most vicious of the vicious former Special Ops forces. They went on a killing spree so insane and undiscriminating, that, two or three years in, Afghan President Karzai demanded that the U.S. remove these elite kill squads from the country; too many innocents were being slaughtered in a desperate bid to turn the tide in an unwinnable war.

That was the situation in Afghanistan when Michael Winters went nuts.

Michael paced back and forth as he set the scene. It was early evening, just after sunset, when the rebels go on the move and do whatever damage can be done. That was also the time of day when Michael felt the most scared, when the fear gripped him by the throat and made it hard to breathe. Suddenly, there was gunfire. He had no idea where it was coming from or headed to, he just knew with every fiber of his being that he couldn't stay where he was. He literally felt like his head was on fire.

So when he thought no one was looking, he bolted from his unit and out into the middle of nowhere. He ran far and fast over the desolate Afghan landscape, not having any idea of where he was going or why, until he ended up on top of a little hill, overlooking a small camp.

And that's when he saw Robert Davidson - alive, but maybe not so well.

Instead of his military uniform, Davidson was wearing a muted, blood red uniform with a small "D.S." logo over the front shirt pocket. Obviously the Dark Sky uniform. But the uniform wasn't what Michael noticed first. No, what stood out was the fact that Davidson was missing his left arm – and possibly the left half of his face. It must have been missing, because he was wearing a dark brown leather half-mask thing over one side of his face. The mask did have an eyehole cut into it, which maybe meant his left eye survived, and he also had a shaved head, which made him look like a *Friday the 13th – Halloween – Nightmare on Elm Street* low budget horror movie villain.

And then, not far from Davidson, Michael spotted his BFF. Herman. Or what he assumed was Herman. He recognized the 6'5" body, the menacing stance…but his brown hair was now blonde, and face seemed to have been somehow…changed. He looked like some kind of movie star. Somebody specific - somebody Michael had seen before somewhere?

I asked if he was carrying a rifle.

That literally stopped Michael Winters – whose back-and-forth pacing had almost become violent - in his tracks.

"How the FUCK did you know that?"

"Trust me, we know," I replied.

"That's how General Kraemer died!!!"

I nodded.

Michael took himself back to 2008, back to Afghanistan.

He saw that Davidson and Herman were interrogating a group of Afghans who were tied up at the edge of camp. They evidently weren't telling the Dark Sky boys what they wanted to know, because, while Davidson laughed with menace, Herman raised the rifle to his hip and shot all the men several times over by lowering and raising the lever action repeatedly. It was like something out of that one old TV show, Winters added. I told him we knew the one he was talking about.

Watching all this happen, Michael decided he must be hallucinating, because there was no way what he was seeing could be real. That calmed him down because hallucinating is like dreaming, and, in a dream, you can't get hurt. So he slinked off back in the direction of where he came from, and through some miracle, made it back to his outfit.

But it was clear to the others he had snapped. He couldn't form a coherent sentence, so his C.O. sent him to get examined. The medic couldn't make any sense of his ranting and raving about Robert Davidson having half a face and diagnosed him with PTSD and possible schizophrenia so severe that he had to be shipped home.

Back in Milwaukee, Michael gradually got a little bit better, but his nightmares wouldn't stop and neither would his obsession with First Lieutenant Robert Davidson's inexplicable resurrection from the dead. The more he healed, the more he knew what he had seen was real and that he had been led by the Divine to see what he had seen. And what God wanted from him now was to let the military know what was going on, especially General Davidson. He didn't think he could reach such a great and famous man all by himself, so he worked his way up the chain of command, first writing a letter to Colonel Allen, then to General Kraemer. No response. So he finally got up his nerve and wrote to General Davidson himself. He might never get the letter, but he had to try.

And one day, when Michael was doing some of his usual pacing back-and-forth in the backyard, the phone rang. His sister called to Michael in disbelief - it was General Davidson on the phone. Michael had put his phone number in the letter.

Michael got on the line and stuttered, he stuttered and repeated himself as he did since his brains had gotten scrambled overseas, but the General was very patient and very understanding. He wanted to hear every word of what he had to say, every detail of what he had seen. And when Michael finally managed to relate everything he knew, the General thanked him very much and told him he would look into it.

Michael Winters thought, at that moment, he would finally be vindicated, that the phone call he had just finished was the start of uncovering the truth.

Instead, as he said to us in his backyard, "That was the last I heard from anybody. Anybody. *Anybody.*"

As those words hung in the air, his sister stuck her head out the back window and yelled at us that we had had enough time with Michael.

Oh, and that we should get the fuck out of her yard.

Last Stop

The kid was hungry. He hadn't eaten since yesterday and he had been up most of the night. If I was going to be honest, he smelled a little. But I didn't mind the stink, if he hadn't shown up when he did, I wouldn't have gotten anywhere with Michael Winters. He deserved a decent lunch, so we drove off in search of a place to eat.

We were quiet. We were both taking in what we had heard from Winters. Then PMA spoke.

"You believe him?"

"Yeah, I do," I answered. "But I don't think anybody else would. Which is why he's probably still alive."

It was true. If they did know about Michael Winters, they wouldn't have bothered to kill him, because it would be easy to write him off as a traumatized freak. If I hadn't personally witnessed Not-Quite Connors in action, I might have joined the club. But that detail, the Lucas McCain rifle, made the rest of it plausible.

The question was, where did that get me?

For the moment, it got me to a Panera Bread near the motel where I still had a room. I watched the kid wolf down two turkey Paninis, but my stomach wasn't taking any food requests at the moment. Between mouthfuls, PMA remarked that this was some weird shit we were sinking in. I agreed. And he wondered what the hell we were going to do now.

I had to figure out where we stood before I could answer.

I had worked out a likely chain of events that had led to this point. After General Davidson talked to Michael Winters, he called his old pal Andrew "Uncle Andy" Wright, the king of the spooks, to look into Winters' story. And for whatever reason, Andrew Wright didn't want the story verified. So he went back to the General and said Michael Winters was just off his nut and not credible. That wasn't a hard conclusion to peddle and the General probably seemed like he bought it.

But he didn't.

Why? Who knows? Of course the General desperately wanted his son to be alive. So maybe he thought Andrew Wright hadn't done enough and went directly to the CIA to have them find Kraemer and Allen. That would be when I got called in the first time a couple of years ago. And even though I found them, they must not have done the General any good – which means either they didn't know anything or they were intimidated into keeping their mouths shut.

But the General still didn't buy it. At least not totally. Because when his health started failing and he realized he was running out of time, he came back to me to see if I could find out anything else about Robert Davidson. It was a random shot in the dark, but he had nothing to lose except some money he didn't really need, so why not?

Unfortunately, he once again turned to Andrew Wright to find me and hire me, and we already know Wright wasn't too keen on his buddy the General getting any closer to a reunion with his long-lost boy. Wright probably figured I wasn't going to find anything, but he also wasn't going to take any chances, so he used the flash drive, the credit card and the burner phone to track me - just in case. When he saw I was heading to see Allen and Kraemer, he probably panicked and called in Herman, and maybe Herman went a little further than Wright would have liked to get rid of the officers and scare me off.

Did they really have to kill those two retired officers? It seemed way too extreme for what pieces of the puzzle I had.

In any event, they must have thought that would be enough to make me turn back and give up. But they didn't know Kraemer had handed me Michael Winters' name. They didn't know that Herman, AKA Not-Quite Connors, had given away the game by confirming the craziest part of Winters' story - the part with the crazy Rifleman in it. So they didn't know I hadn't been scared off – at least not yet anyway.

But again – what good did all that do me? Or, as the kid had asked me, what the hell were we going to do? I was in some kind of no man's land, a limbo that I didn't know how to escape from…

…unless I gave up the case entirely.

That would mean doing what everybody kept telling me to do - go back to General Davidson and very politely and quietly talk him into accepting that his son was dead. That was the easy out. But what if he started asking me what happened to Kraemer and Allen? He had to know they had been killed.

The kid asked me again – what the hell were we going to do?

I didn't have an answer.

We went back to the motel, where PMA instantly crashed on the bed and caught up on some of the sleep he had missed out on the night before. As for me, I couldn't nap at that moment even if I was on a date with Bill Cosby and had just sampled one of his special cocktails. I was having an existential crisis, I didn't know where I was or who I was anymore. I sure as hell wouldn't have taken on this job if I had known I'd get caught in the middle of some weird top-secret death squad shit.

I missed my apartment, where undoubtedly UPS had been repeatedly trying to deliver my new *Fantastic Four* trade paperback which reprinted issues forty through fifty-five, perhaps Lee-Kirby's finest run on the comic, including the introduction of Galactus, eater of worlds.

More importantly, I missed Jules - and thinking about her made me feel like a giant piece of shit. Her operation was in a week and I had just completely thrown her always-tentative emotional equilibrium into a tailspin by taking on this insane assignment.

General Davidson sent me out his door with a sense of duty – but that sense of duty was very quickly dissipating in a cloud of psycho killers and official deceptions. I didn't need this. I didn't need any of this. This wasn't the time in my life where I wanted to transform into Max Danger, solver of deadly mysteries.

I had to get out of this.

And Howard had to be the guy to cut the cord for me. He got me in, now he needed to take me out. As I watched the kid sleeping, I couldn't believe how many times I had risked his life – not to mention mine – on this quixotic quest that only led to a guy with half a face and a twisted heart.

It was time to stop playing Secret Agent Man.

I picked up my magic CIA phone and went out to the motel's pool area. As it was late afternoon in early May, I'd have all the privacy I wanted – and I could make the call without waking up the kid, who would undoubtedly try to talk me out of what I was going to say. I laid back on the dirt-caked lounge in front of the empty pool and hit Howard's number.

"Yeah?" came his voice on the line. It sounded tight.

"I'm in Milwaukee."

"What happened?"

"It doesn't matter. I'm through."

"Through?"

"I want you to get me out of this. Now. I'm agreeing with you. I'm in way over my head. So – how do we do this?"

"You want to get out of this." I heard another voice in the room. And then Howard said, "Hang on a second."

He began quietly talking to whoever else was there. I couldn't hear what he was saying, but who would he be telling all this to? I heard him hand over the phone, so I wouldn't have to wait long to find out.

"M-Max…?" said that other person.

Oh, shit.

Mr. Barry Filer.

Oh, Howard.

"If you w-want to wrap this up, we're amenable to doing that."

"How nice for you," I said with steam coming out of my ears. "Does that mean you're sending over a couple of guys with a body bag to take me home in?"

"Th-there's no need to be unpleasant, Max. Y-you know, y-you haven't been in contact with me…"

"Because the fucking PHONE you gave me was tracking me everywhere I went! Because the fucking FLASH DRIVE you gave me was loaded with spyware! Because the fucking CREDIT CARD you gave me left you a beautiful paper trail! Because YOU SET ME UP. So I'm glad you're ready to wrap this up – I AM TOO."

I heard him make one of his almost burps and then I went on.

"By the way, what's your real name, Barry? I couldn't find you in the phone book."

"M-Max, we're fine with ending this contract and we'll even pay you the rest of your fee, but we n-need you to make one last stop."

"So the body bag's not coming to me, I have to go to the body bag?"

"I assure you, y-y-you will not be harmed in any way."

"Said the man who has done nothing but lie to me."

"I-I really haven't, Max, if you want to review…"

"I don't. Let's just call it a day. I keep the half you paid me and I get to go home and not get killed."

Pause.

"I need you to travel to a specific address in Montana, I-I-I'll text you the address…"

"*Montana?*"

"I'll be meeting with you there…"

"You want me to pay a call on Dark Sky? Am I correct?"

"I expect you to finish out the c-c-contracted job."

"Do you think I'm crazy? Well, obviously you do. You just invited me to my own murder."

"I-i-it's not in anyone's interests to kill you, Max. That's why you're not dead. Go to Montana and it will all be over."

He hung up.

It will all be over. What did those words mean?

I looked at the empty pool ten feet away from me and considered what sound my skull would make while hitting the bottom of it.

"He told you to go to Montana?"

The kid was awake. Wide awake after I told him about the next destination.

"Yeah, and he promised I won't get hurt."

"You believe him?"

"Good question." I sort of did, but no part of my heart, soul or brain felt good about going to Montana. Just thinking about it made me feel choked off by an overpowering darkness. And I wasn't the only one. For the first time, I saw real fear in the kid's eyes.

"I bet I know who we'll find there," he said.

"Maybe, maybe not. We should let your mother know where you are."

He understood the subtext of that statement.

"If you're going, I'm going."

"Did I say I was going?"

"If you're going, I'm going."

I knew how good the kid was at arguing he was going someplace where the other person said he wasn't going and I wasn't in the mood to spend a few hours playing "You Say the Opposite." So I dropped the argument for the moment and wrote out the information Mr. Barry Filer had texted me on the cheap motel notepad.

I then moved over to the Chromebook and checked the address into Google maps. The location was a few hours north of Missoula, above the Flathead Reservation, in the middle of fucking nowhere. I had a hunch the town, named Sonnenrad, would make Booneville seem like Manhattan. It lay at the edge of the Rockies, not far from the Canadian border. Anything would be game up there and I had a hunch that's exactly why Dark Sky had picked this particular location for the Black Sun facility.

The kid stared at me as I stared at the map.

"So – are we going?"

I looked at him.

"No other options are coming to me."

Yeah, we were going.

Tuesday morning.

We boarded a flight from Milwaukee to Missoula, which would take a little over five hours. Our shopping bags were beginning to shred, so, the previous evening, I bought the kid and myself a couple of pieces of legitimate luggage. We now had matching carry-ons, which was cute as hell.

I didn't argue with PMA anymore about him coming along for the ride. He had earned his spot and, besides, as a Davidson blood relative, I thought he had a much better chance of coming out of this in one piece than I did. He even might be an insurance policy for me – they wouldn't know he was coming and they wouldn't want anything to happen to him or there would be repercussions.

I was still arguing with myself about taking the ride at all - but, again, I was out of options. Knowing that Howard was now definitely under their thumb removed any chance at a safe harbor for me – and it also explained why, on the call before this last one, Howard had seemed so…*nice*. They trickled out a little information through him to keep me trusting him – which, in turn, enabled him to keep track of what I was doing for them.

Was I disappointed in Howard? No. Howard was a company man and Howard wanted his pension. If they told him to cut out my liver and cook it for dinner, he would do the decent thing and think about it for a few minutes before he actually went to work on me with a scalpel. Weak people were weak people and you had to expect them to act badly when the hammer came down.

When we arrived in Missoula, it was chilly, still in the thirties at night even though it was late spring. I used my David Muhlfelder credit card to get my sixth rental car and we headed north. It would be dark by the time we got near our destination, so I thought we'd stop and spend the night in beautiful downtown Kalispell at a Hilton Hampton Holiday Inn. I definitely wanted a whole lot of daylight before we entered hell.

After checking in, we went downstairs and across the street to some pizza joint to enjoy what I was calling our Last Supper, a reference the kid didn't seem to appreciate. At dinner, he wanted to know what my plan was. I had none. He didn't appreciate that either.

Wednesday morning.

I knew we each had a phone call to make before we left the hotel and headed further north.

I gave PMA back his cell phone so he could make his. It didn't matter if he had it now. It didn't matter anymore if anyone had hacked his phone or was tracking our movements through it. As Mr. Barry Filer had said, this was going to be the last stop. I told him to call his mother, not to say too much, but just to tell her he was okay and with me.

I went into the bathroom to call Jules. It was six a.m. our time, which meant it was eight a.m. in New York. Which also meant I woke her up.

"Hlllowww?" she mumbled.

"It's Max," I said. "Don't yell and don't hang up."

"Where are you?" she said sleepily and with confusion.

"Kalispell, Montana."

Pause.

"WHAT?"

"Kalispell, M…"

"I HEARD YOU."

Pause.

"Wait…you're Max again?"

"I was always Max, I…"

She groaned with the pain of the eternally-in-the-dark. I kept going.

"Look, I haven't slept with anybody else. You know I don't lie, unless it's about something stupid just to keep you from getting pissed off."

"You don't think I would get pissed off about you fucking somebody else? Where the hell is your mind? Oh, yeah, Montana. What the HELL are you in Montana for???"

"Not sure."

"You're really in some kind of trouble, aren't you?"

"Normally I would use this as a punchline, but I'm serious - if I told you anymore, they might have to kill you."

I could feel her tears welling up over the phone.

"What the hell…I thought they just gave you stupid shit to do…what the hell, Max? What the hell is this?"

"I don't know. But I should be home probably day after tomorrow. Don't worry."

"You're doing that bullshit thing where you pretend everything's going to be fine. I hate that bullshit thing, Max, I hate bullshit. Are you really going to get home?"

"If I have anything to say about it."

Another pause.

"I…I don't want to talk anymore. If you can't tell me what's going on, I…I can't do it."

"Yeah, I get it." I stopped a moment. "I love you, Jules."

A pause.

"FUCK YOU!"

Not the reaction I hoped for.

"YOU DON'T TELL ME THAT FOR THE FIRST TIME WHEN YOU'RE GOING TO DIE! THAT'S REALLY FUCKED UP, MAX!"

"Yeah. I guess it is."

She hung up.

I looked at the phone as if it might have some words of wisdom for me, but all it had was a big DISCONNECTED on its screen. I got up from where I was sitting, off the lid of the toilet, and went back out in the living room.

Where PMA was yelling at Angela.

"Goddammit, Mom, I'm okay, stop freaking out already!"

He hung up on her just as my phone rang again. I answered.

"Do you love me because you're going to die or because you love love me?"

"The second one," I said.

"I love you too," Jules said crying. "So DON'T DIE."

She hung up again just as the kid got his mom back on the phone.

"I'm sorry, Mom, I just…I just wanted to let you know I was all right. Don't…don't worry about me. I'll call you again soon."

A pause as she said whatever she was saying.

"Goodbye, Mom." He hung up again.

We looked at each other, two emotionally-stunted males trying our best to deal with women who were scared to death of what was going to happen to us.

"We should get going," I said.

"Yeah," he agreed.

"What do you think they're going to do to us?"

We were heading north on Route 93, north to God-knows-what, when the kid turned to me and asked that perfectly valid question.

And I really had no idea.

"I don't think they're going to kill us. They don't have to bring us to Montana to do that."

"So we shouldn't worry, huh?"

"Well…there are other things you can do to a person."

He looked at me in confusion.

"What does that mean?"

I shrugged, because I didn't really know. It was my gut talking. And my gut was screaming at me to turn the car around.

It was going up to the low sixties today, the kind of weather I liked the best. The big sky country was beautiful, the mountains on either side of us were magnificent.

I'd have to come back here another time when my life wasn't completely fucked.

Black Sun

Jan told us to turn left off the state highway and take a small gravel road that seemed to disappear into the woods. I thought my cyber-beloved was double-crossing me, until I saw a marker to the side reading, "Sonnenrad, 8 miles."

The road made for a long and rough ride - it was narrow and not in very good condition. A beat-up pick-up came from the other direction and we both had to get over to our respective shoulders to allow both of us to occupy the same patch of road at the same time. If this was designed to look like a road to nowhere, it succeeded in its aspirations.

Soon, however, we saw some small buildings in a clearing in the distance. As we got closer, we could see that they were all shapes and sizes and, together, they made up a strange hodgepodge that resembled a community. Some homes looked like they had literally been constructed from nearby trees and shrubs. Some looked like the kind of prefab houses you could order online. Then there was a modest gathering of mobile homes all parked to the side, as if the owners had decided to consign themselves to their own movable ghetto.

The streets, such as they were, were mostly made of mud and the parked vehicles ranged from bright new shiny 4x4s to old battered trucks that looked like they were made of more rust than metal. There was a single massive electricity line traveling overhead with smaller wires hanging down from it like some sort of power spaghetti, spreading every which way - some to junction boxes and some directly to the homes themselves.

"Is this a town?" asked the kid as I wondered how many septic tanks were buried in the immediate area.

"Your guess is as good as mine."

Neither of us could tell what the hell it was. It obviously wasn't a planned community, but it *was* grandly posing as a gated one – because, blocking our way ahead in the road was the kind of red and white tapered horizontal beam you'd find at a train crossing - and to the left side of it, a small makeshift guard booth made of tin or maybe just aluminum foil, who the hell knew?

We stopped a few feet from the gate and a big burly hairy man in his thirties who looked like Tony Soprano crossed with a bear came out of the booth. He wasn't wearing a uniform, just a large brown sweater with a hole or two in it, black work pants with a hole or three in them, and muddy boots. I rolled down the window to meet today's very first special guest.

"Good day, gentlemen," he said in dramatically-courteous fashion as he waddled up to our rental. "And how are you doing today in all of your endeavors?"

"Not bad, how about yourself?" I answered sweetly.

"Oh, I'm doing AMAZINGLY well. It's a beauteous day every day here in God's country."

"Yeah, I suppose it is. I'm here looking for Black Sun…"

"Are you, sir?" He gave me a skeptical and suspicious look.

"Yeah, is there a problem?"

"Well, sir, very few non-official vehicles make their way down this road. Can you provide any documentation as to the nature of your business?"

I began counting the holes in his clothing. I was up to six when I decided this was really a whole of lot of horseshit.

"I don't know, can you provide me with any documentation demonstrating you have any official connection with Black Sun? That you actually have the power to detain me?"

He blinked back at me.

"Sir, they entrust me with the…"

Horseshit.

"What's your name?"

"Claude Bachman."

"Well, Claude, I'm Max Bowman, currently on an assignment from the CIA. This is Jeremy, he's General Donald Davidson's grandson. And I've obtained the maximum insurance possible for this rental vehicle, which means I don't give a shit if I ram it through this plywood gate of yours."

It took him a few seconds to process all that, so I kept counting. Nine holes. I was about to ask him to turn around so I could continue, when Claude suddenly broke out into a huge laugh.

"Well, Mr. Bowman, you won't have to resort to that sort of measure, believe you me! Very good to meet you – and an honor to meet young Jeremy here, a descendent of such a great man!"

He offered a hand. I shook it. He squeezed way too hard, just like he did everything way too hard.

"Black Sun is two more miles down the road, through our lovely little town here. I hope you'll forgive me, we just have to be TREMENDOUSLY careful around here. The government, you know. They want to burn our little hamlet to the ground."

"Why's that?"

He lost his tremendous and amazing joviality in a heartbeat.

"Because they know we oppose them!"

"In what way?"

"In all ways! They want to defile our purity. Take our country away. And we, sir, are not going to allow that to happen."

"Well, as long as you've got it under control."

"That's why we've come here, sir. We've put our trust in The Dark Sky people. We know that when our time of need comes, it is THEY who will be standing on the side of righteousness.

"So…this town is here because of them?"

"Word gets out, sir. We would be tremendously honored to join them when the Day of Struggles begins."

"The Day of Struggles."

"Absolutely. We all know it's coming."

We stared at each other a moment.

"So, can you open the gate…?"

"ABSOLUTELY, sir!"

As he waddled back to the booth, I looked inside its open door and saw a giant Samurai sword standing in the corner. He hit a button that raised the gate. I called to him.

"Nice sword!"

"It's AUTHENTIC!" he boomed proudly.

Of course it was. I nodded and drove on.

The faces of the residents of Sonnenrad watched us with curiosity and suspicion as we slowly made our way down the main "street" of the "town." There was a grocery store, a pharmacy, a dry cleaners and some kind of rickety café, which looked so filthy that the food probably killed any rodents that might threaten it. There was also a church of sorts with a nailed-together wooden cross over the door – oh, and more than a few confederate flags flying proudly over homes.

"This place is freaky," the kid said in the understatement of the millennium.

The faces kept staring at us like we were aliens - the outer space kind, not the Hispanic kind. If we were the latter, I had a feeling our car would have been on fire.

"Yeah. When that Day of Struggles comes, I'm not sure this will be a viable first line of defense."

Then we saw it.

Down the road, maybe another mile or so, nestled in a small valley, appeared a large five-story black building surrounded by a large grouping of modern army barracks.

"Black Sun?" the kid said.

"Don't know what the hell else it would be." I answered.

As we got close, we approached another checkpoint, a checkpoint much different than the one occupied by the tremendously good gentleman with the samurai sword. This was a full-on for-reals military-style checkpoint, the kind that made you frightened even though you hadn't done anything. The high-security booth was manned by two bad asses wielding submachine guns - and wearing the very same blood-red Dark Sky uniforms that Michael Winters had described from memory.

The gate itself was composed of two giant, twenty-feet high sliding doors made of solid metal fencing – the same kind of metal fencing that encircled the entire, seemingly-endless perimeter of the Black Sun complex. At various points along the fence, towering high in the air, were guard stations where what looked like trained snipers perched, ready to take out whoever needed to be taken out.

This didn't look like a training facility. It looked like a prison.

The main guard at the checkpoint lacked the ebullience and élan of Claude Bachman. He didn't inquire as to the state of our health. Instead, he curtly looked us up and down with a severe expression. He wasn't too much older than PMA.

"Yes?"

"We're here to see a Mr. Barry Filer. I'm Max Bowman."

He hit his tablet with his finger a couple of times.

"You're expected, Mr. Bowman, but alone."

"I have Jeremy Longetti with me."

The guard looking inside at Jeremy Longetti for a long minute.

"Does he have ID?"

"No sir, he flushed it down a toilet."

The guard had nothing to say about that. Instead, he walked away from our car as he whipped out his small walkie-talkie device. When he was out of earshot, I saw him start talking to whoever was on the other end. It was a very short conversation.

He came back and asked us to get out of the car. Then he and his partner searched us thoroughly. Another guard seemed to appear out of nowhere and began searching through our car. He even used one of those mirrors-on-a-pole to look underneath the rental to make sure we didn't have any bombs strapped there. These people didn't take chances.

When all that was finally done, the main guard handed us two badges that said "Visitor" in blood-red letters.

"Pin these on. Drive straight ahead to the tall black building and check in at the front desk. They'll know what to do with you there."

I handed the kid his badge as the gates creaked open. He mouthed "What – the – fuck" at me and I shrugged.

We drove through the facility, past Dark Sky officers drilling young recruits. It reminded me of Parris Island, the Marines facility located down in South Carolina. My brother signed up with the USMC during the Vietnam War and my parents took me to his graduation from boot camp. There were a lot of angry drill sergeants yelling at a lot of sweaty recruits everywhere on the base. This was similar, only this was no official military organization, this was a private company playing soldier, getting ready for their own for-profit wars.

The streets here were paved, wide, pristine and clean. In fact, everything was pristine and clean at this place, since it couldn't have been more than a few years old. Andrew Wright had certainly directed a few billion towards its construction and, at the same time, made sure it was so far off the grid that people could easily disappear here. The Day of Struggles wouldn't have a chance.

We arrived at the black building, which had a huge Dark Sky logo rotating on the roof. I parked in front of it. A few seconds later, the entrance doors automatically opened and we entered the belly of the beast – and it was a magnificent belly, I had to say. The lobby was three stories tall with a giant black metallic – what else? - American Eagle covering the forty-foot back wall. Under the eagle, a receptionist sat at a long black granite desk, patiently waiting for us to cross the length of a football field that stood between us and him. He was another humor-deprived young man in a blood-red uniform.

"Mr. Bowman and Mr. Longetti?"

We nodded in unison as we walked towards the desk.

"So, that town or whatever it is down the road," I began. "What's…"

"Mr. Bowman, I'm going to ask you to turn around and walk back out of the building. You're to be taken to The Barn."

"The Barn?" I asked. "Are we to be milked?"

"It's the name of the building in the back of the facility." He craned his neck to look past us and through the glass entrance doors. "As a matter of fact, your vehicle is here."

We turned. It was a black SUV identical to the fleet we encountered in Branson – not exactly a surprise to either of us. We turned and started to head back out the way we came in.

"Um, no, Mr. Longetti, you're to remain here."

PMA turned back to the receptionist.

"You'll be…" The receptionist reviewed his computer screen with a slightly confused expression, then looked up again. "…someone will be meeting you here shortly."

The kid looked at me.

"It's their ballpark," I said. "Wait here. I'll be okay."

I turned and headed out to the waiting SUV. I really didn't know if I was going to be okay. It wasn't a good sign that they were splitting us up, but I assumed this was to safeguard the kid, which I was all in favor of.

The driver of the SUV was yet another young gentleman in a Dark Sky uniform with a serious case of being serious. He had me get in the back seat and drove towards the back of the facility, past all the barracks, a mess hall, a few other one-level office buildings, a gymnasium, their equivalent of a PX store…and then, into the weeds. We had driven through a back gate in the tall metal fencing and were now driving through the wild grass, because there was no real road back here, just vegetation that had been run over a couple hundred times until it formed a path of sorts.

The only thing back here was The Barn.

We came over a small hill and there it was, all by its lonesome, about a hundred feet or so ahead. I assumed it was The Barn, it sure as shit was shaped like a barn, even though it was jet black and appeared to be made of solid steel. We drove around the back of it to where two other lookalike SUVs were parked, pulled up beside them and stopped. My driver helpfully pointed out a nearby door, I got out of the vehicle and thanked him. He said nothing in return.

I had the feeling the Dark Sky support staff knew that a trip to The Barn never meant anything good.

As the SUV backed up, turned around and headed back towards the main facility, I breathed in some of the Montana air. It was clean and refreshing. I took in as much of it as I could.

I was stalling. And frankly, I wished I smoked. This would be the time to have one last cigarette, fuck the clean and refreshing Montana air.

A couple of moments later, I headed for the door and knocked on it when I reached it. I wasn't sure what else to do, there wasn't a doorbell, an intercom, written instructions, or even a welcome mat.

A voice from inside yelled, "It's open!" So I opened it and walked inside.

It took my eyes a minute to adjust to the darkness inside after the bright sunlight outside. When I could finally see clearly, the first thing I locked on was a glass display case mounted on the wall to my right filled with…

…tomahawks?

That's when something rammed me in the gut and drove me to my knees.

The party was starting.

When I looked up to see what had hit me, the same something whacked me in the back of the head and took me all the way down to the floor on my stomach.

That was going to leave a mark.

My eyes had to refocus yet again from the attack to my skull. When they did, I looked up at the walls of the Barn and saw that they were festooned with all sorts of mounted medieval weaponry. Battle axes, maces, quarterstaffs, war hammers…and a lot of other scary things that I didn't know the names of. I also noticed the floor I was lying on had the occasional dried stain here and there. The stains looked like they were comprised of dried blood. And the more I looked for them, the more I found.

I got up on my elbows to see what had walloped me. My guess was right - not that I was happy about it.

There was Not-Quite Connors leading with his rifle butt, which had doubled me over and then knocked me down. He repositioned the weapon so he was holding it in one hand, rifle barrel pointing at me.

"Hello, Herman," I said weakly.

That seemed to startle him for a moment. But he quickly snapped back into angry psychopath mode.

"Get up," he snarled.

He flipped his rifle around to cock it and make a point. I adjusted my rumpled Banana Republic jacket and slowly got to my feet. I felt behind my head. A little blood? I tasted my fingers.

Yep, blood.

Herman looked at me with his piercing blue eyes.

"How do you know my name?"

"To be fair, I only know half of it. By the way, who's your plastic surgeon? Can he make me look like Chuck Connors? Actually, I think I'm more of a Mike Connors guy. Remember him? *Mannix*? Great theme song."

He approached me, pushing his rifle barrel towards me threateningly.

"Remember what I told you in Branson? You answer to me," Herman said with his jaw set, apparently by a very talented plastic surgeon. "I told you to stop. You didn't. Now you're mine."

"Herman, I know you're not going to kill me. I don't know why you're not going to kill me, but you're not."

He seemed to want to convince me otherwise and in the worst way possible. He dropped his rifle down against his hip, Lucas McCain style, and shot towards me. The bullet whizzed by my ear so closely it felt like a gentle whisper of a breeze. Whatever the wall was made of behind me, it absorbed the bullet like a sponge.

More proof that anything goes inside The Barn.

He kept shooting.

One bullet went by my other ear, another by my left arm, another by my right arm and another over my head.

I didn't actually piss my pants, but a few drops might have snuck out.

"H-H-Herman, stop. We've discussed this."

Emerging from the darkness was none other than Mr. Barry Filer, wearing one of his Joseph A Bank suits. I was actually happy to see him, and it took him stopping someone from shooting me in the head to elicit that positive reaction.

"Barry, what the hell? You said I wouldn't be hurt and I'm bleeding from the back of my head," I said with more than a little irritation. "And where did you take Jeremy?"

"WE ask the questions," said Herman.

"D-d-don't worry about the boy," said Mr. Barry Filer.

"Worry about yourself," said Herman.

Mr. Barry Filer tentatively reached over and pushed Herman's rifle barrel down so that it wasn't pointing at my head. Which I appreciated.

"Y-y-you were told not to be so aggressive, Herman."

Herman took a few steps back, but he wasn't done with me.

"Why'd you bring that kid with you?" he barked. "What the FUCK are you up to?"

"Not a whole lot, cowboy," I replied, "And you?"

My abdomen ached and my head was killing me, but I wasn't going to let them know, that would give them some power. I learned that early on, when my oldest brother hit me in the stomach as hard as he could for no damn reason. That's when I made a promise to myself not to let him see me cry and he left the room looking empty and disappointed. So I was going to put on a show here as long as I could. If they saw I was scared, they would try to get away with anything they could.

I again eyed all the bizarre and cruelly primitive weaponry mounted on the walls.

"What do you boys do in here anyway?"

"W-w-we have advanced weaponry classes here, if that's what you mean," said Mr. Barry Filer. "W-w-we pride ourselves on providing training at the highest level here at Black Sun. That can get a little n-n-nasty."

"I could tell by the bloodstains. So did Claude Bachman get his samurai sword from you guys?"

Herman laughed again. Who knew he had a sense of humor?

"That loser?" he said with a roar.

"I-i-it was a gift," Mr. Barry Filer replied quietly. "To reward him for watching the road."

"To get him to shut the fuck up," was Herman's version.

"You've acquired quite a following down the road there," I went on.

"They're harmless," said Mr. Barry Filer. "P-p-people understand what we represent."

I once again eyed the bloodstains, the instruments of death and Herman glaring at me with his rifle ready at his side to blast me full of holes the moment management gave him permission. And I couldn't help but think all that was represented here was some kind of sadistic nightmare.

And that's also when I saw a figure come out of the shadows behind Herman – a figure holding a mace.

A mace that came slamming down right on top of Herman's Stetson.

Mr. Barry Filer turned with a start as Herman fell to the ground. His turn to bleed from the head.

That's when I noticed the figure holding the mace only had one hand to hold it in.

He looked exactly as Michael Winters had described him. A leather covering over the left side of his face, the left arm missing, head shaved and, unlike Herman who was into Western cosplay, wearing an official Dark Sky blood-red uniform. He had a Browning Hi Power 9mm pistol resting in a holster on his right hip – and – of course – the mace in his hand.

He turned to Mr. Barry Filer, who was in the middle of experiencing a severe almost-burp.

"Where's my nephew?"

"Richard, I-I-I have no idea of what you're talking about."

Richard?

"Filer, I can access the entry logs, I know he's here." He turned to me. "You Bowman?"

I nodded slowly.

"Let's get out of this torture chamber."

Robert Davidson threw the mace to the floor, and grabbed me by the arm, ushering me towards the exit. Once outside, we got in his SUV and I rode shotgun.

"Why did you bring my nephew here?" he demanded to know as we drove up over the ground Rat Patrol-style back to the base.

"Your nephew doesn't take no for an answer. He's a good kid. You'd know that if you were still alive."

He gave me a hard look.

"But I'm not, am I?"

He stopped at the back gate and talked to the guards, asking them if they knew the kid's whereabouts. They shook their heads with their serious faces. Nobody knew anything. He had them call the reception desk in the big black building. All they knew there was Herman had picked up PMA.

Herman.

Robert Davidson revved the motor and took a few turns until we were suddenly in a small neighborhood of modest bungalows. He screeched to a halt in front of one of them and got out. I followed, not sure what to do and still a little goofy in the head from Herman's rifle butt, not to mention the insanity that was swirling around me. This was like one of those nightmares I had been having before I got here, only there was no way to wake up from this one.

Robert marched up to the front door. Locked. He pulled out his 9mm pistol and fixed that problem with a well-placed shot, then kicked the door in.

And then came the real nightmare.

The kid was in there all right, sitting on the sofa and looking stunned for good reason. He was the only visitor to what was for all intents and purposes the world's only Rifleman museum. There were framed pictures of Lucas McCain all over the living room - stills from the show, framed Rifleman comic book covers, and a wall-length poster of Chuck Connors himself shooting at an onlooker. Not only that, but there were large mounted video screens on each wall, each playing a different episode of *The Rifleman*, as well as a display case of old Rifleman toys from sixty years ago – which included a board game. I wondered what you had to do in order to win, make it out alive?

"Let me guess," I said. "Herman's place."

But Robert Davidson didn't respond. He was staring at the kid, the kid he hadn't seen in over a decade, staring at him as if he were mentally measuring everything he had lost by playing dead all these years.

"Uncle Robbie?" the kid said tentatively.

Uncle Robbie couldn't bring himself to speak. He motioned to the boy to get up and follow him back out the door. We got back in the SUV, drove not far down the same street and stopped at another bungalow, his bungalow.

Inside the small modest home, he motioned for us to sit down. We did.

"You shouldn't have come here."

"I didn't have much of a choice," I replied. "Management was insistent."

"Management," he muttered.

And then he looked down at the Dark Sky shirt he was wearing and, with one savage move, used his one hand to physically rip it apart, leaving the shredded cloth hanging on his torso like he was an old Doc Savage paperback cover.

"Why did you bring my nephew here?" Robert asked again. "Why did you bring family into this?"

"I made him bring me," said the kid.

"Besides," I said, "Isn't this all about family?"

He glanced out the window with a sigh.

"I'll never have a fuckin' family. I'll never have a fuckin' life."

"They called you Richard back there. That your name now?" I asked.

"Yeah," he said bitterly. "Herman suggested it. Richard Kurtz."

"Like Colonel Kurtz – *Apocalypse Now*."

"That's what I thought until Herman started calling me 'Dick.'"

"Dick Hurts," I said with a wince. "Oh, shit."

"Yeah. Herman thought it was a pretty funny joke," Robert said, nervously glancing out the window again.

"Speaking of Herman, what's the deal with that guy? Why is he allowed to run around beating and killing people whenever he feels like it?"

Robert said nothing. He kept staring out the window.

"Why does he have so much power around here? I would think a loose cannon like that – okay, a loose *rifle* like that – could bring a place like this down."

Again, nothing.

"And what, are you a prisoner here? Why not just leave? Your father wants you home. That's why he hired me, you know."

That made him turn back to me.

"Think my father wants to see me like this?"

He pulled off the leather covering that hid half his face. The kid and I both let out an involuntary gasp.

What was under there wasn't pretty – it was gnarly, like he had smeared cheese on that side of his face and then dropped some rats on it to chew it to pieces. It was something you wouldn't let the kids see because it would give them nightmares.

"You know, there are plastic surgeons. Herman must know a pretty good one," I offered, trying to pretend I didn't want to turn and look in a direction where his face wasn't.

"You don't understand. We both choose to look like this."

"Why…"

"Because of the plan."

"Plan?"

"We were going to run a campaign of psychological terror in Afghanistan. We would change our appearances to become living embodiments of evil. We'd be so scary that the rebels would shit their pants if they even saw us. We called ourselves 'The Demonic Duo.' Clever, huh?"

"Yeah, but how come you had to be the…"

"The ugly one? The one that would send kids running screaming into the night? Because I was the one who was lucky enough to step on the roadside bomb."

He leaned against the wall and put his hand up to his head as if he had the migraine to end all migraines. I looked at PMA to see how he was coping with all this. The answer? Not well.

"I'm a sick fuck, Bowman, a very sick fuck, and I have been for a long time. But Herman said we'd be sick fucks for America, and that seemed like a good use of my talents.

"But why The Rifleman?"

"The Rifleman could go out and massacre a half-dozen guys, then go home and teach his son good family values, all in thirty minutes, not counting commercial breaks. Meaning you could be a really fine, upstanding, moral sick fuck. That's why Herman loves that show, Bowman, that's why he decided to make his face look like The Rifleman's, so he could feel like a hero, no matter what kind of sick shit he and I did. And we did a lot of it, let me tell you, a whole lot of sick shit."

Well, shit, maybe TV did cause violence, like the experts used to say back in the seventies.

I stared at Robert Davidson, who was again staring out the window, waiting for the inevitable to come crashing through his door. I had a feeling his mind looked a lot like his face – half-normal and half-scarred beyond belief. You couldn't feel sorry for Herman, but Robert Davidson was a different story. This poor guy had come through the fog of the violence of his younger years and now could see clearly what he had allowed himself to become. I couldn't help but pity him – because I couldn't imagine how he was going to live with everything he had done with his life for much longer.

"Look, Robert," I said softly, losing all the wiseass from my voice. "We should work together and get you back home. Your dad's not in good shape and he wants to make things right."

"What's wrong with him?"

"He's had a few strokes," PMA said, finally able to join the conversation. "He's very weak. Mom will do everything she can for you, I'm sure."

Hope flickered in his eyes for a second, then it seemed to vanish without a trace.

"I belong here. I'm fucking dead inside. I belong here."

Then he sat. And then he cried. And he cried and he cried.

The kid and I looked at each other. That's when the men in blood-red jumpsuits burst in, led by the hunk who had played bartender in Branson. He glared at Robert with sheer hatred.

"If Herman doesn't recover, I'll kill you - and this time you'll stay dead."

Then his men took me and the kid away, leaving Robert sitting there, still sobbing uncontrollably.

The Tank

"L-l-let's try this again," said Mr. Barry Filer.

The kid was locked away in a room nearby, presumably safe and sound, while we sat in a small conference room inside the main five-story black building, a room they called The Tank. The Tank. I knew that was the name they called the room in the Pentagon where the President would come and talk with the Generals about their most secret secrets, so it made sense that the powers-that-be would bring that same sensibility here to Dark Sky.

The Tank in The Barn. I thought it was all The Stupid. It all smacked of boys who had built their own forts in their backyards and defended them with BB guns, at least until they were old enough to get erections. Places like this were monuments to arrested development.

"Okay," I replied. "And let's start with us all agreeing that Robert Davidson isn't dead. Because I just spoke with the guy."

"W-well…" Mr. Barry Filer stopped there, because at that moment, the door opened. In walked a well-dressed older man with a cane, which he used to support his right leg.

The last missing piece of the puzzle.

"Hello, Andy," I said, looking him up and down, realizing he wasn't the king of the spooks at all. He was the king of the sick fucks.

He blinked at my familiarity.

"Mr. Bowman."

He almost smiled and sat down.

"I have to give it to you," he continued. "You were never supposed to get this far. We completely counted on your failure."

"Usually that's a safe bet, sorry."

"When you hire some aging freelancer who quit the Agency over a dozen years ago, you assume he won't want to make waves. You assume he won't even *know* how to make waves. By the way, I wanted to ask…Daniel Bowman…?"

"My father."

Andrew Wright nodded. "One of the Agency old-timers. He was there at the beginning. Didn't seem to make much of it, did he? Not very ambitious?"

"More in the self-defeating business. Like me."

"I see. Well, first of all, I'd like to apologize for everything you've been through."

"Maybe you should also apologize to Colonel Allen and General Kraemer. Oh, wait, you can't, one got blown to charred little bits and the other has twelve rifle bullets in his heart."

"That shouldn't have happened," Wright said after an uncomfortable moment of silence. "Herman shouldn't have done what he did in Kentucky and Missouri. He keeps acting like he's still in Afghanistan."

"Shouldn't you put that guy in a cage?" I asked Wright. "Or will the mace to the head keep him down for good?"

Wright bristled. "Herman is going to recover, don't you worry. And you should also know that Herman is a patriot, a very valuable asset to Dark Sky, and…"

"Wait a minute. You're implying he killed Kraemer and Allen just for kicks. And you're just going to let him back out there?

I noticed out of the corner of my eye that Mr. Barry Filer was stifling a smile. Evidently, I was saying something he liked hearing.

"W-well," stammered Wright defensively, suddenly sounding like Mr. Barry Filer, "To tell the truth, Afghanistan was hard on Herman. War does things to people. You saw what it did to Michael Winters."

"With all due respect, Andy, I think Herman is the type who causes what happened to Michael Winters, not the type who suffers from it."

Another uncomfortable silence.

"Herman is my son, Mr. Bowman," said Wright.

Oh.

"I know he seems a little…extreme. But he only has his country's best interests at heart as well as those of Dark Sky. Barry here may run the organization, but Herman is the soul of Dark Sky."

Wow. Andrew Wright just might have been the most deluded dad since Adam bought Cain's story about Abel stabbing himself in the chest repeatedly.

"W-w-we're not here to talk about Herman," Mr. Barry Filer broke in to save his boss from further embarrassment.

"Then let's talk about Robert Davidson. Why is he still alive?"

Wright took a deep breath.

"In 2005, Robert Davidson was killed in Afghanistan - although, of course, he wasn't. However, the I.E.D. did a lot of damage. His facial injuries…the loss of his left arm…tragic. But instead of becoming a victim, Robert looked at what happened to him as an opportunity. He and Herman were already in discussions prior to the incident. He wanted to join Dark Sky and their efforts rather than continue to serve in a neutered military subject to shifting political winds. So we saw this as the perfect opportunity to "kill" Robert Davidson and reincarnate him as Richard Kurtz, a high-level Dark Sky operative."

"Dick Hurts."

"Well, yes, we didn't see that at the time. Herman really pulled one over on us."

"Such a scamp. Anyway, who's in the ground at Arlington under Robert Davidson's name?"

"Some other unfortunate soul who was shot in a firefight. We told his family he was MIA and we shipped his body home in place of Robert's. I told General Davidson Robert's remains were too gruesome for him to be put back together and he accepted that reluctantly. No open casket at that funeral."

"Why pretend to kill him?"

"We were going to do some very dirty work in Afghanistan, Mr. Bowman. Counterinsurgency, you know. Robert was anxious to be a 'COINdinista,' as we like to call ourselves, but he was rightfully afraid of what his actions in that arena would do to his father and the entire family's reputation. Plus, after the blast, he did not want his father to ever see him looking…well…"

"So how did he and Herman hook up in the first place?"

"Well, he and Robbie were in the Army Ranger program together – they became great friends. Great friends."

He hit "friends" a little hard.

"More than a bromance?" I asked.

Wright smiled. "Yes I had a little more trouble accommodating myself to the notion…but it takes all kinds. The gay thing was another reason Robbie wanted to go underground. He didn't think his father would accept…who he is."

"He might've been right about that."

"Anyhoo," Wright continued, "I had already helped Herman make the transition from the Army to Dark Sky. He took to it like a duck takes to water. So…while Robbie recuperated, the boys talked about what they could do with the new mandate to make some aggressive moves in Afghanistan - after the success of the surge in Iraq. Their idea was to find a way to make a substantial psychological impact on the Taliban fighters. Become frightening legends that would strike terror in the hearts of the enemy."

"I heard. The Demonic Duo. They should have their own comic book."

"Yes, Robbie's appearance would obviously have an impact. But that left Herman feeling like he was at something of a disadvantage, and he's a very competitive boy. So he thought about how he could change his own face – and that gave him the idea of assuming the persona of his childhood hero, Lucas McCain. We flew in a top plastic surgeon for the facial reconstruction, we had a few of those special rifles fabricated for him, and the transformation was simply astonishing. He really did become, in his own mind, this mythical assassin. The two of them were remarkably successful in terrorizing the Afghan rebels. Psychological warfare is the most effective, Mr. Bowman."

"Okay, Andy, you lost me. Do they show *The Rifleman* on Afghani television? Do they have their own TV Land channel over there? How would they even know who Herman was pretending to be?"

"It wouldn't matter, Mr. Bowman. You've seen for yourself how terrifying Herman's roleplaying can be. In any event, the two of them together moved fast and worked quietly. And they did some damage, let me tell you."

"C-c-cleaned out more than one village," grinned Mr. Barry Filer, while he was looking at the folding chair to the side. Oh, wait, wrong again, he was looking at me.

"So why are they here in Montana – there's still plenty of shit going on overseas, right?"

"Our government lost the appetite to continue with the mission. The Afghan government objected. Everyone wanted to cut and run like cowards. So…we left. And wouldn't you know, Iraq and Afghanistan are in chaos again. ISIS is the threat du jour. Now, we're in Syria. Inevitably, the political winds will blow back in our direction – at which point, we will return and do what we do best."

"And if those winds don't shift?"

"We'll find our way."

Mr. Barry Filer spoke up again – and forcefully. "This country has to find the will."

"The will?" I asked.

"W-w-we act like we don't want to be a world power. Like we don't want to c-c-conquer. We start things, we don't finish them. We ran away in K-K-Korea. In Vietnam. In Iraq and now in Afghanistan."

"Patton, you know, wanted to go right into Moscow with the tanks at the end of World War II," added Wright helpfully. "Imagine if we had let him. Imagine if we hadn't had a Cold War or an arms race to attend to. Our already incredible prosperity would have been magnified a thousandfold. We run away from empire-building, because it's not politically correct. But who else is qualified to run the world? Who else has our values and our morals? All we lack is the will to admit to ourselves this is what we need to do and do it. We are capable of making the move, you know. We're still the only country that's used an atom bomb against another."

"We should have used a lot m-m-more," Mr. Barry Filer chimed in. Wow, what a fun guy.

"Barry's a true believer, Mr. Bowman," chuckled Wright. "And so am I. For decades, I've had to attempt to control the world through secret plots and silly underground conspiracies. They wanted us to kill Castro with an exploding cigar, for God's sake. We're all after the same thing – we just can't bear to be seen doing it in broad daylight. That's why Dark Sky was built, Mr. Bowman. Our government will call on us again and we will be more than ready – and yes, we'll do it in the dark if we must. You can't have progress without conflict. If we all agree the American Way is a great thing, why not apply that template to the rest of the world and create a marvelous and productive earth?"

Andrew Wright made genocide seem positively positive. He was Hitler crossed with Dale Carnegie – *How to Conquer the World and Influence People.*

"That's all wonderfully inspiring, Andy. But why are you trying to sell me?"

Wright leaned forward. Time to close the deal.

"General Davidson is a great, great friend of mine, has been for decades. We trust each other. I'm a loyal man, Mr. Bowman, and I have a hunch you are too. When that lunatic soldier wrote to General Davidson…"

"Michael Winters." I didn't like him to be casually dismissed.

"…yes, Michael Winters, when he wrote to General Davidson, the General was very upset. I tried to calm him down, because I knew that if he found out about Robbie, it would literally kill him. But he wouldn't stop. He went after Kraemer and Collins, who did some digging of their own. I had to convince them to stop to protect the General."

"And then you ended up killing them."

"As I said, that was a mistake. Herman went a little too far…"

"A little too far? Andy, you got a blind spot that's the size of Kim Kardashian's ass…."

"Judge me as you will, Mr. Bowman, but let's discuss your role in all this."

"My role?"

"All we're asking you to do is go back to the General and tell him you tried and you tried, but you could find no evidence that Robert is alive. He'll believe it coming from you and that will put an end to all the unpleasantness. We'll pin the deaths of Kraemer and Allen on some unhinged friend of Michael Winters. We'll provide you with the back-up documentation. That will make your job easier, right?"

"Why does it have to be me?"

"The General hired you because he trusts you, Mr. Bowman."

"And he doesn't trust his friend of multiple decades?"

"Sadly, in this area, I believe he might not. In our last conversation, he kept bringing up the whole closed casket thing at the funeral. It's getting to that difficult place. But, if you make a good show of it, I think he might finally accept things. Create a good story, so he feels it's all credible. There's no point in breaking the old warrior's heart at this point in his life, is there?"

"Angela Davidson laid out the exact same plan for me. Any idea why?"

"I won't get into private family matters."

That shut me up. Being a giant idiot usually did. Of course she knew what was going on.

During that expanse of quiet, Mr. Barry Filer pulled a very thick envelope out of his jacket pocket, an envelope of approximately the same thickness as the original envelope given to me at our first meeting. He shoved it across the table in my direction.

"The other half of your fee, M-M-Mr. Bowman. If you'll agree to finish the assignment as we've suggested."

I pushed the hair back on my head. We had hit the crossing in the road. I stalled. Becoming an unofficial member of this murder machine wasn't appealing.

"If I say no, you kill me? Is that it?"

"No, Mr. Bowman, we want you to show up and talk to the General in person. If we killed you, that wouldn't happen, now would it?"

"But if I said no, Andy, it also wouldn't happen. So why not kill me? Let Herman do it, it could be an early Christmas present for the boy."

Wright's face tightened. He was done being my Dutch Uncle. I didn't care, I went on.

"And if you're going to try and blackmail me by saying you're going to pin Kraemer's and Allen's murders on me, I'm not scared of that. I know Herman tried to set things up that way, but I know too much - and you wouldn't want me starting a conversation with the authorities, would you?"

"We don't have to kill you, Mr. Bowman. And we don't have to frame you. We have other means."

Mr. Barry Filer reached into another jacket pocket and pulled out a folded photo. He handed it to me with a knowing smirk.

I unfolded it and looked at it for a long time.

It was Lorie's mug shot.

Retreat

I wasn't in the mood for Claude Bachman.

Not that there ever would be a time when I was in the mood for Claude Bachman, but this was the worst possible moment for me to encounter a dopey survivalist who had thrown away any semblance of a normal life to play Checkpoint Charlie for a bunch of murderous psychopaths who happened to have a huge billion-dollar playground in the middle of nowhere.

"You better slow down," PMA said. He knew I had lost my shit but he didn't know why. What he did sense was, as my car approached Claude Bachman's makeshift gate at way too high a speed, I was seriously considering slamming the gas pedal to the floor and ramming through it – mostly because I desperately wanted to get to the next bar without having to engage in conversation with a moron who couldn't even afford clothes that moths hadn't made their mark on.

But I stopped. I didn't want to…but I stopped.

Claude was a little taken aback by the sound of squealing brakes, so he quickly waddled out of his shack in a dither. He saw us and recognized us, so hope briefly flourished in my heart that he would simply raise the gate and let me go on my way. But no, I had been to the enchanted land

and, like a munchkin who had been denied entry to Oz, he wanted all the secrets of the magical center of his demented universe.

He waddled over to the driver's side. Wonderful. I quickly lowered the window, so I could finish this quickly.

"Good day, sir!" he bellowed as he approached.

"I'm in a hurry, can you raise the gate?"

He didn't do that. What he did was lean into the open window. The price of passage was having to talk to him.

"Well, most certainly. Just wanted to ask if I may, how was your visit? How are things in the Dark Sky community?"

"They're getting ready to make the world safe for white people like you. So don't worry your pretty little smelly head."

He looked at me with some confusion, not sure if I was joking or actually tuning in on his wavelength.

"I'm not sure what you mean, sir."

"I mean, you and the rest of your paranoid bigoted subhuman clan of pussies who piss their pants at the thought of progress in any form are going to be fine. You can continue to claim to own Jesus, the Bible, the Constitution, the Declaration of Independence and, of course, the American flag and you can continue to pretend all of those things are full-on in favor of you keeping your foot on the throat of every person of color, condemning to eternal damnation every sexual act outside of heterosexual marriage, despising and invalidating every other religion outside of yours and teaching your children that America has never done anything remotely wrong in its entire two-hundred-and-thirty-nine year history."

A couple of beats. PMA was staring at me as though I was experiencing a complete psychotic break.

"What?"

"RAISE THE FUCKING GATE."

He waddled back as fast as he could to the booth.

"AND SHOVE THAT SWORD UP YOUR ASS!"

The gate went up and I hit the gas pedal. In my rear view mirror, I saw him standing there like a poor faithful dog who had no idea why his master had just kicked him across the room. I briefly felt guilty, but only briefly. I didn't have room for any more emotions.

The Dark Sky assholes had gotten all the files out of my computer, every last one of them, through that goddam flash drive. That included all the documents I had stored on Lorie's arrest. That's how they knew right where to hit me and they took their best swing. Wham, home run.

I still remembered the call.

It was a slow morning at the Agency when my phone rang. A voice identified itself as being from the sheriff's office in Salisbury, Delaware.

"Are you Lorie Bowman's father?"

"Yes."

"We have her in custody."

"For what?"

"Murder."

You don't forget anything about that kind of moment.

After I left Allison - for nobody, that's how bad it was – the kids didn't take it well. No kids do. I did my best, taking them on weekends, but a part-time dad wasn't a real one. The split affected them both in very different ways. Grace became more and more of a steel-eyed machine, suppressing any feelings, while my youngest, Lorie, went the other way – she melted down and became an emotional basket case.

I knew Allison was badmouthing me to all her friends in front of them. Grace was receptive to the poison, but Lorie was more than a little conflicted. One day, she asked me why I hated babies, and that's when I knew she had found out about the abortion, which Allison and I had supposedly agreed to hide from the kids. In the end, I couldn't fight the constant stream of anti-dad propaganda they were fed Monday through Friday – and, as the kids grew older, they began cancelling the weekends. And then they barely saw me at all.

Allison, meanwhile, had gone back to working at the Agency, where she quickly found her next victim, a repressed shlub named Edgar who had little experience with women and even less with children. Unfortunately, it turned out he hated kids – but Allison turned the other way when he started raining verbal abuse on ours for such severe sins as having the TV volume up too high. Grace, the tough one, merely let it bounce off her steel skin. That left Lorie, who took most of his heat and took it to heart.

When she hit her teens, Lorie went into full rebellion, piercing her nose, dying her hair and embracing the emo culture of the time. She also cut herself. When she got out of high school, she moved out as fast as she could and not to college, because she didn't keep up her grades and hated school. Instead, she moved in with a local rock guitarist.

That relationship didn't last and she was devastated.

Unable to cope, she moved in with Grace, who had already graduated from college and had a staff job at an internet company in Delaware. But she was still obsessed with the rocker. She talked him into spending one more night with her - but when the morning came, so did her wake-up call: The relationship itself was over as far as he was concerned.

I saw her a few months later and noticed her stomach was a little big. Was she…? "No!" she yelped. She had always had weight issues and I should keep my mouth shut. I did, thinking no more about it. A couple of months later, I got that call from the sheriff's office and found out they were holding her for suspected murder. And I had the sensation of falling off a cliff I didn't even know I was standing on.

She had indeed been pregnant – and, after she had given birth in a bathroom at a party at a friend's house, she dumped it into the trash can outside on the curb.

The next morning, the cops picked up Lorie at Grace's place, where she was alone – her sister was at work. Lorie, when she was booked, for some reason gave the cops my number. Maybe she didn't want Edgar to find out. Maybe she wanted to see what I would do. Who knows, I didn't.

Allison got her out on bail, because I was still dead broke from the divorce. But then there was the defense attorney, who wanted a huge retainer to take on Lorie's case. I was expected to contribute half. I didn't have it. That's when I made the mistake of going to my father.

I had already borrowed some money some years earlier because I just couldn't make it when I was paying both alimony and child support. So far, I had been unable to pay him back – I was up to my neck in credit card debt. But I thought he might understand this situation. It wasn't about me, it was about my daughter, his granddaughter, and doing what we could to keep her out of jail for the rest of her life. But he was still pissed off about my divorce, even more pissed off about the money I already owed him and he made it clear nothing else would be forthcoming. I fought a little because this was the kind of situation when a family came together instead of pointing figures and resurrecting old grudges.

That's when he blamed me for the dead baby.

A screaming match ensued, and my part in it wasn't anything to be proud of. When my father passed away from cancer three years later, I discovered that I had been disowned. By that time, I was also persona non grata with Allison and my kids. She had gotten the money together through other means but never stopped telling everyone around her how I had failed when my daughter needed me most.

The ironic part was that the case against Lorie had come to nothing – it seemed like the D.A. had overreached by charging her with murder in the first when he would have a hard time proving it. The case went away and Lorie moved back in with Allison and Edgar.

I had lost my parents, my kids and a grandson, all in one fell swoop. I started drinking and didn't stop. I showed up late for work on those days when I showed up at all. My work got sloppy. And finally the CIA and I agreed on the fact that I shouldn't work there anymore. I got a decent severance package and Howard said he would do what he could in terms of throwing me an occasional freelance job. He couldn't be too open with his support, because his lovely wife Janet was close friends with Allison, but he still ended up coming through for me on the sly. Which was why I couldn't hate Howard for the betrayal. He was put in a position where he didn't have much choice. Just like I was now in a position where I didn't have much choice.

Andrew Wright had made it clear during the rest of our talk in The Tank that he had a lot of clout with the law enforcement community. He told me what I already knew, that there was no statute of limitations on murder. And he let me know in no uncertain terms that he would see to it that the Salisbury D.A. would go ahead and press formal charges against my daughter unless I did what he was requesting. Of course, the charges might not stick. Of course, Wright might be bluffing about the whole thing. It didn't matter. What mattered was any chance of the dead-and-buried case being brought back to horrifying life. My daughter would be traumatized all over again. Expensive lawyers would have to be hired again. Headlines might pop up in the newspaper again.

And it would all be my fault.

"Are you okay?" PMA asked me, shaking me out of my self-pity. "What'd they do to you in there?"

I didn't answer, because I finally saw, up the road, a ratty old bar that had a "CASINO" sign in front of it. Turned out, in Montana, you could call yourself a casino even if you only had one old slot machine that only took quarters sitting in the corner. I ordered a double Jack on the rocks. And it was gone quicker than you could lose twenty-five cents in that one-armed bandit.

"So what's going on?" PMA sat at the bar, staring at me knocking back my drink, and getting increasingly agitated by my state.

I slammed my empty glass on the bar and motioned for another. "I don't want to get into it. But we're going back to your house and I'm going to lie to your grandfather."

The kid didn't object. "That's probably the best thing. My uncle…his face… He's so messed up."

"Yeah. Join the club," I said as my next Jack arrived. "By the way, you're driving from here on, I don't care if you don't have an ID, because I'm getting fucked up as fast as I can."

"Where are we going?"

"Back to Missoula. We'll fly back tomorrow."

"But, Jesus, Max, we have to do something about this. We have to do something about Dark Sky, nobody knows what they're up to. I mean, shit, how much money is the Pentagon feeding them?"

Money.

Andrew Wright wanted me to believe all this madness was just about one old man not wanting to hurt another old man. He wanted me to believe there was indeed a shred of human decency in him and to trust in fairy tales that never had a happy ending. Well, of course, the truth was good ol' Andy wasn't worried at all about General Davidson's well-being. He was worried about *his fucking funding*. If this shit got out, and it might if the General made a big media stink about all this, Congress might turn off the spigot – and Dark Sky might really go dark.

Money and power. It was always really about money and power.

"Kid, you and I can't do anything about it."

"We could tell our story…"

"We can't."

"Why not?"

I just shook my head.

"We just can't."

We spent our last night on the road in the same hotel in Kalispell where we crashed the night before. I took the last two pain pills I had from the Booneville pharmacy and washed them down with the rest of the bottle of Jack, then spent the night delirious in bed as the ghosts came out of the walls to scream at me. My ex-parents. My ex-wife. My ex-children. My ex-life.

Jesus.

Thursday morning.

I got up in the middle of the night, drunk, tired and wired. The kid was asleep, so I went over to the desk in the room, fired up the Chromebook and, just for fun, started researching the so-called COIN warfare in Afghanistan a few years back just to see if I could find if there had been any sightings of a crazed killer with a trick rifle. There were none that I could find.

Instead, I found out about the tomahawks.

Night raids in Afghanistan were conducted with, according to a *New York Times* article, "primeval tomahawks." Holy shit, really? And the tomahawks were custom-made by a guy in North Carolina, Daniel Winkler, who also provided the Native American weaponry for the 1992 version of *The Last of the Mohicans*. According to the article, the tomahawks were financed by "private donors." A Seal Team 6 member confirmed that he himself witnessed some "hatchet kills."

I recalled the tomahawk display case in The Barn, the handmade instruments of primitive death carefully preserved and under glass – the way fetish items for perverted killers should be. And I wondered if any women and children were involved in those "hatchet kills." After all, Mr.

Barry Filer had proudly proclaimed that Herman and Robert had cleaned out a few villages.

I turned off the laptop and turned on the TV with the sound down, so I didn't wake up the kid. And then I watched infomercials about juicers and genie bras until dawn, the dawn of the day when I would be ending this fiasco once and for all.

When the kid finally woke up, we drove down to the Missoula airport and returned the rental, then we grabbed the next flight to Washington D.C., where, upon arrival, I rented my seventh and final car of this hell trip and drove it down to Virginia Beach. The voice at the gate intercom was a new one, a male voice. PMA told me it was the butler. I gave my name and he buzzed me in.

As I pulled in and parked in front of the General's mansion, I noticed a few more vehicles parked on the roundabout driveway than there were previously. One of them had a little red cross on its bumper. Uh oh.

Before I went in to face the latest fresh hell, I took care of some unfinished business. I turned to the kid and pulled out a few thousand dollar bills from the latest envelope from Mr. Barry Filer.

"Take this. You earned it."

"They make thousand dollar bills?" PMA looked at the bills, and then looked at me in confusion. "You sure? That's a lot of money."

"The only reason I took it is so I could give you some."

That was kind of a lie. I didn't have any qualms about taking their blood money. It was a little less that would be left in their pot and more that would be in mine. That wasn't going to make me lose any sleep.

The kid shrugged and took the money.

We got out of the car and walked over to the mansion. PMA opened the front door like he lived there, which he did, and I was once again in the Four Seasons lobby.

I yelled, "Hello?"

A minute later, Angela came downstairs in her bathrobe, the same bathrobe she was wearing the first time I met her. I resisted the urge to return some of the slaps she had applied to my face a few days ago and instead put all the violence in my glare. She ran over and hugged her boy, then turned to me.

"Hello," she said quietly.

"Good afternoon and you knew the whole fucking time," I replied.

She said nothing. I noticed she looked like hell, but I'm sure I wasn't exactly radiating good health and vitality myself.

PMA looked at Angela in horror. "You knew what? That Uncle Robbie was alive? You knew the whole time?"

"We'll talk about this later," she said in an almost-whisper.

"Let's get this over with," I said, giving the kid a look that indicated he should leave it all alone.

She led us upstairs, which was a surprise. I hadn't been up there before. We got to the top and then walked down the hallway. She opened the door at the end of the hall.

And that's when I saw this was not going to be over today.

General Davidson was in a hospital bed, attended by a few nurses. They had installed a whole hospital room set-up, the machines, the monitors, the IV, everything. The General was out like a light and didn't look like he was about to wake up anytime soon. He made my paleness look like a Miami suntan.

"Oh my God," said PMA with real sadness.

"We really shouldn't be in here," she whispered to me, "but I knew you wouldn't believe me if you didn't see it for yourself. He had a massive stroke the other night and he's been in a coma ever since."

"Prognosis?" I asked in a little shocked voice.

"They're not sure…" She didn't say more. She didn't have to.

She and I went back downstairs, leaving the kid alone with his Grandpa on his probable death bed. She stopped when we got to the front door and turned to me again.

"I'm sorry…Robbie began calling me a few years ago. I hope you understand."

I didn't want to.

"I'm assuming you – or someone else - will contact me when the General is able to communicate. Then I'll finish the job."

She nodded and opened the front door. As I took a few steps towards the outside, she said softly, "You know, I really did like you."

I turned back.

"Did? I'm not dead yet."

She slowly shut the door.

Homecoming

I arrived back at Roosevelt Island Friday afternoon and not in a good state. Hungover and defeated, I realized just what it had cost me to leave my apartment and go to meet Mr. Barry Filer in that hotel lobby almost two weeks ago. The cost was discovering what was underneath the tips of a few very ugly icebergs.

For example, the all-American persona of General Davidson that the country worshipped. The immense darkness lurking underneath that persona was a narrow belief system and an ingrained intolerance that caused Robert Davidson to deny who he was and embrace a violence that wasn't natural to him. Would Jeremy Davidson end up doing likewise?

Then there was Dark Sky, the unseen arm of the Pentagon, attempting to win wars without anyone in the country knowing how they were really being fought. Andrew Wright built his own, personal rogue branch of the military and then created the ultimate soldier to fight for it – his own son. Herman and Robert were crown princes, royalty expected to live up to their lineage. The former didn't have a conscience to get in the way of that, the latter, unfortunately for him, did - no matter how hard he tried to destroy it.

Finally, there was me, dragging my own condemned past behind me like Marley's chains, sitting in my apartment year after year avoiding any significant engagement with the human race or my own destiny, medicating the pain by sheer denial of its existence. Wright had shoved my worst failures in my face, forcing me to look at them for the first time in years - the son that was lost in Allison's abortion and the grandson that was tossed away by my daughter. Because I had broken up a marriage that was bad to begin with and because I couldn't find a way to heal my daughter's heart in the aftermath, I was considered a double murderer. That was what they all believed - and that was what I was afraid was true.

I hated myself and I hated the world too much at that moment to face anyone – which was why I couldn't call Jules when I returned to my apartment on Friday. Instead, after I took the tram over to the city and deposited my blood money into my bank account, I walked over to T-Mobile and finally got a replacement for my original iPhone. Then I texted Jules on the way home and pretended I was still out of town. I wrote that everything was okay and resolved, and to send me the information about her surgery, and that I would definitely be there to pick her up afterwards.

In the meantime, I would be incommunicado. I would explain everything later.

Instead of receiving a profanity-laced reply, I received a text containing only information – I was to pick her up at three p.m. Tuesday at her doctor's office in Midtown, it was an outpatient procedure. She didn't call me a dickhead without a dick, or some other charming and obscene slur in all caps. That meant she knew I was up to my neck in it and didn't want to bother me - or she was incredibly pissed but still needed my help.

I almost cried while I wondered which one it was.

I finally got back to the island around dinner time. I was standing in the hallway, unlocking the door to my apartment, when somebody emerged from what had been Leg Sore Larry's door. I had already noticed that all the Scarlett Johansson pictures were gone, even though you could still see where the tape had taken off some of the paint – but I had no clue somebody had actually moved in so quickly.

The new neighbor was tall and musclebound, maybe early thirties, with red close-cut hair and a scar or two on his forehead. He was wearing a tank top and sweat pants and he seemed vaguely threatening, even though he was trying his best to give me a neighborly grin.

Of course, something was wrong with this picture. Leg Sore Larry had only been dead for a week and a half – and somebody new was in the apartment? Wouldn't it take a month of constant Lysol treatments to just make the place fit for human habitation? Now I had to wonder if Larry's demise was perhaps engineered. Could you be too paranoid? I didn't think so.

"The name's Skip," he said, offering a hand. "Skip Skipperson."

"Skip Skipperson?"

"Real first name is Mike. 'Skip' is a nickname."

"Figured." I shook his hand. "Can't believe they moved you in here so fast. Where you hail from?"

"Here and there. Were you on a trip?"

I looked him over. "Just a long lunch." Then I took a glance out the hall window at a small storm that was gathering. "A real dark sky out there, huh?"

I came back and met his eyes just to find out what being too cute would get me.

"Yeah," he said. "Very dark sky." And his eyes never left mine.

I opened my door and said "Nice to meet you," then I slammed it behind me and went down the flight of stairs into the apartment. I walked around opening a few windows to get some air circulating, because what was around was stale and humid.

For the next few days, I drank. It wasn't enough for me to call it a bender, but I was mildly pickled the whole time. I had a few delivery sandwiches and not much else, while I watched baseball and the news, where I learned there was some kind of tropical depression forming in the Atlantic around Jamaica that showed signs of being something serious. I didn't see how it could be all that serious, I knew from my couple of years in Miami that hurricane season didn't even start for a few weeks. But television reporting was all about making everything as dramatic as possible, which is why I wasn't about to buy their Chicken Little act this time around.

Tuesday morning.

I showered and shaved for the first time in a couple days and checked the news, because Chicken Little was screaming louder than ever. The meteorologists had a giant storm-watch hard on, the bottom line being that the former tropical depression, which had since morphed into a full-on hurricane, just might hit Jersey again the way Sandy did in November of 2012. And if it did, it would probably be tomorrow evening.

And, by the way, its name was "Mel."

I don't know who was in charge of naming these things, but it was going to be hard to get people to get scared of something named Mel. It was like nicknaming the Apocalypse "Cuddles."

In any event, I headed over to Jules' doctor's office to pick up the patient. I had texted her earlier that I would be there as promised, so she didn't worry. She texted back a simple, "k," which again worried me that World War III was right around the corner. I got there a few minutes early, so, as an act of good faith, I started a few new Words with Friends games with Jules' unattended phone and then waited.

Finally, the doctor led her out. She was wearing a simple black dress and flats and looked good. She was the first nice thing I had seen in a while.

"Are you Max?" the doc asked. I nodded. She came over and hugged me and held on for a while, and I didn't mind at all.

"Julie's pretty much out of the anesthetic, but maybe still a little groggy. She's been told about a million times – but I'll tell you too – she is to do NO talking until she comes back for her follow-up visit this coming

Monday. She should drink a great deal of water – no caffeine, no alcohol."

She made a frowny face at that last instruction. The doctor turned to her.

"Julie, you have the reflux medication? Remember, you need to take that every day."

She pulled it out of her purse and showed it to the MD like she was his star student.

"Okay, if there's any severe pain or discomfort, you let Max know, Max, you call me and get her back in here. All clear?"

She nodded. I nodded. We got the hell out of there.

I didn't want to subject her to the subway in her condition, besides, it was too far a walk to the F train, so I grabbed us a cab and told the driver to take us to 2nd and 60th, where the tram station was. Inside the cab, she put her head on my shoulder. She was still a little sleepy. At one point, she made a little heart symbol with her two thumbs and forefingers and gave me a questioning look. I gave her the finger, and she knew everything was okay. She put her head on my shoulder again.

As we got off the tram, we caught the little red bus that traveled the length of the island and back again. I had been avoiding the thing for years, but, again, I didn't want to make Jules walk. I caught her looking at me, studying me as if she knew something bad had happened to me. I wanted to save it all until we got back to the apartment.

However, as I helped her off the bus in front of my building, I saw, sitting on the bench inside the small glass-encased area that was between the entry door and the inner security door, someone who was going to delay our catching up with each other.

PMA.

With the new carry-on I had bought him on the ground next to him.

Jules saw my reaction and looked back and forth between PMA behind the glass wall and my face with a look of pure WTF. I opened the entrance door.

"What the hell are you doing here?" I asked. I should have been happy to see the kid, but I wasn't happy to be reminded of anything that had happened while I was with him.

"Sorry, Max…I…is this Julie?" he asked.

She nodded in a big cartoonish way.

"She just had the surgery," I explained. "She can't talk for a few days." I turned to Jules. "This is Jeremy, but I call him 'PMA.'"

"Nice to meet you." He extended his hand and she shook it.

I looked around to make sure Skip Skipperson or anyone else questionable wasn't watching us, then I unlocked the security door and got everybody to the elevator. We were the only ones in there, so PMA told me how he lit into Angela about lying to him, not to mention me. She claimed she didn't know about any of this Dark Sky business, just that Robbie was working for some private military organization and wanted her to make sure the General didn't find out he was still alive. According to her, Robert just needed to talk to somebody, he thought he was losing his mind being so isolated and confined to that Montana base. For her part, she was worried about him staying there, but more worried about what would happen if he got out.

Jules had a hard time following the conversation.

We got back to my apartment. I got Jules a glass of ice water and put her in my bedroom with the TV tuned to HGTV. I had a hunch she'd be asleep in about three minutes. Then I came back out to the living room to talk to the kid.

The General wasn't improving, he said. But he couldn't stay in that house anymore, not with everything he knew, not with a mother who was complicit in this whole deception. He was wondering if he could crash with me for a few days. I told him he was welcome to use the queen bed in my office – but he should know I was being watched. I told him about Skip Skipperson and he knew enough to be as paranoid as me.

"Max, it's like I said, we need to do something about all this," PMA said.

"Why don't you write a letter to the Times?" I asked, shutting down the discussion.

A little later, as the kid and I were watching the bombastic hysteria over the approach of Hurricane Mel, Jules came out wearing my bathrobe and texting with her phone. My phone buzzed and I read her message as she pointed to PMA.

HE'S CUTE – CAN WE KEEP HIM?

"I still haven't agreed to the dog," I answered. She sat down next to me on the couch and kept the text talk going.

WHO IS HE

"He's the grandson of General Donald Davidson."

Her eyes went wide open.

"Yes, THE General Donald Davidson. His uncle, who's supposed to be dead, is actually alive in Montana with half a face. It's pretty fucked up."

PMA turned to Jules. "Max is a good guy," the kid said, warming the cockles of my heart. "He got us through a lot. You're lucky you have a guy like this."

NOW WE HAVE TO KEEP HIM

I shook my head. She texted again.

MAX CAN YOU FUCK ME NOW IT'S BEEN DRY DOWN THERE FOR TOO GODDAM LONG

That message wasn't for the family, so I didn't read it out loud. I just got up, excused myself and escorted Jules to the master bedroom. After she did that thing she did with her vagina and I laid there enjoying the memory, she motioned excitedly to my ancient clock-radio and I didn't know why.

"What, it's ten after seven, that why you're pointing? What, you want to get some dinner in here?"

She shook her head and grabbed her purse from the chair next to her side of the bed. And she pulled out a CD with no label.

"You want me to play that?" I asked. Then I remembered – oh yeah, that ancient clock-radio had a CD player built into the top. I put the disc in and waited to see if the thing still worked.

A beautiful voice began singing *Moonlight in Vermont*. I listened for a minute or two.

Then I looked at her questioningly.

She nodded and pointed to herself.

I couldn't believe it. "That's you? Holy shit, really?"

She nodded vigorously. I was starting to think I had just fucked Marcel Marceau, because she was becoming a very talented mime.

"I didn't even know you had a CD of yourself. How come you never played it for me before?"

She shrugged and looked a little embarrassed. Julie Nelson, shy? A new one.

"Wow. And you're going to sound that good again?"

She teared up and nodded. If I had been a younger man, I would have done her again right then and there. I had to be happy just knowing I didn't need boner pills yet.

We ordered some dinner for ourselves and the kid. Over the Chinese, Jules texted me a question for the kid that I couldn't quite believe I hadn't asked him in all the time we spent together.

"Jules wants to know if you have a girl."

He looked a little embarrassed.

"There was somebody, but then I got the CIA summer job thing."

"She disagreed with that move?"

"We had a huge fight about it."

"So I guess your dad's not the only one who disapproves."

"People need to stay out of my fucking business."

We moved on to less volatile subjects and it ended up being a very nice night. God knows I needed one.

But it didn't last long. I woke up around three a.m. worrying about the kid and Jules. I didn't know why Skip Skipperson was next door – maybe just as insurance that I would do what I was supposed to do if the General recovered. But it bothered me. Jules was sleeping like a rock, so I got up, put on my bathrobe and went into the closet off the hallway. And I dug in the back of it until I found what I was looking for.

The small box with the handgun and the bullets that went in it.

Howard, who believed that no household was complete without firearms, had sent me his old gun as a joke when he traded up to a newer and more powerful model. I had taken some shooting classes while I was with the CIA, so I knew the basics, but that was all I knew. I started to take the box into the living room, then remembered something and doubled back to the bedroom, where I quietly unplugged the clock radio and took it with me. I had only listened to a couple of Jules' songs and I was anxious to hear the rest.

As I checked out the gun, I listened to the CD at a low volume. Son of a bitch, on the next track, she sang *Nice and Easy* and did a good job of it. The gun itself was in its original packaging, so it was clean and ready for action. I carefully loaded it, leaving the first chamber empty so I didn't accidentally shoot myself. Guns made me nervous and I wasn't afraid to admit it, but I had to get past that so I could at least try to protect Jules and PMA from whatever might happen next.

When I was done, I put the handgun in a pantry in the kitchen, on a high shelf behind a bunch of shit I never used. Hopefully, I would forget I ever put it up there.

Then I sat back down on the couch, turned on the TV but kept it muted, because I was still listening to Jules belt out the standards. Hurricane Mel was looking big and monstrous on the CNN radar – they were still holding to their Sandy-sized prediction. It would be making landfall in fifteen hours or so. Tomorrow afternoon, we'd start seeing rain here on the island.

Meanwhile, on the CD, Jules started singing *Good Morning Heartache*, the Billie Holiday standard. Gutsy move taking on a legend, but Jules held her own. As the song went on, the melancholy got to me. She found the profound unhappiness in the lyric and injected it straight into my heart.

Then I heard a noise and wondered why I had hidden the gun in the kitchen. That wasn't very practical if something happened fast.

I turned. It was just Jules standing there in the hallway, wearing that godawful *Anchorman* T-shirt and nothing else. I saw it in her eyes – she wanted to know what had happened to me. She knew me too well and she knew something had changed. So she came over and sat next to me, and I told her about my daughter and what she had left in the trash, and somehow I made it all the way through without breaking down. She hugged me and held on. She was going to stay with me.

That was all I needed to know.

The Hunt

Wednesday evening.

Outside the wind was howling and the rain was pounding. Mel was launching his assault on the shore, which meant many television reporters standing by beaches on the coast of New Jersey were hoping things would get bad enough to get them on YouTube - but not bad enough to kill them. I was somewhere in the middle - maybe just a few bloody noses or near-drownings. It was a win-win; I'd get some entertainment value and they'd get a few million online hits.

Along with the gusts and the downpour, it was also dark as night outside, even though sunset wasn't due for another hour; the thick clouds were blocking out whatever light was left in the day. It was around seven p.m. and Jules was searching the kitchen in a panic. I watched her, not sure why she was spooked, as she picked her phone up off the counter and started typing furiously. I pulled mine out of my jeans and waited for my latest communication from headquarters. It was a good thing I had an unlimited text plan or I would have gone completely broke in the past twenty-four hours.

THERE'S NOTHING TO EAT IN THIS FUCKING CAVE

"I'm not going out in this shit!" I yelled as I headed into the living room, where the kid was waiting for the Weather Channel reporter to get picked up by the wind and thrown into the side of a building.

YOU HAVE TO. STORES MIGHT CLOSE MORON

I sighed at my phone screen. More incoming.

I'M NOT GOING TO LIVE ON MOLDY SALTINES AND WATER SHITBIRD

"Make a list," I wearily said. I really didn't have to make the suggestion, because text after text started coming through of all the things I needed to buy. Milk. Eggs. Chocolate-covered pretzels. Bananas. Ben & Jerry's. Basil. Chocolate-covered potato chips. Cheese.

I turned to PMA. "Get your shoes on, I'm going to need help."

As we rode down in the elevator, I asked the kid if he had heard from his mother. He said he had had his phone off since yesterday morning because she was calling constantly and he didn't want to talk to her. I asked him to turn it back on in case we needed to know anything. He wasn't happy about it, but he did it.

Maybe I made more of the trip downstairs than I needed to, because we were literally out in the harsh weather for about ten seconds, the time it took to run from the exit from my building to the entrance to the bodega. On a covered walkway. I didn't even put on a coat and neither did the kid, which turned out to be a mistake, because Mel's winds turned the rain horizontal, so we were soaked by the time we got in the store.

Inside the bodega, chaos was in full swing. Everybody and their brother and their mother and their brother from another mother was in there thinking what Jules was thinking, that if this storm was as bad as the media said it was going to be, anybody without supplies would be SOL come tomorrow morning. We each grabbed a shopping basket to gather up what was left on the shelves and when we were done scavenging, we made our way back to the end of the long, long line that wound its way from the front counter all the way to the back of the aisle with the cookies and the cereal. It would be a while.

After what seemed like most of the rest of my lifetime, we had made it almost halfway through the line, inching our way up a couple of footsteps every so often, when my phone vibrated with a new text. What, did we need Nutella too? I pulled it out and checked the screen.

IS THAT YOU GUYS

I stared at it a moment, then wrote back.

Is that us what? Still in store

I turned to the kid, who was staring at his phone, which had finally fully rebooted and was buzzing like there was no tomorrow. Somebody had been trying hard to contact him.

He looked at me.

"My grandpa died this morning."

My heart stopped. I turned back to my phone – another message from Jules.

THEN WHO DO I HEAR

I dropped the basket and ran, and the kid followed suit, even though he didn't know what was going on. We pushed our way out of the bodega and back into my building. Luckily, the elevator was already sitting on the ground floor, so I jumped right in with the kid, hit the 13 button, then repeatedly hit the button to close the doors.

"What's going on?" asked the kid.

I didn't have an answer.

We got to my floor, I punched the button to open the elevator doors repeatedly and we ran out and down the long hallway. As I passed the door of Skip Skipperson, I noticed it quietly closing, but not closing all the way, as if he was avoiding making the sound of that final "click." And then I noticed my door, which I had left unlocked like a dope, also in the same not-quite-closed position.

I opened it and flew down the stairs, almost killing myself in the process. I yelled Jules' name, even though she couldn't yell back.

Then I saw her.

She was down on her stomach on the carpet in the living room, as if she had just taken a few steps away from the sofa when she was hit and fell forward. There was blood coming from the right side of her head, where there was a vicious wound, too big to be caused by a knife. She was unconscious.

I ran to her motionless body, yelling to the kid to call 911 and get an ambulance over here. First aid was a prominent part of my collection of things I did not know anything about, so I had no idea how to proceed. She was breathing, but it seemed a little weak to me, who, again, didn't know anything. As I heard the kid finish up the call, I ran and got an old towel out of the closet, then I ran back to her and put the towel up against the wound to try and slow the bleeding.

"They said it would take a few extra minutes because of the storm, but they'll be here soon."

I nodded and motioned for him to come kneel by her and take my place. When he had, I got up and headed to the kitchen.

"Who the fuck did this?" he yelled over to me.

"Guess," I said grimly, as I reached into the back of the high shelf where I had stashed the gun. I grabbed a bullet out of the ammo box and put it in the first chamber.

The General was dead. If we had been watching anything else other than The Weather Channel, we might have known that and had some warning. As it was, the moment I had been dreading was here – the moment when I was no longer useful and just a loose end to be tied up.

Which is why I had a new neighbor.

When Skip finally got his marching orders, he most likely took a peek outside his door and saw mine was open, then came in to quietly take care of me with one of Dark Sky's specialty items, a handsome, handmade tomahawk. Jules heard him coming in – but the only person coming in should have been me and I would have said something, because I always did. That's when she texted. When she got confirmation that it wasn't me, she got up to see who was there. And when Skip turned the corner and saw a figure, he let the tomahawk fly. Maybe he saw it was a woman in the moment before he made the throw, maybe that's why he just missed making a clean kill, who knows? But he quickly knew how badly he had fucked up and he just as quickly got out of there.

"I'll be back," I said as I headed for the stairs.

PMA saw what I was holding. "Max, a gun? Where'd you get that?" he said with extreme surprise.

"Stay with her," I said quietly as I went up the stairs.

I pushed my front door open – it had never closed all the way. Skip's door, however, was now shut tight. I gently tried his doorknob. Locked.

I hit the doorbell over and over like the world's most persistent Jehovah's Witness and waited.

After a few moments, he pulled the door open, but stayed mostly behind it, firing a couple of shots into the hallway. He was taking a chance I'd be standing there like a human target and that I'd go down fast. But all he got out of that move was mystified, because the shots only knocked a couple of chunks out of the white bricked wall opposite him.

As he stepped into the open doorway and looked up and down the hallway, he didn't know I was lying on the hallway floor to his left, opposite the door hinge. I was shaking so hard, I was lucky to hit any part of him. What I got with my shot was the right leg, which went out from under him and sent him falling back down the stairs into his apartment. Then I got up as fast as I could with my ancient aching joints to make sure I got to him before he got his equilibrium back.

It was almost a tie. He was on the almost side.

Skip Skipperson lay sprawled on the landing below. But damn if that Dark Sky training didn't work – he had reflexively moved into a position where he could return fire. So he quickly shot back at me, but a little too quickly, like a shortstop who stretched to make an amazing catch but blew the throw to first because he was off-balance. The shot went into the inside wall beside the stairway as I fired back and got him in the shoulder. He was down again and I put three more bullets into him. Then, not particularly caring where they landed, I quickly backed up and slammed his door shut, locking what was left of him inside.

I fell against the hallway wall, feeling the heat of my discharged pistol on my hand. I had never killed a man, or even come anywhere close to it. I thought I would I have been more upset, but instead I was just relieved. He was a fucking killer so fuck him. Besides, I didn't have time to dwell on how I was feeling because I suddenly saw, at the other end of the long hallway, the EMTs getting off the elevator. I hid the gun behind my back and yelled to them, so they wouldn't waste time looking for the right apartment.

While they bandaged Jules and got her ready to move downstairs to the ambulance, I went and got my old raincoat, which was bulky enough to disguise a pistol sitting in its pocket. Then I went into the kitchen and grabbed the ammo box and put it in the opposite raincoat pocket. Mel might stop anybody else from coming after me tonight, but no way was I taking chances.

There was only room for me to ride along in the ambulance with Jules, so I threw the kid an old windbreaker I also had in the closet and told him to meet me down at the hospital at the north end of the island. If the red island bus was still running, he could catch a ride on that and stay relatively dry. Whatever he did, I told him not to stay in the apartment, because some other unwelcome guests might show up.

The good thing about living on a tiny island was that it was only a mile drive to the Coler Hospital, the last building before Lighthouse Park at the very north end. And good thing it was close, because the street was already flooding and the wind and the rain were getting insane. We made it down to the emergency entrance, but it looked like we might be the last vehicle to do it without a struggle. Almost instantly, Jules disappeared down the hall into a treatment room.

I'm not a praying man, although I do on occasion try to talk to whoever's in charge. And I was doing a lot of yakking in my head at the moment. It was some kind of sick joke to do this to Jules right before she regained her singing voice. As usual, I blamed myself. I never should have let her stay with me with the possibility of this going down, but she was depending on me to take care of her. Not that depending on me was ever really a great idea.

Everybody inside the hospital was scrambling. The basement was already filling up with water and the staffers working that night were worried about the parking lot flooding and their cars getting an inside rinse job, which is exactly what happened during Sandy. Surges of water were crashing over the sea walls along the walkways on both the east and west sides of the island. Mel was going to be a great, big son of a bitch, maybe even a bigger bastard than Sandy. I remembered back then flooding got so bad, it was impossible to get to the northern end of the island, where the hospital was.

Maybe that's why the kid hadn't made it here. Maybe the hospital was already cut off from the rest of the island. It had been a couple hours and I was starting to worry as much about him as I was about Jules – I texted him more than once and got nothing.

Finally, a doctor came out and said Julie had suffered blunt trauma, a concussion and a skull fracture. It was touch-and-go at the moment. They'd keep me posted.

A few minutes later, I finally got a text. But it wasn't from PMA, it was from a number I didn't recognize.

We found your neighbor.

Skip Skipperson's friends had arrived. Here we go.

I sat there a moment, taking in those four words, then I finally got up and went to the nurses' station. I left my cellphone number with the head nurse in case anything happened and told her I was going to take a walk. She naturally looked at me as though I was insane.

But I didn't care. Every part of my body was tingling. I knew I wasn't safe and I knew it was better to go find the danger than have it come find me. I had to tap into my own PMA and get us all out of this unholy mess.

As I headed for the hospital exit, I tried calling the Roosevelt Island Public Safety department, which was what they called the island's police force. I got a busy signal. Either their lines were down or Mel was keeping them tied up. Of course, I wasn't sure how I would explain what was going on if they did answer. Were they really going to believe that trained killers who might be armed with tomahawks were coming after me?

Then came another text from the same strange number.

Still at the hospital?

I had been afraid they knew where I was and I was right, not that that was anything to pat myself on the back about. Maybe Skip wasn't all the way dead, maybe a neighbor told them the EMT crew had been in the building, there was no way to know how they figured it out, I just had to deal with the consequences. So I worked my way through the hallways, towards the north side of the building, the parts that were no longer much in use. The back of the building, the side facing the northern end of the island, the side opposite Lighthouse Park, was virtually empty from disuse. I couldn't make it all the way there, the doors were bolted shut, but I came out the side as far north as I could. As I opened the exit door, a rush of water came in over my feet.

I shut the door behind me and faced Mel like a man. And Mel almost knocked me right back on my ass.

The wind was so strong I had to lean back against the hospital wall to adjust to its power. I had exited the hospital on the western side of the island, and as I looked toward Manhattan, I saw how bad things had gotten. Huge waves were crashing over the fence at the edge of the walkway, which was now under a few feet of water. I imagined the walkway on the east side of the island was in the same condition. That meant I wasn't getting to Public Safety on foot.

I had to switch to Plan B. Which wasn't going to be a whole lot of fun.

I started heading north, staying on the highest ground possible. The area at the very back of the hospital was already flooded - in the small parking area, I saw an ambulance with water up to the top of its tires. Meanwhile, I was already soaking wet, and the rain was nowhere near over.

I headed north to Lighthouse Park and sloshed up one of its small, grassy, tree-covered hills, where I grabbed a tree for support and scanned the sky. I thought I saw some clearing to the east - a good sign, except, just at that moment, all the streetlights around the park went black.

The power on the island was out.

I turned back to the hospital. The lights flickered, then came back on. The emergency generator was working, which meant they could still take care of Jules.

I kept moving forward across the park, avoiding the mammoth lakes of water that had formed over the low areas of grass and heading for the very the tip of the island and the lighthouse that anchored that tip.

It was slow going. The ground was saturated along with my feet and every once in a while, I sunk down into a pit of mud. The wind was so strong I kept having to stop and grab a tree to keep from blowing away. I probably looked just like one of those idiot television talking heads I loved to make fun of – the Kens and Barbies who stayed outside when the NWS told everyone to stay inside, desperately clutching their hand mikes and hoping their immaculately sprayed-down hair wouldn't get too mussed.

Except this wasn't about me making it on YouTube. This was about me making it to tomorrow.

Finally, I made it all the way north to the paved walkway that led directly to the lighthouse. It was under a foot of water, but, as I saw it at the time. I had no choice. Whoever was coming for me was probably already staked out somewhere by the hospital. They had to know I couldn't make it back to the main part of the island.

If I was going to make a stand, it had to be someplace where I could see everybody before they saw me. Where I could control as much of what was about to happen as I could.

That place was the top of the lighthouse.

The lighthouse wasn't much – it was just fifty feet tall and maybe fifteen feet across. It had been built out of stone, legend had it, by an inmate of the old asylum about a hundred and fifty years ago.

That was appropriate, because there was a lot of madness coming its way.

I made it to the building's too-short-by-a-foot entrance, which was padlocked. That meant I finally got to do something I had always wanted to do – bust it off and see what was inside. I took out my gun, stood back a few feet and shot it – just like they do in the movies. Turns out I'm not Tom Cruise. First of all, I don't buy Scientology and second of all, it took me three shots to shatter the lock. But the important thing here is that I did, in fact, shatter it, and opened the door and ducked inside. It was cold and clammy, but it still felt like paradise after my evening with Mel.

It was also time to make my presence known.

I took out my phone and replied to the last text from a few minutes ago.

Meet me in lighthouse park – north end of island.

And I climbed the narrow rusted iron ladder straight to the top.

There was another too-short door up there that led out to a small octagonal balcony that surrounded the lighthouse crown. I hunched down, opened the door a crack and looked out. It was definitely clearing to the east now and the rain was starting to let up. The worst was over, but I could see the East River was still churning like a million motorboats were racing through it, sending ever-higher waves of water crashing onto the island.

A text came in answer to mine:

Is he with you

"He?"

Did they mean PMA? I didn't know who they were talking about and I didn't answer it.

Even though the park lights were dark because the power was out on the island, the lights of the skyscrapers across the river on the Upper East Side were still working, and gave me some visibility to see out over the park. The sky continued to clear in patches and that helped a lot too, because the moon was close to full. I reloaded the gun to replace the bullets I used on the lock and waited.

Then I saw them.

Three figures emerged way back from the side of the hospital and began slowly walking over the grassy park area that I had just passed through. All I could tell at first was that one of the figures was being forcibly held by another — and the remaining person's silhouette indicated a rifle being held by his side.

Even a mace to the head couldn't keep a good man like Herman down.

And the sick bastard was wearing a Stetson in a hurricane, holding it down with his free hand. You had to admire the guy - he had a look and he was going to stick to it.

As they came closer, I was able to figure out who the other two figures were. One was the bartender hunk from Branson — and the person he was forcibly holding onto was, unfortunately, PMA.

This, of course, complicated things.

They stopped on one of the small hills in the park, where the bartender hunk started tying the kid to one of the trees, while Herman furtively looked all around, in all directions, not knowing who was where.

Meanwhile, I was confused. The text asked, "Is he with you?" If they already had the kid, who the hell was "he?"

I wished I had Herman's rifle, something I could shoot accurately from a distance. They were over a hundred yards away, if I tried a shot with the handgun all I'd do was give away my position. So I stayed hidden inside the crown of the lighthouse, peeking out through the crack in the door, hoping they'd come close enough for my pistol to do some damage.

But it would still be hard to make a decent shot from where I was.

They left the kid tied to the tree and started walking towards the tip of the island - towards the lighthouse. Towards me. I stayed in the darkness behind the door. They paused and the bartender hunk turned his back to Herman – and I saw that he was wearing some kind of backpack. Herman dug into it and pulled out something, which he held up to his eyes and looked through in all directions.

Shit. Probably infrared binoculars.

I reacted like a scared little bitch and too-quickly slammed the door shut. It was too big and too loud a move. I waited a couple of minutes – and sure enough, another text popped up on my phone.

Incoming.

I cracked the door open again, because that's one word I don't like to see.

That's when I saw something else I don't like to see.

I saw Herman pulling out something else from the bartender hunk's backpack.

A rocket launcher. And it wasn't hard to guess where that rocket was going to come calling.

Time for an orderly retreat. I quickly texted back.

>*Coming out.*

The reply came back just as quickly.

>*I don't give a fuck.*

I stuck my head out again just in time to see Herman hand the phone back to the bartender hunk and position the rocket launcher on his shoulder. I wouldn't have time to get down the ladder inside before this whole lighthouse was rubble. That meant I would have to get down the hard way. I crawled out on the balcony as fast as I could and looked down at the flooded paved area below me. It was a long drop. I looked up.

Herman was firing the rocket right at me.

That was all the motivation I needed to throw myself over the balcony guardrail.

I was feeling everything in slow motion again as the heat of the explosion seared my skin, bits of stone ricocheted off of my body and the thunder of the blast seemed to blow out my ear drums as I fell towards the ground. I strained to stay conscious as I landed on my left leg with a splash and a crack.

Turns out a few inches of water doesn't really do much to break a fall. I was pretty sure my leg was broken, but I'd have to deal with that later. Right now, there was a big man with a big rifle heading towards me. A man so focused with venomous hate that he didn't even notice when his Stetson blew off and revealed his bandaged head. Guess the mace left its mark.

"WHERE IS HE?" he bellowed.

I blinked back the tears of pain, shook off the fragments of stone that were covering me and tried to figure out who he was talking about.

"Where's WHO?" I yelled back. "You have the kid…"

He raised the rifle. He was about fifty yards away.

"Where is he?"

"I…"

He shot the ground a few feet away from my arm. We were going to play this game again.

"I don't know…"

He shot the ground a couple of feet away from my broken leg. He kept advancing.

"Herman, darling…I don't know who you're talking about…"

He shot the ground a foot away from my head. Twice. He was coming to the part where the grass ended and the paved area began. He would reach me soon.

"Herman, I swear, nobody is…"

Three more shots. I didn't know how close they were, because my eyes were closed. Fuck.

Then another shot rang out – but it wasn't from Herman's rifle. No, this shot was much further away. I opened my eyes to see the bartender hunk, standing guard near PMA, crumple to the ground like a sack of potatoes.

Herman's eyes widened in hatred and horror as he twirled around and shot five more times all in the direction of where the kid was tied to the tree.

"COME OUT, ROBBIE!" he screamed. "I KNOW IT'S YOU!"

Oh. That's who "he" was.

They had come hunting Robert Davidson, not me.

Robert must have fled the premises and came here – but why? Whatever the reason, they sure couldn't let that cat out of the bag for long, so Wright had no doubt dispatched Herman to come and take care of him once and for all - unless I could do something about it, and it turned out I could.

"Hey, Herman," I quietly said.

He didn't turn back to me, he was too scared of what was out there. He just kept scanning the park and growled, "What?"

"You're out of bullets."

That got his attention. He turned to me – and slammed the rifle lever home. But I had counted correctly.

I pulled the trigger on my pistol in my coat pocket, the one Herman didn't know was there. The shot blasted through the fabric and into Herman's side.

Boy, the look on his face…

He went down hard with the rifle flying out of his hand and barrel-first into the nearby wet dirt.

I looked over to where the kid was tied up and saw, emerging from behind the tree, Robert Davidson.

His leather face covering was back in place and he had an oversized knife in his hand, which he used to slash the ropes and free the kid. Robert threw the knife into the trunk of another nearby tree and pulled his 9mm handgun out of his holster. Then he started heading down the hill towards us. The kid lingered behind him, not sure what to do. I was hoping he wouldn't do anything.

Herman, still down on the flooded ground, strained for his rifle and reached it. Lying on his stomach, he pulled the shells out of his shirt pocket and began to reload his weapon with a vicious intent. Even though I was the one who had shot him, he was totally focused on Robert. I didn't exist.

"You killed him on purpose, didn't you?" Herman spat the words in Robert's direction. "You couldn't stand me being with him, could you?"

The bartender hunk was Herman's new squeeze? Well, to be fair, at least he had a whole face.

As Robert approached, he raised his gun to finish the job on Herman. I thought that was a swell idea.

But then he lowered it again.

Even Herman was like, what the hell?

"I can't do it anymore," Robert almost whispered, as he continued walking towards us. "I can't."

It was a nice sentiment, it was the timing I was questioning.

Herman got up on his knees, rifle in hand. He had enough bullets in it to do the job. Then he got up onto his feet with a grunt, reflecting the physical strain. The blood from the wound I had given him was started to seep through his shirt. He acted like it wasn't happening. He aimed the rifle Robert's way with a sinister smile.

"Then leave the killing to me, Robbie. I'm happy to do it."

"You always were," said Robert, tossing his gun to the side.

"We were the elite," said Herman with a touch of pride. "Our fathers were the elite. You destroyed it."

That's when I saw the kid coming up behind Robert and picking his discarded pistol up off the ground. I couldn't yell at him to stop or I would have given Herman another target. Fucking PMA, why couldn't he stay out of this shit?

"We were SICK FUCKS," replied Robert, continuing to walk forward, leaving the grass of the park for the pavement. "Sick fucks killing for the sake of killing. I can't sleep because I see their faces at night. Every night. The faces of the people we killed."

"Allow me to end your suffering," Herman said with dripping sarcasm.

He raised his rifle.

"Go ahead, Herman! Blow the rest of my face off!" Robert shouted back at him.

I clenched the pistol in my pocket. I wasn't so crazy about killing either, especially shooting a guy in the back. Like Herman, I had watched too many bad Westerns.

"Robert, duck!" PMA yelled. "I got him!"

Oh Jesus.

Robert turned, but he didn't duck. He yelled at the kid, "PUT IT DOWN!" and blocked the kid's shot, so the only thing he could hit was his uncle. The two of them started shuffling around, with the kid trying to get around Robert and Robert blocking him every time.

"Jeremy, you don't want to do this!" exclaimed Robert.

"Somebody has to do this!" was the kid's response.

"Not you!"

The whole thing was infinitely amusing to Herman, who actually chuckled. Which left it up to me.

"Herman, I still got a few bullets here," I said to his back. "Put down the rifle."

Herman, aiming straight at either Robert or the kid, I couldn't tell, simply said "Fuck you," and slammed down the rifle's lever.

And then came a big surprise, Herman's second bad one of the night.

The gun barrel blew up.

Herman screamed in pain – his face had powder burns and the end of the rifle barrel was split apart like a noisemaker. And I realized what had happened. Herman's rifle was shoved in the mud when he fell – and the end of the barrel was stuffed with wet dirt. Which blocked the shot and blew up the end of the rifle.

Herman, momentarily blinded, staggered back, spewing venom.

"You're a goddamn coward, Davidson! A fucking pussy, your father knew it! A fucking pussy bitch!"

Robert wasn't having it. He shrieked some animal war cry and ran at Herman, who was blindly backing up against the sea wall. Robert ran into him with such force that they both fell back over the fence, down the embankment and into the flooded East River, which was raging like the Mississippi.

PMA came running down the hill, falling a couple of times in the watery mess, getting right back up and barreling down the watery walkway to the edge where the two men had fell.

He looked down over the sea wall for a while, then turned back to me.

"They're gone. I don't see them."

Then he looked me over.

"Are you all right?"

I asked him, "What do you think?"

Recovery

My apartment had become a hospital ward.

There was me with my broken leg in a cast and there was Jules with her bandaged head. Yeah, the good news was I didn't get her killed or even brain-damaged, she was going to be all right. I could tell nothing was wrong with her head just by watching her dance between being pissed off at me for luring a tomahawk-wielding maniac into the building and being giddy about having a great story to tell on Facebook.

Our nurse? PMA. I paid him to stick around and help out for a few weeks, even though I think he would have done it for free to avoid going home. It wasn't good with him and his mom, especially after what had happened in the aftermath of the events in Lighthouse Park.

As I had laid there by what was left of the lighthouse, soaking in the flood waters and waiting for the EMTs, I wondered what story I was going to tell to explain all this. And I went back to John Ford, the General's favorite filmmaker and my father's. I knew exactly how he would have handled this plot development.

He would have me pretend that I didn't know Robert Davidson had just been killed for the first time. Instead, I would tell the cops that the dead man who had washed ashore on the Queens side of the East River next to Herman Wright was Richard Kurtz, an operative who worked alongside Herman at Dark Sky. Why not? Andrew Wright no doubt had Kurtz's identity planted in the intelligence files just for this happenstance. So I could preserve the lie that Robert Davidson was a war hero who had been dead for a decade. After all, America needs its myths to continue to grow and thrive.

But I called bullshit on the whole idea.

When you don't tell the truth in situations like these, you institutionalize deceit and corruption as the norm. You perpetuate the illusion, like the government tried to do with Jessica Lynch and Pat Tillman, that war is always glorious and heroic, that there is no down-and-dirty side, that military purity is, in fact, pure, when in fact war is a bloody, messy business that can't help but get sidetracked into savagery.

I wasn't going to be the guy to prop up the lies that had already caused so much chaos and death.

So I told the cops that Robert Davidson was, until a short time ago, alive and well and had escaped from the Dark Sky compound. I told them that Herman Wright, son of the king of the spooks, had come here to kill him as well as me so we would keep our mouths shut. Of course, the kid backed up everything I said. When the authorities verified he was the General's grandson, that certainly helped.

The resulting national headlines and internet chatter did the damage Andrew Wright feared. Congress put a temporary hold on Dark Sky's funding until a full investigation into their activities could be completed.

Now that the beast had been dragged out into the light, now that they knew that Wright's psychotic son was a part of the murder spree and had personally killed General Kraemer himself, they could no longer turn a blind eye. So Andrew "Uncle Andy" Wright was forced to resign from his DOD position and disappear into the shadows for a very lonely, sad and disgraced retirement.

And all of that becoming public knowledge caused Angela Davidson to feel deeply humiliated and betrayed – by her own son and by me.

She didn't understand that we were doing her a favor. That the only way to shake off a family legacy that, in the end, was more destructive than productive was to break the cycle and be who you were meant to be, rather than who your forefathers and/or your foremothers wanted you to be.

Robert Davidson had finally found the strength to break his cycle when he heard his father was dying. He broke out of the Dark Sky compound and drove one of the base's trademark black SUVs night and day to get to Virginia Beach, to try and have a final reconciliation with the General before it was too late. Unfortunately, when he arrived, the old man was already sinking into his final coma - and, when Angela told him PMA was with me, he knew we would both be targeted before the ink on the death certificate was dry. That's when he probably realized there was no second chance for Robert Davidson - and that's when he came to Roosevelt Island to protect us from whoever was coming after us.

What he hadn't expected to do was save his nephew from beginning his adulthood with blood on his hands. It was a sacrifice that maybe brought him some peace at the end, because he had freed the kid to live his own life the way he wanted to. Jules liked PMA and spent a lot of time talking things through with him, which was good, because he needed some counseling from someone who could hold a touchy-feely conversation, which left me out. And, I have to say, she gave him good advice when she wasn't calling all the other members of his family fucking assholes. Go to college in the fall, she told him. Go do what you want to do. And maybe dump all that Andre Gibraltar crap in the garbage.

Break the cycle.

I had to do the same. I had to let go of all the past damage that involved Allison and the girls. I wasn't perfect, but Allison had made an extra effort to keep the kids united against me and she was very good at it. Andrew Wright had done me a perverse favor of sorts by forcing me to look it all with cold, clear eyes and realize everything that happened was because I had been too young and dumb to make a good choice when it came to women. I had lost all my money and almost my mind trying to make things as right as I could without staying married to her, and I had come up empty. It was time to move on.

Which is why I was allowing myself to be happy with Jules for maybe the first time ever. It was a good time for it. As her vocal cords healed, she was getting more and more excited. She tried singing a few notes here and there and said she hadn't sounded that good since she was twenty. She was working on getting a gig next month and then, she boasted, she would show me what singing was all about. I told her from what I had heard coming out of her mouth, she better start practicing a lot more. Then she told me to hop off her tits and leave her alone.

Our love was here to stay.

As for my future, I decided I should take advantage of my recent publicity blitz and expand my client list beyond…well, just Howard. So I was studying for the test to get my Private Investigator license. I could no longer dabble in the self-defeating business – I needed to try and be a grown-up at the age of 58. Jules was all for it as long as nobody else with a tomahawk showed up at my place.

To apply for the P.I. license, however, I needed to get a reference – so I gave Howard a call after my interview on *The Today Show*. I began by asking him if I looked a little less pale on the boob tube. He was shocked to hear from me. He had it in his head that I would never talk to him again after Andrew Wright forced him to knuckle under to the notion of fucking me over. I told him I understood and I felt the weight fall off his back by the way his voice lightened. I didn't feel wonderful about what had happened, but I was willing to let the damage heal over time. We always had a complicated friendship, but it was a friendship and it would endure.

And besides – like I said, I needed the reference.

As my leg healed, I did my P.I. homework while cable news played in the background. As usual, there was a lot of sound and fury about how we should put some troops in the latest Middle Eastern problem country and straighten shit out, even though it seemed to always be the worst possible solution to what was essentially tribal warfare that had been going on for thousands of years. It wasn't our culture, it wasn't our right and it always made things worse.

And that brought me back to John Ford, who sometimes did get it right. I remembered the scene General Davidson had been watching when I had my one and only meeting with him, where soon-to-be-retired cavalry officer John Wayne and Native American elder Pony-That-Walks agreed on the idea that old men should stop wars, not start them.

Unfortunately, it was still an idea whose time had not come. But maybe, someday, when I looked at my nice new silver watch, it would be that time.

Max Bowman Will Return in

Blue Fire

A missing comic book genius. An all-powerful hallucinogenic designer drug.

Max Bowman is haunted by both of them – and he just might lose his mind as a result.

When Max takes on the mission to find the long-lost creator of cult superhero Blue Fire, he ends up secretly dosed with a chemical that upends his sanity just when he needs it the most. Now he's got to contend with zombies on the Upper East Side, a cult run by a clueless pawn, a hipster rapist who knows her way around a knife, a secret CIA spook program left over from the Cold War and powerful old enemies who are out to destroy him – all while trying to keep his mind from crashing and burning for good.

Blue Fire's mantra in the old comic books was, "For good to be purged of evil…Blue Fire must endure." But now it's Max Bowman who must endure – and he's as far from a superhero as you can get.

Blue Fire now available on Amazon.com.

About the Author

A novelist, screenwriter and ghostwriter, Canfield has lived in New York City, Chicago, Detroit, Miami Beach, Auckland, New Zealand, and his own personal Pennsylvania trifecta, Pittsburgh, Wilkes-Barre and his hometown of Bethlehem. He now resides in Long Beach, California with his favorite blondes, writer-editor wife Lisa and dog Betsy, but he will undoubtedly move again, because that's just what he does.

Canfield's books include *Dark Sky*, *Blue Fire* and *Red Earth* (the first three books in the Max Bowman series); *What's Driving You???: How I Overcame Abuse and Learned to Lead in the NBA* (co-authored with Keyon Dooling and Lisa Canfield); *Pill Mill: My Years of Money, Madness, Sex and Drugs* (co-authored with Christian Valdes and Lisa Canfield); and *226: How I Became the First Blind Person to Kayak the Grand Canyon* (co-authored with Lonnie Bedwell. *Blue Fire* was a 2016 Silver Honoree in the Benjamin Franklin Digital Awards as well as a semi-finalist in the Book Life Prize in Fiction competition. *Red Earth* was a 2017 Gold Honoree in the Benjamin Franklin Digital Awards. He has also co-written two television movies, *Eat, Play, Love* and *Yes, I Do* with Lisa Canfield.

Receive the latest updates on the Max Bowman book series at
www.Facebook.com/MaxBowmanBooks.

Printed in Great Britain
by Amazon